Tactical Revival

COASTAL HOPE
BOOK FOUR

JESSICA ASHLEY

B.A.D. PUBLISHING CO

believing in the power of reading

TACTICAL REVIVAL

A Coastal Hope Novel

By Jessica Ashley

Copyright © 2024. All rights reserved.

Scripture used in this novel comes from HOLY BIBLE, New International Version®, NIV® Copyright ©1973, 1978, 1984, 2011 by Biblica, Inc.® Used by permission. All rights reserved worldwide.

Edited by HEA Author Services
Proofread by Love Kissed Books, LLC
Cover Design by Covers by Christian
Photographer: Wander Book Club
Model: Andrew

Tactical Revival

A detective struggling to put down roots. A single mother fighting to make ends meet.

Former homicide detective Jaxson Payne knows a thing or two about starting over. His marriage imploded after he broke his back serving as a Marine overseas. He was told he'd never walk again. However, he was back on his feet within months, proving his resilience is only outmatched by his faith.

After moving to Hope Springs for a fresh start, he's hoping to finally close the door on his past. But it seems the ghosts that still haunt Jaxson have followed him here, bringing danger to his front door.

Margot Anderson had her entire life planned out. Then her husband left her and their thirteen-year-old son. She's spent the last year holding their lives together with prayers and a positive outlook, and then a former Marine moves into her B&B.

Jaxson Payne is everything she should avoid. He's handsome. Strong. And her older brother's best friend. But as danger sets its sights on her, Jaxson is her shield, making it clear that there is nothing he won't sacrifice for her and her son.

If you're looking for a sizzling (but not spicy!) romantic suspense with a protective Christian hero, a small town that protects their own, and a team of wounded veterans turned private security officers, then Tactical Revival is for you!

This Christian Romantic Suspense deals with:
-Coping with trauma
-Discovering your worth
-Seeking God in everything
-Healing from your past

The Coastal Hope series can be enjoyed in any order!

There are times in life when it feels like the hits just keep coming. Like no matter how hard we try to get ahead, we're continually dragged right back down into the pit of anxiety, depression, and stress.

The groceries are expensive.

Bills are sky high.

Mortgage has to be paid on time.

Oh, and the car needs new tires.

The AC went out.

Kids need new shoes.

Round and round we go, constantly trying to keep up with a world that seems bent on destroying every bit of joy we have.

It's easy to get sucked into the day-to-day, focusing only on how you're going to make ends meet instead of remembering that we're not alone.

Even when we find ourselves crying in a dark corner,

hiding our pain from those who rely on us, we are NOT alone.

Jesus is always there.

He hears our cries.

And He can move those mountains right out of your path if you just let Him in.

When you feel like you have nothing.

You have Him.

You have love.

You have the salvation He bought for you with His blood.

And you have the promise that better days are coming.

JESUS IS KING.

REDEEMER.

CHAIN BREAKER.

-Jessica

To all those who feel like they're at the end of their ropes.
Keep hanging on, you're not alone.

Psalm 34:17-18

CHAPTER 1

Jaxson

Sweat beads along my skin despite the brisk March morning, but I continue pushing myself, pumping my arms harder as I sprint down the beach, the fast-paced tune of Brandon Lake's "I Need a Ghost" blasting through my headphones.

The sand is soft beneath my bare feet, making it well worth the risk of accidentally stepping on a shell. There's just something about running barefoot on the beach that makes the start of a day perfect. I drop down and knock out thirty push-ups, then jump back up to my feet, wipe the sand from my hands and start running again.

In another mile, I'll repeat, just as I have every single mile since I started running forty minutes ago. It's a morning routine I've maintained—even in the rain—since I got clearance from Doc to be active after being shot and nearly bleeding out on the floor of the local high school almost a year ago.

I've been at full functionality for seven months now, but even still, I don't feel strong enough. Fast enough. I'm a Marine. A man who has seen more combat than I care to focus on. And after that, I'd been a detective at the LAPD for a decade. Ten years of chasing down bad guys and solving murders.

But after a few months in the small coastal town of Hope Springs, Maine, working private security with a group of other Veterans I've come to see as brothers, I nearly died. The sound of that gun going off haunts my nightmares, as does the look on Reyna Acker's face as the man abducting her forced her out of my sight.

I hadn't been able to protect her then.

But I'm going to make sure I don't fail on my next job.

I pump my arms and legs faster, as though picking up speed will force the memories from my mind. The nightmares that still wake me from a dead sleep.

A beep in my ear signifies another mile down, so I drop down and knock out another thirty push-ups, then push up and take off running again. My muscles burn with exertion, but I know that it's these last miles that truly make me strong. When I feel like I can't go anymore, that's when I find my strength.

I've made it another half mile when I see a familiar brunette standing at the edge of the ocean, her bare feet in the sand. The sight of her steals my breath, and I come to a stop, heart beating heavily for a whole new reason.

The breeze toys with her dark hair, gently caressing the strands that have come free from her loose bun. Her jaw is strong, her features elegant as she stares out at the crashing waves. She's wearing bright pink shorts and a white T-shirt beneath a pale pink cardigan.

She's beautiful. Breathtaking. And not for me.

I start to turn around, head back up the beach, but then she glances my way, and I note the troubled expression on her face even as she offers me a wave and a soft smile.

So instead of bolting the other way, I continue toward her. Stopping at her side, I remove my headphones and shove them into my pocket. "Surprised to see you out here this early."

Margot O'Connell—or rather Margot Anderson, as she's officially divorced now—sighs and brushes some of the strands of her thick, dark hair behind her ear. She's the younger sister of Michael, one of my closest friends and coworkers. She also happens to own the B&B I've been staying in for the past year. "I wanted to see the sunrise. Matty stayed with Michael last night, so I'm flying solo."

I turn to stare out at the sunrise alongside her, enjoying the way the world wakes up. It's my favorite time of day because it's the only point where everything is starting fresh. The day is a blank canvas, so many different opportunities awaiting.

I steal a look at her out of the corner of my eye. Her jaw is set, her shoulders stiff. It seems that for Margot, the day is going to be anything but a fresh beginning. "Everything okay?"

She sighs and runs a hand over the back of her neck. "I'm tired."

"Margot." I know her well enough to see that something is truly bothering her.

"Chad called."

Anger surges through my system. In fact, the amount of fury I feel for a man I've never met should probably concern me.

But Chad O'Connell left his wife. Abandoned his son. And even if I didn't know what it feels like to be left by the people who are supposed to love you most, I'd still see the man as absolutely useless. "What did he want?"

"According to him?" She scoffs. "A relationship with Matty."

"You don't think that's what he wants?" I may have been a homicide detective with the LAPD before moving here to Hope Springs to work at a security firm, but it doesn't take a cop to hear the skepticism in her voice.

"No. I think he wants money. Or more of my dignity. Who knows, really. I just— I wish he would stay gone." A tear rolls down her cheek, and she quickly wipes it away.

Seeing her pain guts me.

I wish I could drive to whatever hole her ex crawled into, drag him out by the collar of his shirt, and tell him he'd better back off or I'd throw him in a cell and toss the key. Unfortunately, that would be assault no matter which way you spin it.

Margot is a good person. Her son is a good kid. Chad will bring nothing but problems back into their lives.

So, unable to do anything other than be here for her, I cross my arms and continue staring straight ahead. Getting involved in personal business—especially the personal business of my best friend's sister—might be a mistake, but I can't keep myself from trying to help where I can.

Margot has been more than kind to me. She's allowed me to stay in the maintenance apartment of the B&B for such low rent it should be criminal, and she cooks me dinner most nights, even though I tell her it's truly not necessary since I'm just as happy to occupy a booth in the diner.

Truth is, I prefer her company. Which is dangerous. Because the more time I spend with her, the more I want to be around her. The beat of her broken heart haunts me because all I want to do is be the one to put it back together.

The problem is, mine's in pieces, too.

Clearing my throat, I face her. "What can I do to help?"

"Oh, nothing." She waves her hand as though she's dismissing me away. "I'll get it figured out. I just thought I was done dealing with him when the divorce was final and he took off for good."

I have no idea what really happened between them, though according to Michael, Chad skipped town one night and never came back. I have my suspicions that there's more to it and Margot likely doesn't want to give her older brother any reason to let his temper loose.

The former boxer has a reputation for a reason.

Given that I have my own divorce I try to avoid talking about, I haven't pressed and have no intentions of doing so. Sometimes bitter business is best left buried.

"Do you have a busy day?" she asks me, then turns and starts walking back toward the path that leads to the B&B.

I follow, even though I wanted to get another few miles in. I sense she needs the company, and since she's been a friend when I needed one, it seems only fair to return the favor. Then there's the whole *I love her company* piece of it.

"Michael and I are headed to Smith Harbor for an install." The town is about a twenty-minute drive from Hope Springs, and while we didn't have any business there before, we just picked up a handful of clients after some teens broke into a bunch of neighborhood vehicles.

"You guys have been out there a lot lately."

"Yeah. We've done a couple installs a week for the past two months."

"Good for business." She heads up the stairs, then drops her sandals at the top and slips back into them, her coral-colored toenails peeking out of the ends.

"What about you?" I ask.

"The Butlers are checking out today, so I'll be getting that room ready for the Greys, who will be arriving sometime this evening."

Her tone is already exhausted. She'd had to let her cleaning lady go last week, so she's been doing it all. The books. The cleaning. At least Lilly, the local diner owner, and Kyra, our town's baker and the wife of Pastor Redding, have stepped in to help with providing breakfast until Margot can get someone else hired.

She's drowning, though, and too proud to ask for a rescue.

"Well, if you need help—"

"You've done plenty for me already," she interrupts.

"Doesn't feel that way," I reply. "Changing out a light-bulb here and there hardly seems fair in exchange for room and board."

"Trust me, it's fair to me." We reach the B&B, so I rush around and pull the door open. Breakfast is in full swing already, with muffins, donuts, and fresh coffee out and set up in the dining room.

After waving at a few of the guests, I follow Margot back into the kitchen where she pours us each a cup of coffee. She pours a bit of creamer, some honey, and a splash of cinnamon into her cup, then turns and leans back against the counter.

"When Chad and I bought this place, he was supposed to handle the maintenance while I ran the rest of it. It was my dream, so when he started to skip certain tasks, I just let it go. I'd felt so guilty for asking for help." She shakes her head, and my contempt for her ex-husband grows. "Anyways, thank you for your help. And I'm sorry to lay it all on you first thing this morning."

"Don't apologize. I hear venting is what friends do for each other."

She grins at my joke. "I'm worried about how Matty will take it if Chad decides to come around and really does want to start trying to have a relationship with him. Truthfully, they didn't get along even before Chad bailed. Matty isn't into football or baseball. He likes to box, but only occasionally when he can get in the ring with Michael.

Really, Matty loves to play chess. It's one of his favorite things to do, and Chad just couldn't understand why. He told him it was the hobby of a weak man." She shakes her head angrily. "Who tells their son that?"

"Someone who has a small brain and doesn't understand the game."

Margot laughs, the happiest sound I've heard from her all morning, and it brings me a dose of joy I hadn't been expecting. "You know what? He most certainly does have a small brain." She takes a drink of her coffee.

He'd have to, if he left you both behind. I run a hand over the back of my neck, uncomfortable at the track my thoughts have jumped onto. "I like to play chess, and I'm pretty good, too. So let me know if Matty ever wants a run for his money."

Her expression completely lights up, and for a moment, it steals the air from my lungs. Margot is my friend. My best friend's sister, so there can be no romance between us. But I can certainly appreciate the beauty she absolutely radiates. Especially when a smile from her brightens every aspect of my day. "Matty would love that so much. I'll have him get with you about setting up a game."

"Great." I finish my coffee, then rinse the cup and stick it in the dishwasher before turning to Margot. "I'll see you later. Let me know if you have a to-do list for me once the Butlers check out. I really can help if you need me."

As I head upstairs, I mentally tally everything I need to accomplish today, from grabbing breakfast at the diner to updating my paperwork, the installation, and one final follow-up with Doc. It's been nearly eight months since I was shot, but because of the fact that my back has already been broken once and is pieced together with a rod and pins—thanks to an IED that nearly killed me overseas—he's been monitoring my recovery a bit closer than he would have anyone else.

According to him, if the bullet had been a centimeter to the left, it would have blown out the rod and likely paralyzed me permanently, given there wouldn't have been enough bone left to stabilize me. Thank God it wasn't.

I'm just getting out of the shower when I hear my phone ding. Wrapping a towel around my waist, I cross over and note the name on my screen. My heart drops, and my stomach twists into knots.

Not again.

Rosalie: Hey, I'm just checking in again. It's been a few weeks since we talked, and I would love an update on your care. Talk soon.

I cringe at the message. I'd accidentally answered *one* phone call because I hadn't been paying attention to the caller, and it opened a door I closed a *long* time ago.

Still, I suppose there is some irony in the fact that both Margot's ex-husband and my ex-wife decided to try and make contact on the same day.

My phone rings again, and I half expect it to be her calling, but thankfully it's my brother's name on the screen. I have a moment of hesitation but shove it aside to put the phone on speaker. "Hey, Tyler, what's up?"

"How you feeling, bro?"

"Back to normal. How are things with you?"

He sighs into the phone, Tyler Payne's code for bad news delivery. *Great.* "Not too bad. Sherry is about ready to pop any day now." His wife of two years is pregnant with their first child, a little boy due next month.

"I bet." But I don't buy into the good news. It's his typical delivery method. Hit me with the good news, then slam a right hook of bad straight into my jaw when I'm not looking.

"So listen—" He trails off a moment. "Dad's been trying to get in touch with you."

"Not interested."

"Jaxson."

"Not interested," I repeat. "You want a relationship with him? Good for you. I, however, want nothing to do with the man."

"You can't hate him forever. He's all we've got."

"No. He's all you've got. I have you, and I don't need him." Our dad left us when we were young. Bailed on our mom, who was already struggling with being a parent as it was. She wanted nothing to do with us, so she dropped us off at a shelter and never came back. I was sixteen, and my brother was nine.

It's why I have no tolerance for Chad. My father abandoned me, too.

Tyler and I barely scraped by, living on the streets until I turned eighteen and could legally adopt him. And that was a fight in and of itself. Two years of stealing food, sleeping in alleys or shelters, and hiding from the authorities who would have thrown us in different group homes. We likely never would have seen each other again.

"What happened to forgiveness?" he asks me, knowing I've been on a journey to grow my faith for the past few years.

"I can forgive him and want nothing to do with him," I reply. "Is that all you had to say?"

He sighs again. "He wants to talk to you. To air things out."

"There's nothing to air out." The familiar anger climbs up the back of my neck, and I have to force it down and remind myself that it's not Tyler's fault. He'd been young then, younger when our dad bailed.

He doesn't remember all the fighting.

The horrible words spoken.

But I do.

And while I am working to forgive, forgetting is not something I'm sure I can do.

"Jaxson, he's our dad."

"I have a Father," I tell him. "And He will never leave me. I don't need Bradley Payne."

"You've got to let the past go, or it's going to drag you down," he argues.

"I'm not being dragged down by it," I tell him truthfully. "I just don't have the same interest to share a meal with the man who bailed on us." My phone beeps, so I glance at the screen and note Lance's name flashing. "I have to go. Work is calling."

"We're not done with this."

"We are. Love you, Ty, tell Sherry I said hi." Without waiting for a response, I swap lines. "What's up?" I ask, phone still on speaker so I can pull on my boots.

"How soon can you get into the office?"

"I'm just getting dressed now, so fifteen minutes? Why?"

He sighs into the phone, which tells me whatever news he has is not good. "We've got a missing person," Lance says. "And Sheriff Vick is requesting our help."

CHAPTER 2

Margot

"You are more than welcome, Mrs. Fry." I smile despite being alone in my office, so happy that I could accommodate a date change for her and her husband's sixtieth wedding anniversary trip.

Sixty years.

What is that like? I couldn't make it thirteen.

"You are a darling, Margot. We're looking forward to seeing you again. It's been far too long!"

"It really has. Two years, right?"

"Oh my! It's been that long, hasn't it?" They'd had to cancel their annual trip last year because of their great grandson being born. But she'd made sure to call and tell me that the little boy and his mother were doing great, and I'd even sent a bouquet of flowers to the new mother.

And this time they have to move their trip out because her husband came down with something.

Chad never understood my desire to connect with

those who stay here. My need to make them feel cared for. He saw people as dollar signs, while I see them as family. Close friends. People who trust me to make their trips special and stress-free.

Even as I'd given him credit for supporting my dream of opening this place, I knew he only quit his job because he'd hated it and thought this place was going to be an instant moneymaker. When it hadn't been, and we'd started struggling, he'd gotten angry and resentful.

Perhaps that's part of what tore my family apart.

"I can't wait to show you pictures of little Bobbie! He has gotten so big!" she exclaims, pulling me out of the darkness of my thoughts.

"I'm looking forward to it. I'll see you next month, Mrs. Fry. I hope Mr. Fry starts feeling better soon. Let me know if there's anything I can do between now and then."

"Thank you, dear. We will see you and your sweet boy next month. Goodbye!" She ends the call cheerfully, and I set the receiver down, then lean back in my chair and close my eyes.

Sweet boy. Matty hasn't behaved like a sweet boy since Chad left. He just keeps getting more and more volatile. Honestly, the closest I've seen him to his true personality is when he jumped to action, saving Jaxson's life.

He'd applied pressure to the gunshot wound the former detective sustained, then called 9-1-1 before calling me. I'd arrived right as Jaxson and Silas Williamson, a former Navy SEAL they'd brought in to find my brother when he'd been missing, were brought out on stretchers.

Seeing Jaxson Payne looking so weak was far more difficult than I could have anticipated. While I don't know the former Marine well, he's a powerful force to be reckoned with. Anyone who spends more than ten seconds in a room with him can sense it.

My thoughts drift back to the beach this morning. To seeing him standing in the sand, barefoot, muscles slick with sweat, the light breeze toying with his dark hair. Attraction swirls in my gut, but I shove it back down.

He's one of my brother's best friends and one of his business partners.

And I have a thirteen-year-old son to worry about. The last thing I need is a romance that will likely fizzle and burn out, just like the marriage that was supposed to last me a lifetime did.

My gaze lands on the worn Bible sitting on the edge of my desk. Tears fill my eyes as I look immediately to the right of it and take in the stack of bills piling up. Some of them are pink.

Final notices.

And I have no idea how I'm supposed to pay them.

As it so often does when this happens, my mind fills with intrusive thoughts.

I'm not smart enough to run a business.

I'm not capable of keeping this place afloat.

I might as well quit now, before I lose what little savings I've managed to put away for Matty's college fund.

No. I will *not* let Chad into my head. Not ever again.

Knowing I can't deal with these thoughts on my own, I bow my head.

God, please help me. I can't do this without You. I know I can't, and I know You are here for me. Please keep me strong. Amen.

The bell above the front door dings, so I push to my feet and slip out into the front, a smile plastered on my face. That is, until I see the bane of my existence standing on the other side of my counter.

Seems the devil is working overtime to drive me out of the peace I fight so hard to maintain.

The last year hasn't changed Chad at all. He still looks every bit the jock he'd been when we were in high school, with the years only adding a few more lines to his otherwise youthful face. When he sees me, he shoves his hands into his pockets. "Margot."

I cross my arms. "What do you want, Chad?"

"You won't answer my calls."

"Because I have nothing to say to you."

His cheeks turn red. "You don't get to decide that."

I can practically smell the alcohol on his breath, which makes me even more nervous. Chad was never violent unless he was drinking. The alcohol completely changed him, turning him into the monster haunting our home. I try to make myself look busy by rearranging the stacks of Post-its on my front standing desk. That way, maybe, he won't sense the nerves. Being alone with Chad is something I never wanted again. Not after I'd finally had it with his violent outbursts. It started with screaming and throwing things…and then he slapped me.

It was the first and last time he ever put his hands on me.

"I do get to decide that, thanks to the divorce decree. Now leave. This is my home and my place of business." My gaze drifts to the entryway security camera, and I try to breathe. I know Knight Security monitors it, so even as it's just Chad and me, I know I'm not truly alone.

"I'm not going anywhere until you let me see Matty." His tone picks up that all-too-familiar flash of anger.

"*Matthew* doesn't want to see you." Hearing him call our son by his nickname makes me nauseous. He lost that right when he chose to throw everything we'd worked for away.

"Because you've poisoned him against me." He tightens his hands into fists at his sides, and my gaze flicks to the letter opener on the check-in desk to my right. It might be the only thing I can use to defend myself.

"I didn't do anything. That was all you, Chad."

He places both hands on the desk between us, and I stiffen. Surely he wouldn't do anything here. Not in the middle of the day when anyone could walk in…but I still can't put my nerves at ease. All the guests have checked out.

No one is due to check in for another two hours.

What if— The door opens again, and Silas strolls in. Standing just as tall as Jaxson, the man is over six feet of solid muscle. And while the former Navy SEAL is a man of few words, his expression speaks volumes. He's pissed that Chad is here, and I send up a thank you to God for my brother pushing to install the security cameras.

"You are not welcome on this property," Silas says, crossing his arms.

Chad doesn't even give Silas a glance. "This is none of your business. Margot is my wife, and we're discussing personal matters."

"Margot is your *ex*-wife," Silas corrects. "And she, her son, and her property are all under the protection of Knight Security, which makes it my business."

Chad looks from me to Silas, then back to me, his expression even more furious—if that's possible. "You hired your brother's toy security company to keep me from my son?"

"Toy security company?" I let out a humorless laugh. "I'll be sure to tell Michael that. He'll get a kick out of your appreciation of his company. Either way. What I do and who I hire is none of your business. Get out."

His expression softens, and he runs both hands over his face. "Fine. But can we please talk, Margot? I'll meet you at the diner. I really just have some things I want to discuss."

"I don't—"

"Please," he says again, his tone a bit more anguished than before. "I really messed up with our son, and I want to make it right."

The part of me not completely obliterated by his betrayal understands his need to make things right with Matty. And even as I know our son cannot stand his father,

I also know there's a part of him that wishes things were different. "I'll hear you out," I tell him. "But I won't make Matty do anything he doesn't want to. And that includes seeing you."

Chad smiles, flashing that boyish grin that once had me weak in the knees. "Done. Diner tonight? Seven?"

"Fine."

Chad turns and leaves, completely ignoring Silas. When the door closes behind him, the newest addition to Knight Security moves closer to my desk. "Are you okay?"

"Annoyed. Angry. Grateful you showed up."

"Elijah called. He's on monitor duty since Michael, Jaxson, and Lance are with Sheriff Vick right now. I was close, so I was able to get over here quickly."

A bite of panic pushes past my anger at Chad. "Is everything okay?"

"I haven't gotten the update yet," he replies. The man is all business every time I see him. Except when he's out with his four-year-old niece, the little girl he's been raising ever since her parents passed. "You good, though? I can hang out a little longer if you're worried he'll come back."

"No, it's okay." I wave him off. "Thanks, though. Chad got what he wanted. He won't be coming back."

Silas offers me a single nod, then turns and leaves the B&B. The little bell over the door jingles as it closes behind him. Taking a deep breath, I lean my head forward and try to steady my nerves.

Surely Chad isn't coming after me for partial custody. Not after he already gave up his rights. Can he do that? Can he come after me now that our agreement is finalized? Anxiety fuels my panic, so I head into the kitchen for a glass of water.

No. Chad cannot have Matty. I told myself that I would never stand in the way if Matty wanted a relationship with his father, but I will fight tooth and nail to keep my son from being forced to share a space with his cheating, abusive alcoholic father.

Not that anyone knows about the abuse. I never told a soul—especially not Micheal. My brother would have killed him.

The former Army Ranger would have made my ex-husband disappear, staining his soul with the blood of a man undeserving to even breathe the same air as him.

It was not a risk I could take, so I kept it to myself.

The bell dings, and a stab of panic shoots through me. Is he back?

"Mom?" a familiar voice calls out.

I press a hand to my heart and take a deep breath. "Back here!" After setting the water down, I head out of the kitchen and meet Matty near the front desk. Anthony Bell, Matty's best friend since kindergarten, is with him. "Hey, boys. You got here early." I glance at the clock, surprised that it's not actually that early.

"We ran." As evidenced by his red cheeks and breathless smile. "Mom, can I stay the night at Ant's? We've got a science fair project due in a month and we both really want to get working on it."

I study him closely, looking for any tells that it's a lie,

but get none. Anthony is a good kid. One of the only boys Matty hangs out with who is an actual good influence on him. Is it possible my son is finally getting back to normalcy? Back to the study-loving, happy boy he was before his world imploded?

A wave of hope flushes through me.

And then the remnants of Chad's desire to get close to him seeps in. What if Chad ruins it? What if seeing him reverts Matty to the troublemaker he was right after Chad left, tagging police cars and stealing candy from the corner store?

"Your parents are home?" I ask Anthony.

"My dad will be. Mom is working the night shift at the hospital. I can have him call you if you'd like, Mrs. O'Connell."

I try not to wince at him calling me by Chad's last name.

"Anderson," Matty corrects, elbowing his friend lightly.

His cheeks turn red. "Mrs. Anderson. Sorry."

"No worries, hun. It's a hard habit to break, trust me." I smile. "If you could have your dad call me, that would be great. You guys will just be working on the project then? Not going anywhere?" I hate that he won't be home tonight—that I'll be alone, but Matty behaving like a typical thirteen-year-old is a balm to that wound.

"Yes, Mom." Matty rolls his eyes. "I'll call you right after dinner and before I go to bed, too."

"And you better not be late for school tomorrow. If you are—"

"I know, I know, trouble city." He laughs.

"You got it." I open my arms, and he steps in closer, wrapping his around my waist and hugging me. I breathe him in, enjoying every second of this moment before he pulls away. "You guys have fun. I love you, Matty."

My boy grins at me. A sideways smile that reminds me of his father at that age. Before he became the womanizer he is now. *God, please let my boy stay kind.* "Love you, too, Mom."

CHAPTER 3

Jaxson

"You said your daughter is home visiting?" I ask, jotting down a few impressions on my notepad. The way the parents are behaving, the feel of the home we're standing in. This one is nice and tidy, though well-lived-in.

These people love their daughter, and it's clear from the photographs adorning the mantle that she loves them too. Which means she most likely didn't just leave in the middle of the night or walk out without saying goodbye.

Dread coils in my stomach, but I shove it down to focus on the facts.

"Yes," the mother—Mrs. Finch—replies. "She got back home Thursday night since she has no classes on Friday." She sniffles, her gray eyes red and glassy. "She's getting her master's degree in physical education." Her voice breaks. "I never should have let her go out for that run this morning." She cries. "It was still dark. I should have made her stay."

Her husband pulls her in closer, and Sheriff Vick, who is dressed casually in jeans and a T-shirt today, reaches out to take her hand. "Millie, we'll find her. I'm sure she just got turned around. Besides, she's an adult. You couldn't have made her stay."

"I could have tried. She's never been gone this long. Normally, she's back an hour after leaving. She's been gone eight hours now. Eight hours, Ray!" Mrs. Finch covers her face with shaking hands.

I leave Lance to ask the rest of our questions and turn my attention to the photographs. The cute blonde staring back at me has something familiar about her, though I can't quite place what it is. She has the same gray eyes as her mother, her features soft yet refined.

She's slender, a runner, and every photograph has her genuinely smiling. Occasionally in cases I've been called in on, you can tell that the home life is little more than a façade put on for social media's benefit. But this family truly loves each other.

That familiar sense of dread is back, so I beat it back down again. I spent too many years on the force. Too much time identifying the dead and breaking the news to family members all while promising to hunt down the killer who stole their loved one.

God, please don't let this be another one of those cases.
Please, God, help me find her. Alive.

"Was anything amiss when she left this morning?" Michael questions.

"No," her mother replies. "She got up, drank her smoothie, grabbed her bottle of water, and left."

"Without a cell phone?"

"Kleo doesn't carry her phone often," Millie replies, her voice shaky. "And never on runs. She doesn't like to be tied to anything when she's out. Our girl is all about living in the moment." With that, she starts crying.

"I get that," I reply, offering them a kind smile. Unfortunately, even though I do understand it, it makes it even more difficult to find her. "Did she carry any form of protection? Pepper spray? A knife? A firearm?"

"She carries a knife," her father replies. "After her twenty-first birthday, I tried to get her to start carrying a firearm, but she said it weighs her down. She carries most of the time, but on her runs, she sticks with the knife."

I nod, then close my notepad and stick it back into my pocket. "I'm going to go walk the area. See if I can't trace her steps."

"We did that this morning," her father insists.

"Sometimes a fresh pair of eyes helps," I say, then offer Michael and Lance a nod before slipping outside. They both know I do better with facts than people. Not that I can't handle an interview—God knows I've done enough of them to be decent at it. But once I have the base facts, I do much better from a distance. Where I can be in the quiet of my own mind, retracing the final moments of a victim in order to discern what happened to them.

It's a bright day, the temperature perfect for a T-shirt given our spring weather. I move down the front steps, then head out onto the sidewalk in the direction Kleo's father said she runs in. I don't move much faster than a walk, though, because I want to make sure I don't miss anything.

Even the slightest of details can lead to a break in the case.

Once, a single hair clip abandoned on the sidewalk led us to a woman who'd been missing for three days. And we would likely never have found her if not for the fingerprints on it.

So, as I walk, I look for Kleo Finch's 'hair clip.'

The sidewalk is relatively trim as I keep walking, the grass clipped short on either side of it. The road isn't super busy, though enough so that if she were attacked in broad daylight, the likelihood of someone driving by and seeing the incident is high.

However, it wasn't broad daylight when she attacked. It was five in the morning, and I doubt there were many people out on the road then. No one to witness an abduction. That familiar dread coils in my belly.

I monitor the sidewalk for any scuff marks or anything that might allude to a struggle while also keeping an eye on the houses. If anyone had been out this morning, maybe they saw something.

Definitely worth knocking on doors as I make my way back to the Finches' home.

My phone rings, so I dig it out of my pocket and

check the readout. I don't recognize the number, but it could be Lance or Michael calling me from the Finches' for whatever reason, so I press it to my ear. "Payne," I answer.

"It's about time."

Every muscle in my body goes rigid, and my stomach churns at the mere sound of her voice. "Rosalie."

"So you do remember me. Here I thought that time in the hospital gave you amnesia."

"What do you want?" I pinch the bridge of my nose and stop walking, knowing that if I continue, I won't be paying near the attention I need to be.

"I want to talk to you. It's all I've been trying to do for weeks now."

"And I told you the last time we spoke that I had nothing else to say."

"Jax," she starts.

"No, Rosalie. I am working, and this is hardly the time."

"Listen—" She sighs into the phone. "I want to see you so we can clear the air. I know you're in Maine now, and I'm actually headed to New York in a couple of days for a conference. Can we meet up? I can come to you. See where you're—"

"No. There's nothing to clear."

"There is for me."

"There's not for me," I repeat. "Goodbye, Rosalie." I end the call and take a deep breath. The phone rings again, and I'm prepared to answer it and tell her just how tired I am of her constant phone calls, but the B&B's number appears on my screen. "Hey, everything okay?"

"Hey, yeah, it is now. Silas came and handled it."

Unease climbs up my spine. "Handled what?"

"Nothing important. Chad showed up, Elijah sent Silas. Chad's gone now."

"Are you okay?"

"Yeah, thanks." She hesitates a moment, as though she wants to say something else about it but changes her mind. "Anyway, you know how you offered to help earlier?"

I smile. "Vaguely."

She laughs. "I was wondering if you wouldn't mind grabbing a can of paint from Felix's on your way back? I need to do some touch-up painting later, but won't have time to get it before the hardware store closes. If not, it's okay, I can figure—"

"I don't mind." I can't help the stupid grin that adorns my face yet again, or the way I can picture her twirling the cord of her office phone around her finger because she refuses to go cordless at the B&B.

"Really?"

"Really. We're nearly done taking statements, and I can pick it up for you later. If you show me what you need painted, I can take care of that, too."

"Jaxson, you don't need to do that."

"I don't mind. Seriously. Will Felix know what color you need?"

"He will. It'll be waiting at the front counter. Thank you so much. Seriously, Jaxson. You are a lifesaver."

"It is my job. See you later, Margot."

"Bye."

The call ends, and I shove the phone back into my pocket. I'm just about to start walking again when I glance to my right and note a path of slightly bent tall grass. It's still standing, but not nearly as high as the surrounding area.

All the distractions melt away and my hand goes to the firearm at my hip. I inch closer to the path, stepping carefully so I don't disturb any possible evidence if there is something here.

The hairs on the back of my neck stand on end as a prickling awareness that I'm being watched settles over me. I glance around, trying to see if there's anyone there, but I only spot houses.

No one's on the street. No one's looking out the windows.

Still, I can't beat back the feeling as I return my attention to the tall grass. Everything in my gut screams danger, but I press forward, not wanting to spare the moments I would need to make a phone call until I know exactly why it is I'm making one.

A few feet into the tall grass, hidden away just out of sight, a young woman is lying on the ground, wearing shorts, a tank top, and running shoes. Her blonde hair is streaked with sweat and matted with grass. But I see no blood. I rush forward and kneel at her side.

"Kleo, can you hear me?" I ask, checking to feel her pulse.

Her gray eyes flutter open. "I don't—" Her eyes roll back into her head.

I monitor her pulse, noting that it's far slower than it should be, then use the tactical flashlight I always carry to check the reaction of her pupils. She appears drugged, though uninjured. I pull out my phone and call 9-1-1. "This is Jaxson Payne. I found a barely conscious twenty-one-year-old female and need an ambulance." After rattling off my location, I end the call and tap Lance's contact. "You're going to be okay," I tell her as I wait for him to answer.

"Knight."

"I've got her. About two miles up the road from her house. Ambulance has been called."

"We're on our way."

After ending the call, I shove my phone back into my pocket. Kleo tries to sit up, but she falls right back down, so I offer her assistance while monitoring the way she reacts to movement.

"Do you know what happened?" I ask her, propping her up with my bent leg at her back, the other knee down to hold us both upright.

"No. I—" She rests her chin to her chest and takes a deep breath. "I was running and—I'm so dizzy. Why am I dizzy?"

Sirens wail in the distance. "Can you remember anything?"

"No. I'm so tired." She starts to fall back, so I steady her as the ambulance pulls up right at the same time Lance's truck and her parents' small SUV stop at the curb.

"You're going to be just fine," I tell her, so thankful that it's the truth. *Thank you, God. Thank you for guiding me to this girl so she can get home to her family.*

———

"Hypoglycemia?"

"That's the one," Michael says over my Bluetooth speaker. Since Margot needed me back at the B&B, I cut out as soon as I knew Kleo was going to be okay.

Once they got her stabilized, she was able to tell them everything she remembered, which wasn't much. Apparently, she'd stopped to tie her shoe, and as she was kneeling, got dizzy. Sherrif Vick believes she must have wandered into the brush and fallen over. It's lucky I found her when I did.

While it's the more likely version of the story, especially given that there were no signs of assault, there's something about it that's still bugging me. Then again, it could just be my own case history sneaking into the recesses of my mind.

Unfortunately, there weren't many cases in LA where the pretty missing girl was found unscathed.

"Is that something that happens to her often?" I ask.

"They were all surprised," Michael replies. "So I'd say no. Doctor said it's not uncommon, though. Especially for runners. And Kleo has apparently been preparing for a full marathon and has been really careful of what she's eating. Her mom thinks she wasn't eating enough."

"Man, well, I'm glad she's okay."

"Same. So, listen, Chad was at the B&B today."

"Margot told me."

"Oh?" His tone leaves little to no room for accusation, but it makes me uneasy anyway. The last thing I want is for him to think I'm moving in on his younger sister. "She called me earlier to ask if I could pick up some paint for the B&B. She mentioned that Elijah sent Silas over when he caught Chad on the camera."

"So glad we got that facial recognition update to the cameras. Not that Elijah wouldn't have recognized him anyway. I put his face up like a BOLO."

I laugh. Mainly because Michael showed Chad's picture to each of us when the guy left town. "Same. She okay?" She'd sounded fine when I spoke to her earlier, but it's possible she was just trying to put my mind at ease. Would she have told her brother if she'd been left shaken by the visit of her ex?

"You should know, you clearly talk to her more than I do." He laughs. "Just kidding. Yeah, she's good. Anyway, Reyna and I are headed to Boston for the weekend, you need anything before we head out?"

"Nope. You two have fun."

"Great. See you Monday morning."

"See you."

The call ends just as I'm pulling in front of Felix's hardware store. Climbing out, I take a moment to stretch and breathe in the salty sea air. Living in LA, I was near the ocean, but it was never like this. The air was never quite as crisp, the weather not quite as perfect.

Here, the ocean feels like the center of this town, whereas in LA, the ocean is merely a small part of the big city. You can feel completely alone even as you're in the center of a crowd. Not in Hope Springs, though. Everyone knows everyone here, and you never feel alone.

"Hey, Mr. Payne!" Lanetti Ester, the newest waitress at Hope Diner now that Lilly is on bed rest, jogs up the sidewalk toward me. Her smile is bright, her blue eyes shining with interest.

I'm at least ten years older than her, but the age gap clearly doesn't sway her from the interest she seems to have taken in me.

I plaster a friendly smile on my face—but not too friendly—and offer her a wave. "Hey, Lanetti. On your way to work?"

"I am. You coming in for dinner tonight?"

I wish I had other plans. But as of now, I've got nothing. And the last thing I want to do is assume I'll be eating dinner with Margot and Matty. "I am."

"Great." She grins and begins to toy with a silver cherry blossom on a chain around her neck. "Well, I'll see you later then?"

"Sure thing."

She offers me another smile, then starts down the sidewalk, looking back over her shoulder as she does.

I wish I could find a way to kindly tell her I'm not interested. That even if we were closer in age, I'm still dealing with drama from my ex-wife, and a relationship is just not in the cards for me. But I have no clue how to do that and not completely crush her, so I sigh and head into the hardware store.

Felix glances up from some papers he's reading behind the counter, and a smile graces his aging face. "Hey, Jaxson, how's it going?"

"Not too bad. Margot said you have some paint for her?"

"I do." He sets the papers aside and reaches down to lift a gallon of paint from the floor. He sets it on the counter, along with a wooden paint stick and two brushes. "She doing okay?"

"Why do you ask?"

"I saw Chad earlier. He was headed into the diner."

"He there now?"

Felix shakes his head. "Alex said he left a few hours ago." Alex is married to Felix's daughter, Lilly, and the two of them own the diner. "I just want to make sure she's okay. Chad was always a troublemaker, but him leaving her and Matthew like that—I wish we could ban him from town altogether."

Chuckling, I lift the can of paint. "Maybe someday," I tell him. "Thanks for this."

"So, listen—" Felix runs a hand through his grey hair, so I set the paint can down again. "If you're interested in Margot like that, you should know that we're all really protective of her."

I've been expecting a talk like this ever since I accepted

her invitation to move into the maintenance apartment at the B&B, though to be honest, I expected it to come from Michael rather than the hardware store owner. "I'm not moving in on Margot," I tell him. "I'm not looking for a relationship. Fleeting or otherwise."

Felix runs a hand over the back of his head this time. "Sorry, I didn't mean to assume, I just—I don't want to see her hurt again."

"I get it." I smile so he knows I take no offense, then lift the paint, stick, and brushes. "Thanks again. See you around."

As I set the paint and supplies down in my truck, I stop and stare out at the ocean again. I wish I could have told him that I had no feelings for her. That my not moving in on her is because I only see her as a friend, rather than my own fear of commitment after the divorce that nearly stole everything from me.

The truth is, I feel a lot more for Margot than I should.

And it's getting a lot harder to bury those feelings.

Maybe it's time to find a new place to live.

CHAPTER 4

Margot

Stomach churning with nerves, I step into the diner. It's relatively lean tonight, but I offer a wave at Mrs. McGinley, the town's librarian, who sits in the corner with a group of her friends. All of the women glance over at me and offer smiles, but I can see the curiosity on their faces, and know it's because word got out that Chad is in town.

I received more than a few phone calls about the sightings, with people asking me if I was okay or if I needed anything.

Honestly, that's one of the things that angered me most. I became a victim in the eyes of every single person in this town. I was the poor, unsuspecting wife who waited at home for her cheating husband.

And I hate that they see me that way, even if it is the truth.

My gaze travels around the diner as I look for Chad,

but instead, my attention focuses on the handsome, dark-haired man with salt-and-pepper strands at his temples, sitting in a back booth, his nose buried in a book.

Just the mere sight of Jaxson eases some of my nerves, so instead of taking a seat at an empty booth to wait for Chad, I walk over to Jaxson and slide in across from him.

He sets the book down and offers me a smile. "Fancy seeing you here." His expression turns a bit more serious. "You okay?"

"Yeah, why?" I set my purse down.

"You look upset."

"Stop reading me, Detective," I reply with a half smile.

He chuckles. "Can't turn it off, it's my superpower."

"Fair enough. I'm just nervous. Chad is on his way here, and I have a feeling he's going to try to fight me for custody. I thought I was done with him, but apparently I'm not." I flash a smile. "And now I'm rambling."

"I like when you ramble," he replies, his deep voice making the butterflies in my stomach go feral.

How can one man have that much power with just the mere sound of his voice? "Tell me something good. Anything good that happened today."

"Mrs. O'Connell, can I get you anything?" Lanetti steps up to the table, her notepad out. I don't understand why she seems to have taken such a dislike to me recently, especially since she used to babysit Matty whenever Chad and I would go out on date nights. But lately, ever since she started working here, she treats me like a complete stranger.

And no matter how many times I try to correct her, she insists on continuing to refer to me as Mrs. O'Connell.

"Hey, Nettie, no I'm good right now. Just sitting for a minute. Thanks."

She smiles and turns her full attention to Jaxson. "Hey, Jax, refill on coffee?" Her bright smile answers the question I'd quite literally just asked myself and solves the mystery as to why she doesn't care for me. I bite back my knowing smile.

She's jealous. Of me. Which, of course, is absolutely crazy.

"No, thanks. I'm good," he replies.

"Let me know if you need anything." She turns and saunters away from the table.

I steal one of Jaxson's fries from his plate. "Someone has a crush on you."

"I don't even know how to stop it," he replies. The man looks genuinely distressed which, of course, only amuses me further.

"It'll pass. Just give it time. You're the cute new guy in town, and she's a single girl in her mid-twenties who is looking for her white knight."

"You think I'm cute?" He grins at me, so I roll my eyes.

"Of course that would be what you zero in on." I steal another fry. "Anyway, good things. Tell them to me."

"We went out to investigate a missing girl, and I found her passed out in bushes."

"Drunk?"

"No. Hypoglycemic. She'd headed out for a run in the morning, then passed out."

"Oh, man. Is she okay?"

"Going to be just fine."

"That is good news." I steal another fry, so Jaxson pushes his plate into the center of the table.

"I thought so. How was your day? Other than Chad showing up."

"Not too bad. The B&B is booked solid for the next three weeks, so that's good for business."

"Maybe you'll be able to hire some additional help," he replies. "I know you're tired."

"Maybe," I reply, not mentioning the fact that the money will barely be enough to cover some of the bills piling up.

"That's great." He looks genuinely happy for me, and seeing his interest makes my stomach twist into knots. Why couldn't Chad have been like this? Supportive, interested, faithful. Why did my marriage have to go down in flames and leave me terrified of risking another burn?

"It will be. Thanks again for grabbing that paint, by the way."

"No problem. I plan to search for the areas you need touched up when I get back. Unless, of course, you marked them for me before you left."

I eye him with fake annoyance. "You are *not* doing the labor."

"I like to paint."

"No one likes to paint that much."

"I do," he replies. "And this is me asking if you want my help."

Knowing that I really could use the hand, I take another fry. "Then I guess this is me accepting said help." I smile at him, and our gazes hold. I'm captivated by his hazel eyes, and my breath catches. Oh, God, why does he have to be so beautiful?

A bell dings in the distance. "Your husband is here," Lanetti says as she stops by the table.

I blink quickly, trying to clear the desire I feel for the former detective from my system. "Ex-husband," I correct. "Thanks, Netti."

"Uh-huh." She beams at Jaxson again, then walks away.

I glance back at Chad, who has clearly not noticed me as he slides into a booth a few down from ours, his back to us.

"You going to be okay?" Jaxson asks.

"Fine. If I yell *strawberry*, that's my 'I need help' word. Come rescue me."

He laughs. "Done. You got this. If you want me to stay until he leaves—"

"Actually. I do. If you don't mind. Chad is—"

"You don't need to explain," he interrupts. "I'm here for you." As he picks his book back up, I swallow hard and stand, then make my way over to the booth where Chad is sitting.

"Hey, sorry, were you sitting somewhere else?" he asks, glancing around the diner.

"Just visiting a friend." I move into the seat across from him, and fully focus on my ex-husband. "What did you want to talk about?"

"Mr. and Mrs. O'Connell, so good to see you. What can I get you guys?" Lanetti is far more cheerful now that I'm not sitting with Jaxson, and I can't help but be annoyed.

"It's Ms. Anderson now," I finally correct her. It's one thing to refer to me by that name when I'm alone, but something else entirely when I'm sitting across from Chad. "And I'll take a burger and fries, please. To go."

"A grilled chicken salad for me. Watching my weight," Chad jokes.

Lanetti laughs. "You have nothing to watch, Mr. O'Connell. Still look like you're in high school." She winks and leaves the table.

"I always did like her."

"I'm sure you did." Once again, the alcohol stench is so pungent it makes my stomach churn. He's drunk. Again. Of course he is.

He crosses his arms. "What's that supposed to mean?"

She's pretty and young. Just your type. "Nothing. Can we just get to what this is about, please? I have people staying at the B&B, and I need to get back."

Chad rolls his eyes. "You always have to have control, don't you?"

"Excuse me?"

"I come to you asking if we can talk, and you're trying to control the way I do it. It's so typical."

My throat burns as I try to bite back my embarrassment, noting a few people looking at us. "I'm not trying to control anything. I just don't like my time wasted."

"I haven't even told you what I want to discuss, and you order your food to go, like it's not going to take any more than a few minutes."

Truthfully, I'm not even sure why I ordered anything since the last thing I am is hungry. But it seemed like the thing to do. "As I said, I have things to do. Now what do you want to talk about?" I keep my gaze averted to my hands, something I would do whenever we were fighting.

And why am I doing that now? Why give him the satisfaction of knowing he upset me? I force my gaze to meet his and stare him straight in the eyes.

"Our divorce was filed so quickly I don't feel like I had time to fully process what was happening before it was over."

"You're the one who left. How did our divorce take you by surprise?"

He leans in. "You threw me out."

"Do we really need to discuss *why* I threw you out? Even before that, you were cheating and coming home so drunk you could barely stand."

Anger flickers in his gaze. "We'd been together so long, I thought you'd want to at least give us time to come back around."

I gape at him. I can't help it. How is he blaming this on me? "You cheated on me."

"I apologized. You kicked me out."

"You'd already been on your way out the door when

that happened and we both know it," I snap. The warning is there, the underlying understanding that if he pushes too hard, I have no issue telling everyone what the final straw was that sent him packing.

"Either way. I've had time to think about it, and I realized you made out with everything in the divorce and I got nothing."

"Nothing?" I choke on the word. "You don't pay child support. You don't pay alimony. I had to sell our house to afford to keep the B&B open, and I have worked my fingers to the bone to keep it since. But you got *nothing?*"

"I had to leave my job for you to start your ridiculous money pit. You kept Matty—"

"You left us when you followed *her* out of this town!" I yell, slamming both hands onto the table.

His cheeks turn red as he looks around to see who's watching. "Keep your voice down, Margot. This is not anyone else's business."

I take a deep breath to steady myself, trying to calm the rage burning in my chest. "You cheated on me. You left Matty behind. Do not come in here acting like I threw you out for no reason and slammed the door on you on your way out."

"You got the B&B. I didn't take a cut from you even though selling our house is what helped you keep that ridiculous place. And you kept full custody."

"Because you signed your rights away!"

"I didn't think I had a choice!"

He's lying. I know it. He knows it. Everyone in here

probably knows it. Signing his parental rights away to avoid child support had been his idea. He'd asked me to keep Matty because his son reminded him too much of me. He'd actually told me that seeing Matty would be a reminder of the jail cell I kept him imprisoned in since the moment he got me pregnant.

"I cannot believe you're saying this." I shake my head as tears burn in my eyes.

I will not cry.

Not out of sadness. Or anger. Or frustration.

"I want what is owed to me."

"And just what do you think that is?" I demand. "What do I have that you want?"

"Partial custody of Matty. And half of the profit of the sale of our house."

I gape at him. "No. Absolutely not."

"I thought you would say that." He reaches onto the seat beside him and hands me a manila folder. "Papers that I'm filing. I'll see you in court."

"Here's your food." Lanetti sets his plate and my Styrofoam container down, but I barely register it as I stare down at the manila folder.

"You're taking me to court?"

"Yes. I want what's mine."

I don't even realize I'm standing until I slam both hands down onto the table and lean in, aggression lacing my tone. I could strangle him. Bury him in the backyard or throw him into the ocean, I'm so angry. "What's *yours*? How about what was *mine*! How about promises you made to me and Matty? How about that?" I scream at him, my cheeks heating.

"You're making a scene," he growls, and his hand tightens into a fist on the table. It's not meant as a threat, I get that, but I take it as one.

"You will *not* get custody of Matty. Do you understand me? Not while I'm still breathing, and not even once I'm gone. The only way he will see you is if he chooses to. I swear to you, Chad, you will *never* get another thing from me."

"That's for the court to decide." His gaze lifts to someone behind me, and I know that Jaxson is there. I can feel the warmth of his body, the steady presence of Jaxson Payne. "This is none of your business, Payne," Chad snarls.

"No, it's not. And I'll walk away if Margot wants me to."

"No. I don't." Straightening, I grab my purse. "I'll see you in court, Chad." Mortified that I let my anger get the better of me, I storm out of the diner. I don't have to look behind me to know that Jaxson followed.

Nor do I need confirmation that he walks quietly behind me all the way across the street and toward the pier overlooking the ocean. I grip the wooden railing and breathe deeply, trying to steady my mood.

How can this be happening?

How did Chad even manage to find a lawyer to take his case?

And then I remember—his mistress was going to law

school. Is that what happened? I open the manila folder and glare down at the name of his legal representation.

Chelsea Brogan.

"You have got to be kidding me." I start to fling the papers into the ocean when a large hand closes over mine. Heat shoots up my arm, attraction eating away at the anger. Our gazes meet for a moment, then Jaxson plucks the papers from my hands, releasing me.

"I'll hold onto those." Jaxson slides them back into the folder, then folds it and tucks it into his back pocket.

"He's using his mistress to sue me. He's coming after custody of Matty and twenty thousand dollars that I don't have." A tear rolls down my cheek. "The hits just keep coming. Why do they keep coming? Why is this so hard?" *Jesus, please help me. I can't do this. I can't carry this alone.*

Jaxson is silent a moment, likely processing everything I said, then he turns toward me. "I'm divorced."

It's honestly news to me, since he keeps his personal life under wraps and I never wanted to pry. When Michael told me I could trust him, I did because my brother's words are solid. "I didn't know that."

"Yeah. It was a nasty divorce. She cheated on me—multiple times—and I gave her everything because I kept trying to hang on to what was already gone."

Cheating never made any sense to me. If you make vows, you should honor them. Still, I managed to find faults in myself that I used to excuse Chad's behavior. I put on a few extra pounds. I wasn't available to him as often as he needed me… It was a vicious cycle, and one I still fight with. But the mere idea that anyone would cheat on the man beside me is outrageous.

He follows God, is kind. Strong. Loyal. Everything that a man should be.

So what kind of fool would sacrifice that?

"She reached out to me recently and has been trying to get me to meet up so we can talk ever since."

"So what you're saying is that there's something in the water that's bringing exes out of the woods and back into our lives like the wrecking balls they are."

He laughs. "Something like that. I just wanted you to know that I get it. I get how it feels to fight for that piece of yourself stolen by their infidelity. How hard it is sometimes just to get out of bed in the morning because you can't understand what it was about you that drove them away."

"I came to terms with the fact that I wasn't enough for him. I just don't know why he has to come back and torment me all over again. Why can't he leave us be?"

"Margot."

I turn to face him, and Jaxson reaches up to brush some of my hair behind my ears. I shiver at the contact. The feel of his fingers gently gliding over my cheek. My gaze locks with his, and I lose the ability to breathe for a moment.

"You are not the one who was lacking," he says softly. "Any man would be blessed to have you as their wife. Matty as their son. As far as Chad coming back now? He's bored. Looking for a fight. And probably realizing that he walked out on the two best people in the world when he left you and Matty behind."

His gaze drops to my mouth, and I get the slightest inclination that he might kiss me. Would I pull away? Turn my head?

No. I know I wouldn't. Because even as afraid as I am to get burned again, the pull I feel toward Jaxson Payne is far stronger than my desire to avoid more pain.

He clears his throat and looks away. "So, we have some painting to do?"

I smile. "We do."

He starts to hand me the papers, then hesitates.

I laugh. "I won't throw them in the ocean, I promise." I take them from him. "Meet you back at the B&B?"

"Definitely." Jaxson begins walking, and I fall into step beside him. As I steal a glance his way, I let myself imagine —if only for a moment—how it would feel to be cherished by a man like him.

CHAPTER 5

Jaxson

After a late night of helping Margot around the B&B, working as quietly as we could so as not to disturb sleeping guests, I'd slept better than I have in years. Add to that the great run I just wrapped up and a morning of watching the sun rise, and my mood is pretty solid.

I also received an email late last night from the Finches thanking me again for finding Kleo, and an update that she is back to her normal self, though she did promise to take things easy in the near future.

God was watching over her, and I pray He continues to do so.

With the stress having melted off of me, I head up the steps toward the B&B. Margot will be up by now and probably having a cup of coffee, and if I time it right, I might get to enjoy a bit of her company before having to shower and head into the office to start my day.

Maybe she'll have a better one too. It is a fresh day, after all, and she certainly seemed to be in better spirits when we'd finally called it a night.

I open the door and stop dead in my tracks when I hear the voice of the man standing across from the check-in desk, engaged in a conversation with Margot.

I'll never forget the sound of his voice. Not as long as I live.

"What are you doing here?" I demand.

Margot's gaze lifts to mine, her expression confused.

The man turns to face me, his face aged, yet somehow still the exact same. "Hi, Jax."

"You two know each other?" Margot asks curiously. Her gaze flickers from him to me, then back to him.

"This is Bradley Payne," I tell her, then turn my attention back to him. "You're forcing me to repeat my question. Why are you here?"

"I want to talk to you."

"And I want nothing to do with you. Get out."

"Jaxson."

"No."

"I'm not leaving until you talk to me. So I can either sit right here in this kind woman's lobby until you do, or we can get this out of the way now."

I would love to call him on it. See just how long he'd be willing to sit here before running out like he did last time. But the last thing Margot needs is a scene made in the lobby of her B&B. "Fine. You have two minutes." I turn and head toward the door.

Because I don't want her to see my anger, I don't look at Margot as I walk past the desk and back outside, into the early morning. I don't bother to hold the door for Bradley as he follows me out, nor do I look back at him as I head across the small parking lot and toward the top of the steps I'd happily climbed mere minutes ago.

"It's good to see you, son," he says.

"No. You don't get to call me that." I turn to face him. I stand an inch taller than him now, and he's far slimmer than I remember him being. Then again, maybe that was the terrified boy I'd been, looking up at a man he saw as a monster.

"You're my blood," he replies.

"Which meant nothing to you then, and it means nothing to me now."

"Tyler and I have made amends."

"Tyler wasn't the one you nearly beat to death." I snarl, taking a step closer. "Tyler wasn't the one who had to step up and be a man and provider at the age of sixteen because you and Elizabeth couldn't bother to be parents."

"I was out of my mind drunk when I did that," he says. "I never would have put hands on you sober."

"And that makes it better?" I have to take a deep breath. *Please, God, help me control my anger before I do something I will regret.* "Either way, it doesn't matter. It's in the past. I've moved on, and I suggest you do the same."

"I want to apologize. I want to make things right."

"Fine. You're forgiven. Now leave me alone." I start past him, and he wraps a hand around my arm. I freeze in place as fresh anger washes over me. "I suggest you take your hand off of me, Bradley. I am not the boy I was the last time you grabbed me like that."

He lets me go, then shoves both hands into his pockets. "I just want to make amends."

"There are no amends to be made," I reply. "I've forgiven you because it's what I'm supposed to do. Truth is, I did a long time ago. But that doesn't mean I have to have you in my life."

Hazel eyes, so like my own, fill with tears. "I'm dying."

The confession hits me harder than I'd have guessed it would. "Then take your deathbed confession to a preacher, Bradley. Get right with God, and leave me be." I push past him and back into the B&B, leaving him standing down by the cliffside.

My chest feels like someone dropped an anvil on it, so I don't even notice that Margot has followed me into my apartment until I'm turning to close the door and she's moving inside.

"I am so sorry. I didn't know his name. We hadn't gotten that far. He just came in asking for a room and we got to talking about the beach and—" She stops talking and stares up at me. "I am so sorry, Jaxson. I never would have let him in the door if I'd known who he was."

But we both know she would have. Not to hurt me, but Margot is far too kind to close the door fully on anyone. It's why Chad has managed to get a foot back into it.

"It's not your fault." I head over to the small mini

fridge and withdraw a bottle of water. She shakes her head when I offer her one.

"Are you okay? What did he want?"

I haven't told her anything about my past until last night, and I've no plans to start opening myself up further. Not when the wounds are far too raw from being ripped right open this morning. "We had a falling out, and now he's dying and trying to get back in my good graces."

She covers her mouth with a hand and her eyes go wide. "Oh, Jaxson, I am so sorry!" Before I can stop her—not that I would—she wraps both arms around me and holds on. Slowly, I return the affection, mainly because holding her feels as familiar as breathing, even if this is the first time.

I never want it to end.

She pulls away and looks up at me. "Are you okay? Do you need to talk?"

"I'm—" My phone rings, the shrill tone cutting through the moment. I start to ignore it, but then see Lance's name on the readout. "Payne," I answer gruffly.

"We've got a break-in at the Pillar residence. Can you meet me at her place?"

"Sure thing." I end the call. "I'm sorry, work calls. I have to go."

Margot smiles softly at me. "I'm here if you need me, Jaxson. I hear venting is what friends do for each other."

Her repeating words I spoke to her just yesterday warms my heart. "I know. Thanks."

She offers me a smile, then leaves my room, shutting

the door behind her. I continue staring after it, recalling the way her arms felt around me. The way holding her made it feel—just for a moment—like everything was right with the world.

"I didn't notice anything," Emigh Pillar says as she bounces a baby on her hip. Her blonde hair is twisted up in a messy bun, and she's still wearing her scrubs from her shift at the hospital.

She's a single mother, her daughter just turning one. She lives alone, so no one set off the alarm by accident, and as far as she knows, no one was trying to get in. "It just started going off, so I grabbed Ollie and ran into the closet to get my gun."

"Elijah is running security camera footage now," Lance tells her as he closes his notepad.

"We didn't see anything when we pulled up," Deputy Wallace says. He was Lance's first call since they're closer than we were. "No one was fleeing the house, and we were here within minutes once we got your call."

"I'm going to take another walk outside," I tell them, then head out the front. According to Elijah, it was a window tamper alarm that went off first, so I head around the back of the house through a side gate.

The yard is small, though green. There is no mud, so no footprints to track, and the gate that backs up to a creek is locked from the inside. So either it's a faulty sensor, or someone managed to get in and out of the back or side gate undetected.

I start at the window closest to the side entry gate, noting that there are no signs of tampering.

Then I creep along the side of the house, checking the windows, looking into the living room and the half bathroom.

It's not until I reach Ollie's window that I sense something off. The curtains are partially open, so I can clearly see the crib and a basket of toys on the rug in the center of the room.

Slipping a glove onto my hand, I lean in closer, noting tiny scratch marks on the corners of the windows, right near the sensors. To set them off, the perpetrator doesn't even have to fully open the window. Any type of unnatural vibration will set them off.

If someone tries to pry the window open? The alarm goes off before they manage to make progress.

Which is exactly what looks like happened here. I turn in a slow circle, trying to track the easiest route out of here. Maybe they got caught on a branch as they were fleeing the scene. Definitely hoping for some DNA or torn fabric. Anything that could lead us closer to whoever was trying to get into baby Ollie's window.

My stomach churns with unease.

How sick do you have to be to target an innocent child?

Or was it the mother they were after, and they figured the baby's room was the easiest way in?

Using the half wall to hoist myself up over the fence, I

drop down onto the other side near the creek bed. Here, the trees and brush are thick, but there are a few paths that teens are likely using to sneak in and out of houses.

I turn toward the gate—and freeze in place.

Taped to the outside of the gate is a two of hearts.

My blood runs cold, every single nerve in my body firing at once. I draw my weapon, then reach into my pocket with my free hand and call Lance. It's all I can do to keep my movements steady.

"What is it?"

"Get the key and come out the back gate. Now. Keep Emigh inside with the deputy."

He doesn't ask questions. Doesn't demand clarification. "On it." The call ends, and I shove the phone back into my pocket as I study the tree line. Is the person who left this watching me now? Admiring the fact that they got my attention?

"I'm going to find you," I call out to whoever left the card. "This will not end well for you."

"You good?" Lance calls out from the other side of the gate.

"Yeah. Don't open it yet." I turn back toward the gate, scanning the sides, top, and bottom for any kind of trap, then call out, "Okay, you're good."

Lance unlocks the gate and opens it slowly. His gaze lands on the playing card. "What is that?"

"It's the calling card of a serial killer I put away. He was my last case before I moved out here. Every card we found was one more than the last. He used them to count his victims."

But why leave it here? Is he trying to get my attention? Freak me out? Or is this just the way it starts?

"Do you think this is him?" Lance questions.

"I don't know. He's serving multiple life sentences, and I haven't heard anything about an escape." I make a mental note to call my former partner Alaric as soon as we leave.

"It's possible it's a copycat."

"The calling card was never made public," I tell him. "The only people who knew about it—aside from him—were me, my partner, and the DA."

"He could have told someone."

Somehow, the idea that there's a second killer on the loose is even more sickening than the idea that Gil Morah got out. The former high school band instructor managed to fly under the radar for months, but now that I've caught him once, I know every move he would make.

If it's him, I have every confidence that I'll find him quickly.

However, if this is a new killer, someone who's only using the calling card and going after—"Blondes." I look at Lance. "Morah went after blondes."

"Emigh is blonde."

"So is Kleo."

"Kleo? The doctor said she was hypoglycemic."

"But what if she's not? What if he drugged her somehow."

"You said the guy is a killer, though. So far, no one is dead."

I look at the card, noting the number two printed in bright red ink. "So far," I say. "But if this is Morah or someone like him, it won't stay that way for long."

With Emigh agreeing to stay with her parents, and Deputy Wallace putting patrols on their house, I finally feel at ease enough to leave and head back to the B&B. Where I've been sitting in the parking lot for the last ten minutes, going over every note I wrote down about Kleo Finch's disappearance and the attempted break-in at Emigh Pillar's house.

Though the more I look at the photos I took of the window, the more I don't think it was an attempted break-in at all. They are too meticulous. Scratches made with the sharp edge of something without bothering to pry at the actual window.

I think whoever did it was trying to set the alarm off to get my attention.

My gut is telling me that whoever is doing this is toying with me. Trying to get me hyper focused on them so I'll miss something.

But what?

Is it possible Kleo wasn't number one, and I've yet to find whoever he went after first? Elijah is looking into missing women who match the description of those he used to target.

My cell rings, so I withdraw it and breathe a sigh of relief at the name on the screen. "Thanks for calling me back," I answer.

"Yeah, of course," my old partner, Alaric Newman, replies. We'd worked side-by-side for nearly a decade before I left LA behind to move out here and join Knight Security. "How are things in your tiny town?"

"Busy. You?"

"Not bad," he replies. "Wrenley is pregnant again, this time with twins, so we're prepping the house."

I laugh. "You did always say you wanted a soccer team."

"You ain't lying, my friend. I'm well on my way there." He laughs. "So what's up? Your message sounded urgent."

"We've had a two of hearts playing card left taped to a gate at the scene of an attempted break-in."

Alaric mutters something under his breath. "Copycat?"

"I don't see how. Unless Morah has had visitors in prison or managed to recruit someone before we caught him."

"I can look into that for you. Pull visitor's logs and everything at the prison. How many bodies?"

"None so far. We only found the one card, but we had a possible kidnapping victim who was found unconscious on the side of a road in some brush and an attempted break-in."

"Which is where you found the card."

"Yeah." I'm operating on the understanding that Kleo was likely victim number one. Maybe he got interrupted before he could grab her. Or maybe she was a way to draw me out—I'm not sure. But I can't help but believe they are connected.

They have to be.

"No bodies, this isn't like Morah."

"I don't think whoever is doing this is trying to kill anyone. Not yet, anyway. I think they're toying with me."

"Brought some LA to small-town Maine, huh?"

My stomach twists. "Apparently."

"Well, listen, I'll look into it for you and let you know what I find."

"I appreciate that. Thanks. Good to talk to you."

"You, too. Try to call me for something other than a case now and then, yeah?"

I chuckle. "Sure thing. Talk soon. Tell Wren I said hi." I end the call and take a deep breath before climbing out of my truck and locking the door, then unlocking the front door of the B&B. Since it's well past eleven at night, Margot has closed everything down, so I'm quiet as I make my way into the kitchen.

A bright green sticky note stuck to the counter catches my eye. With a grin, I lift it, reading Margot's familiar handwriting.

You didn't make it home for dinner, so there's leftover spaghetti in the fridge. I also grabbed a pie from Kira's Bakery and managed to save you a piece. Enjoy! -Margot

The stress of the day melts away at the mere idea that

she was thinking about me after what happened this morning with Bradley. And, with a smile still on my face, I head down the hall and toward her office where I still see a light.

My affection for her grows when I move into her office space and see her sleeping at her desk, her head down, the black-rimmed glasses she occasionally wears partially off of her face. Her hair is braided over her shoulder, and she's wearing green flannel pants and a sweatshirt.

She's beautiful.

Perfect.

It nearly hurts me to see. Moving forward quietly, I stop beside her, then glance down briefly at what she was working on.

I see a manila folder open with the papers Chad brought to her, as well as a list of bills written on a tablet, alongside a bunch of outstanding notices beside her. My heart aches when I note the total cost circled at the bottom. Twelve thousand dollars. Is she struggling more than she let on? She'd had to let go of what little staff she had, I knew that, but is it worse than I thought?

My thoughts drift to the bank account I've been saving money to buy my own place. I could help her. Offer to cover the cost and just stay here for a bit longer. But Margot is prideful. Would she accept my help?

And how would I even begin to offer it?

Reaching forward, I finish removing her glasses. She groans and turns into my touch, and I still, not wanting the moment to end.

How I would love to gather her into my arms and sleep right beside her.

But I can't. She's not for me.

I should leave her here, cover her with a blanket and go up to my apartment to take an ice-cold shower. No, colder than ice-cold. Is that a thing?

But I remember the last time she fell asleep in here she ended up with a tension headache that lasted her three days.

So, even as a voice in my head is screaming *danger*, I reach down and gather her into my arms. As I do, she groans and comes half awake. "Jaxson?"

"Hey, you fell asleep in your office. I'm just taking you to your apartment."

"Oh, okay." Half asleep, she loops an arm around my neck and lays her head against my chest. I want this. Forever. "Did you get the pie?"

I chuckle. "Not yet."

"It's really good." She's still half asleep, so her voice is a bit more gravelly than normal. What I would give to listen to her talk forever.

Carefully, I shift her enough so I can grab the keys off her desk, then make my way through the back of her office. I carefully shift her again so that I can unlock the door without waking Matty up.

Quietly closing the door with my foot, I carry her through her living room and into the back bedroom that serves as her space. I can smell her lavender shampoo the moment I step across the threshold, and desire churns in my gut.

I set Margot on top of her bed, then cover her with a blanket and start to back away. I need space. Distance. Fresh air. Because right now, being in her space, my mind is a foggy mess. I could lean down and kiss her right now, press my lips to hers for just a taste.

But that wouldn't be what either of us needs.

"Wait." She grips my hand, and I stop walking. I couldn't move even if I wanted to. The feel of her slender fingers against my calloused palm is too much. Too overwhelming. "Did you see the pie?" she asks again.

"I saw the note. Thanks."

"Yeah." A bit more awake now, she releases me and stretches with a yawn. "There's spaghetti too. I can heat you up some." She starts to move the blanket, but I quickly cover her hand to stop her.

"I can do it. You get some sleep."

Her gaze narrows on me. "Is everything okay?"

I long to ask her about the bills piling up. About letting me help shoulder some of this burden, but I'm not sure now is the best time. So, I ignore the warning bells going off in my mind and reach forward to brush the hair from her face. "It will be."

Her lips part.

The thought of kissing her assaults me again.

I swallow hard and pull away. "Goodnight, Margot."

"YOU REALLY THINK THIS COULD BE THE SAME GUY?" LANCE asks as he swings on the heavy bag I'm holding.

"It's possible." I step away to grab a swig of water, and Lance does the same. "But my old partner is a great cop. If there's a link, he'll find it."

"Elijah is looking into it, too. He's trying to see if he can find any connections between our current cases and your old ones."

"Great." I take a seat on the edge of a stool. "If I brought trouble here—"

"Don't take too much credit," Lance replies. "Trouble was always here." He smiles at me, trying to put my mind at ease, but all it does is cement my fears. Lance is the best guy I know. The man lives his life by faith. Walking with God and trying to do everything according to His plan. He's a brand-new dad though. What if the danger I brought here puts his family at risk?

"Not like this."

"It'll all be okay," Lance says. "God has a plan, and He will guide us where we need to go."

"I wish I had your faith."

"You do have my faith. You're just struggling to hold on to it right now because you're distracted by the worry." He clasps me on the back. "How are things with Margot?"

"What do you mean?"

Lance arches a brow. "Michael may be blind when it comes to your interest in his little sister, but I'm not. I see the way you look at her."

"She's Michael's younger sister."

"And she's a grown woman with her own feelings."

"No. I'm not going there."

"But you care for her."

"Of course I do. She's a good person. She deserves to be happy. We're—friends." I couldn't help the hesitation, and I know Lance didn't miss it.

"You deserve to be happy, too, Jax. You're one of the best men I know."

"I'm divorced."

"Remember after Eliza's lighthouse burned down and we had that drive for her at the church? You called me out for my feelings for her even as I tried to deny them."

"Because you were wearing them on your face. So was she."

"And I'm only returning the favor. Anyone around you two more than five seconds can sense a connection, Jax."

"We're friends. I'm not looking for a relationship. Not after everything Rosalie put me through."

"Not every woman is out to break your heart."

"She didn't just break my heart. She broke me. I was still in a wheelchair when she left me." Lance doesn't respond. "I had to sign divorce papers while not knowing if I would ever walk again."

"I'm sorry, man. But she wasn't your only chance at love. If you care for Margot, then don't you think you deserve to know if she feels the same?"

"Bradley Payne showed up at the B&B," I blurt. Partly to change the subject, and partly because I'm really struggling with letting go of what he told me, and I'm not sure how to go about moving forward with my life now knowing what I do.

"Your dad?"

"Bradley," I correct. "But yeah." I take a swig of my water bottle.

"What did he want?"

"To make amends and tell me he's dying."

"Man." Lance shakes his head. "You okay?"

"Why wouldn't I be? I haven't seen or spoken to the man since he abandoned Tyler and me. I couldn't care less."

"That's not true, and we both know it."

Always one to call me out when I'm trying to glaze over something, Lance doesn't let me get away with that one. "Fine. I don't know why I care."

"He's your dad. Good or bad, that's a fact that carries its own weight."

"I don't want anything to do with him."

"I believe that," Lance replies. "But that doesn't mean you have to carry the heaviness of anger around with you."

After taking another drink of water, I set my bottle aside. "There was a time I wanted so badly to beat him bloody." The admission feels like a weight off of me. "Honestly, had this happened before I actively started to grow in my faith, I might have."

Lance lets out a laugh. "I guess there's a reason God timed it for now."

"Maybe." I take a seat on a bench ringside. "I don't want to be angry."

"Then give it to God," he replies. "Pray about it, and do what you need to do in order to move past it. We can't change what's happened to us in the past, but we can open our hearts so God can heal them."

"It all sounds so easy when you say it."

"It's not," Lance replies with a laugh. "It will be one of the hardest things you've ever done. But it's worth it."

CHAPTER 6

Margot

"So this is a local beach that's relatively unknown to tourists." I circle a spot on the map and smile at the young couple across from me. They're visiting from Dallas, Texas, a bucket list trip for her on their first wedding anniversary.

"Thank you so much. We're so excited to get some time in the sun." She smiles at her husband, who grins right back. The love between them makes even a cynic like me long for that type of affection.

And why does Jaxson Payne come to mind?

"Well, this is going to be the best place to do it. It's relatively quiet, though you'll have some local teens there as soon as school lets out. The weather may not be hot yet, but it's perfect for beach lounging." I fold up the map and offer it to her husband.

"Thank you so much, Margot. Seriously. You've been so amazing."

The phone rings. "You're welcome, Shelly. Have fun, you guys. We'll see you later." After waving them off, I answer the phone. "Hello?" Nothing. "Hello?" I ask again.

When no one answers, I set the receiver down and make a note for myself to check on the status of Chad's lawsuit with Beckett Wallace, my lawyer and one of my oldest friends. I haven't heard anything since I sent the papers to her, and she promised to make my ex wish he'd never met me in the first place.

Given all that I know she's capable of, I've no doubt she will.

Desperate for a jolt of caffeine, I move around the counter and head for the kitchen. I've only taken a few steps when I hear the bell ding over my front door.

So close. I'm coming for you, coffee. Abandoning my mission to caffeinate, I head back into the main lobby, but the smile I've plastered on turns genuine when I see that it's Jaxson walking in. "Hey, I was just about to grab some coffee. Want some?"

"Sure, thanks."

He's dressed for the gym, looking beyond attractive in dark gray basketball shorts and a black sleeveless shirt, his hair a mess from running his hands through it while he boxed. Which I only know he was doing because I walked past Michael's gym on my way to the bakery for muffins this morning.

I had to stop and watch for a few moments, even though I have no idea how I would've explained ogling him had I been caught.

After grabbing two mugs from the cabinet, I fill each with steaming black liquid, then offer him his and prep mine.

He still doesn't speak.

I turn to face him. "So what's going on? How's your day so far?"

"Margot, are you struggling to keep this place open?"

His question catches me off guard. I stare at him for a moment. "What?"

He sets the mug aside and runs a hand over the back of his neck. "I saw the bills on your desk last night. I didn't mean to. I was just checking on you, and they were right there."

Embarrassment flushes my cheeks, and I have to look away. I can't be mad at him, of course, because it's not his fault they were right there and I'd fallen asleep on them. But why, oh why, God, did he have to see them? "It's nothing I can't handle." I force a smile.

"Margot."

"Jaxson. Seriously. I can do this."

"I'm not saying you can't," he replies.

"Then why are you asking? Are you worried about finding another place to stay if I close my doors? Because that's not going to happen." Suddenly, I'm not spiraling over my debt, but at the idea of not seeing Jaxson Payne every day.

He moves in close enough that I can make out the flecks of color in his hazel gaze. "I'm asking because I'd like to help you. If you're open to it."

"You're already helping me."

"I know, but that's different. I have money saved up, more than enough to cover what you owe and help—"

"Absolutely not." I shake my head. "You will not be giving me a dime."

"Margot."

"Did you tell Michael?" I ask, pride forcing me to feel beyond vulnerable. I hate it.

"Of course not." He steps back. "It's not my place."

"You're right. It's not." I really shouldn't be angry. I know Jaxson well enough to know that his offer comes from a good place. But his desire to help too closely mirrors Chad telling me that I won't ever be able to keep this place going without him.

Which is exactly what he said to me when I told him to get out.

"I only want to help you, Margot. You can consider it an advance of my rent."

"An advance of your—" I do some quick calculations. "That would be fifteen years of rent at your current rate."

"Then raise it," he insists. "I told you when you offered me the maintenance apartment that you weren't charging me enough."

"You help me around here, that more than covers it."

"Some paint here and there, changing out a lightbulb, that doesn't account for the difference, Margot. Please, I'm asking you to let me help you. I can and I want to."

"I have a separate account that I can borrow from if I

need to," I tell him, though only I know that I will never touch Matty's college fund. Not even to save my dream.

"Margot. I'm not asking to be involved in your business, and I promise we'll never speak about it again. You can even pay me back if you want. But let me help you so you don't lose this place."

I consider his offer. The kindness he's already shown me.

And then the front door opens and Matty strolls in. He stops when he sees us, his gaze going from me to Jaxson, then back to me. "What's going on?"

"Nothing, honey. Just a serious conversation."

Matty's gaze narrows on Jaxson. "Is everything okay?" he asks, looking back at me.

"Yes, of course." I force a smile, then turn to Jaxson. "We'll finish the conversation later."

"Of course." Jaxson heads up the stairs to his apartment, and even though I long to look back at him, I don't.

"Hungry?" I ask Matty.

"What's going on, Mom?"

"What do you mean, honey?" I try to keep my tone level as I pull some cookies out of the jar and place them on a plate for my son.

"I know something's up. You keep trying to hide things from me, but I know something's wrong, so what is it? Did Jaxson say something to hurt you?"

My son, my sweet boy, stands and starts toward the door, ready to take on a man twice his size.

"No, no, no, honey. Not at all. Jaxson was trying to help."

He turns toward me. "Help with what?"

I sigh. I could keep it from him. Tell him a half-truth that downplays the entire situation. But it's Matty's life, too. "Remember a few months ago when we had that pipe that broke upstairs?"

"Yeah."

"And before that when the ice storm hit and the old tree that was outside fell onto the house so we'd needed the roof repaired?"

"Yeah," he repeats.

"Well, between the deductibles, the monthly bills, and a few other incidentals, I've got a mountain of debt I'm currently dealing with." I leave out the debt I discovered that Chad took out in my name—the seven-thousand-dollar credit card balance that didn't even make the list Jaxson saw.

"Mom. Why didn't you tell me?"

"The last thing I want to do is burden you with stuff like this. It's mine to figure out, and I will. Jaxson just happened to stumble across some of the bills, and he was offering to help."

"Did you take him up on it?"

"What? No. This is my thing to deal with."

"But, Mom." Matty reaches over and touches my hand. Other than the occasional hug, it's the first time he's initiated contact like this. "Jaxson wants to help."

"He's been enough of a help lately."

"Fine. Sure. But if he wants to help, why not let him?"

"Because these aren't his problems."

"I just don't get it. You tell me all the time if I need help to ask for it. You need help. You're already running this place practically by yourself and you won't let me do hardly anything."

"You have school."

"Yeah, I know, but still. Why can't you accept Jaxson's help when he's clearly offering it?"

I can't bring myself to tell him that it's because even though I *know* Jaxson is not Chad, the idea of allowing a man to have even the illusion he helped get me out of a bind is terrifying. I never want anyone to have anything like that to hold over my head ever again.

"Jaxson isn't Dad, Mom. If he were, he would have bailed already."

I meet his gaze. "What?" Had I said something out loud?

"I'm not stupid. I know that's what you're worried about. I heard some of your fights with Dad. He threw this place in your face over and over again. But Jaxson's not like that."

Jaxson's words come rushing back. *"Margot. I'm not asking to be involved in your business, and I promise we'll never speak about it again. You can even pay me back if you want. But let me help you so you don't lose this place."*

"No," I admit, defeated. "He's not Dad."

WITH A HEAPING PLATE OF COOKIES AND A FRESH CUP OF coffee, I make my way upstairs and down the hall to the maintenance apartment at the very top of the house. Until Chad, I was never prideful. But now, accepting help feels like acid against my skin.

Before I can talk myself out of what I'm about to do, I knock.

A few seconds later, Jaxson is pulling open the door, wearing dark jeans and a white T-shirt, his dark hair wet from the shower he must have just finished. "Everything okay?" he asks, eyeing the cookies then me.

"May I come in?"

"Sure." He steps aside so I can move into his apartment.

I've been in here a few times since he moved in, but with the nerves churning in my belly. I take a moment to study the room, averting my gaze in hopes it will help ease the discomfort that has me wanting to run right back out the door.

"Is everything okay?" he asks, then crosses over and takes a seat on the edge of his made bed to put on boots.

"I want to start by apologizing."

He arches a brow. "You have nothing to apologize for."

"No, I do. You've never been anything but kind and helpful, and it wasn't my intention to make you think I thought little of you or your offer."

"I didn't think you did," he replies. "I just figured you were like your brother—stubborn."

He flashes me a grin that completely disarms me. "I

don't want Michael or my parents to know that I'm having trouble. I never told them about—" I take a deep breath. I have to trust that he won't divulge my secrets. "Chad took out a credit card in my name, and I've been treading water ever since. I made some big payments to it, which drained my savings account, and then I was hit with—"

"You don't have to explain," he interrupts as he gets to his feet. "We're friends and you could use—not need—the help."

"I need it," I reply. "Or I'm going to lose this place."

"Tell me what you need."

"Before we get to that, I want to tell you that if you decide you can't help me, it's okay. I can try and get a bank loan, sell my car, whatever I need to do. I don't want this to affect our friendship."

"Friendship." His tone makes the word feel weighted. Unfamiliar. As though it's not enough to describe what we are together. But before I can think too strongly on it, he nods. "Not a problem."

"Okay. I also would like to invite you to dinner tonight. I'm making baked salmon and vegetables with cheddar biscuits."

"Count me in." His grin is so adorable that I respond with one of my own. "I'll grab dessert."

"Deal."

"And tell Matty to bring out his chess board. I can show him how to really play."

I laugh. "He'll like that."

"Good." Our gazes hold a moment, and I'm unable to

tear mine away, no matter how badly I know I need to. We still have things to talk about, and the way Jaxson is looking at me, the intensity in his gaze, is making me feel things I have no business feeling.

Want.

Need.

Desire.

I clear my throat. "We can discuss details after Matty goes to bed. If that works for you."

"Just tell me how much, Margot. I don't need anything other than that."

"But—"

"Just the amount. I'll grab a cashier's check today."

"Jaxson—" It's happening too fast, right? Like, he's just going to go pick up money now? Shouldn't I tell him what it's for? How I plan to pay him back?

He moves in close enough that the scent of his body-wash fills my lungs. Cedar and a hint of salt. It's intoxicating. "I don't need details," he repeats. "I know you and I want to help. Just let me help."

"It's more than what you saw."

"Not a problem. Give me the amount."

I close my eyes, embarrassment flushing my cheeks. "Nineteen thousand, seven hundred and fifty-two dollars." Opening my eyes, I look up at him, searching for any sign that he's backing out.

But he just nods. "I'll have the check for you at dinner."

"Just like that?"

"Just like that," he repeats. His phone rings, so he reaches down to check the screen. "Michael."

"I'll get out of your hair. Thank you, Jaxson. I'm going to pay you back. I promise."

"No need to promise," he replies. "I'm not worried about it."

CHAPTER 7

Jaxson

"Any word from your former partner?" Michael sits down at his desk, a fresh mug of coffee in hand.

"Got a text from him this morning. He's having trouble getting the warden to agree to send over the visitor logs without a warrant. And as of now, the judge is refusing to grant it on the off chance there's a connection."

"Probably because we're all the way across the country," Elijah says.

"My thoughts, too," I agree. "With the Finches' permission, I drove out to their house this morning and walked their yard as well as the area where Kleo was found."

"Anything?" Lance asks.

I shake my head. "No playing card that I could find."

"I know we don't like it, but is it possible that the card is a coincidence?" Michael questions. "Something some kid taped there?"

"My gut says no," I say. "But I do know that I'm closer to this one because of my past. So if you guys want to look at other avenues, we can do that."

"I'm with Jaxson on this." All eyes turn to Silas. "A coincidence like this would be highly unlikely." The former SEAL crosses his arms. "It's possible Kleo is not victim number one, but that we're missing something."

"I've been running through all of the recent missing persons that fit the description," Elijah replies. "Wrote a script to help eliminate the ones that don't fit. It should be done running today."

"Great."

"Then we operate as though Kleo Finch is a potential victim until proven otherwise." Lance leans back in his chair. "Jaxson, your theory on the window at Emigh Pillar's house was right. We took a closer look today and the scratches were only surface level. Whoever did that was trying to set off the alarm. And they chose the baby's window because it would be the scariest for the mother, would be my guess." His jaw is set, his eyes hard. I imagine he's thinking about what would happen if anyone came after he and his wife's new baby.

"I second that," Michael replies.

Lance sits up straighter. "I looked into the file of the killer you put away. He was methodical and followed a specific process. I can't figure out why there wouldn't be a body if he was behind it."

"I'm not sure if he is," I admit. "Alaric confirmed that

he's still in prison. Once we have the visitor records, we'll be able to discern whether or not he's had any flagged visitors."

"Here's hoping we can get our hands on those records before a body shows up."

Elijah grins at Lance. "On it, boss."

That's how Knight Security operates in high-profile cases like this. They'll try the legal route, and if that doesn't work? They do what they need to do. It's one of the reasons I wanted to come and work here. There's nothing more frustrating as a cop than knowing someone is guilty and being unable to cut through the red tape to prove it.

"All right, that's all I've got today." Lance stands. "If anything pops, let me know," he tells Elijah who gives him a salute.

"I'll see you guys tomorrow." I stand and grab my keys from the top of my desk, then head for the door.

Michael stops me before I can open the door. "How's Margot?"

"What? How would I know?"

Michael grins, amused. "Because you live under the same roof."

"Different apartments," I say quickly.

"You're a bit jumpy today, Payne, everything okay?"

"Fine. Sorry. This case has me worried."

Michael's grin falls just slightly. "I get that. Listen, man, I know she's not blonde, but—"

"I'll keep an eye on your sister."

He breathes a sigh of relief, and I immediately feel guilty. Does he know how I feel about her? How could he? I don't even know how I feel. "Good. Thanks, man. Times like this, it makes me feel better you're there. God knows she wouldn't let me watch over her. Stubborn woman."

I smile, remembering how I'd called her just that this morning. "That she is. Call me if you guys find anything."

"Will do."

I've never been more grateful to not be useful with a computer as I am now. Because not being good with technology means I get to leave early and get ready for a dinner I've been looking forward to all day.

It seems ridiculous to be nervous when I know it's not a date. I mean, Matty will be there. However, I am most definitely nervous.

After making my way into downtown, I pick a spot that will give me a bit of time to stretch my legs in my walk to the bakery, then climb out and take a moment to breathe deeply. Salty sea air fills my lungs, settling a bit of my nerves.

The ocean is a balm to my soul.

"You look happy."

I turn to see Lanetti standing behind me, wearing a colorful sundress, her hair in loose waves around her face. "It's a good day," I reply.

"I'm glad to hear it."

I start down the street toward the bakery, and she falls

into step beside me. "How is your day?" I ask, because not inquiring about her seems rude.

"It's been long," she says softly. "My mom is on me about whether or not I'm planning on going back to college—I dropped out last year because she wanted me to go to nursing school and I have no interest."

"It's important to do something that will make you happy."

"See, you get it." She gently touches my arm. "What made you want to be a cop?"

I shrug. "When I got out of the Marines, I knew that I wanted to do something that would help people. I'd also been injured, so completing the physical fitness portion of the academy was a goal of mine."

"Injured? How."

"IED," I reply.

She gasps. "That's terrifying."

"By God's grace, I made it through."

"And now you're in our small town." She beams at me. "I couldn't imagine leaving a big, exciting city like LA to come here."

"The city is great at times," I admit. "But it can't compare to this place." I reach for the door of the bakery and turn to tell Lanetti goodbye.

"What happenstance," she says with a smile. "I'm coming here, too."

Oh, boy. Opening the door for her, I step aside so she can go in, then step in behind her.

"I'm not sure what I want yet, so go ahead if you do," she tells me.

"Jaxson Payne!" Kyra Redding, the pastor's wife, greets me with a wide smile as she comes up behind the counter.

"Afternoon, Mrs. Redding."

"How many times have I told you to call me Kyra?"

Chuckling, I nod. "Fair enough. How are you doing, Kyra?"

"Fantastic. Got to spend the morning with my grand-daughter, and it was lovely. How about you?" The woman is a literal walking beam of sunshine. It's impossible to not feel at peace in her presence. Which is probably why she made such a good therapist in her pre-bakery days.

"I can't complain."

"I'm glad to hear it." She grins at me. "What can I get you?"

"Any chance you know what Margot's favorite pie is? I promised to pick up dessert, and I have no idea what to go with." I scan the case before me, looking from the apple to a blueberry.

"Lemon meringue," Lanetti says.

I turn toward her, noting that she's smiling, but it doesn't reach her eyes. "Really?"

She nods. "It was always her favorite when I was babysitting Matty. My mom used to send me with one for her occasionally."

"Great. Thank you so much."

"Sure," she replies. "I'm actually going to be right back, that reminds me that I need to see if my parents want anything. See you later, Kyra." She leaves quickly, and I stare after her, knowing that it was me who upset her and hating that I did, even as I know I haven't done anything to mislead her.

I turn to Kyra. "A lemon meringue, then, please."

"You got it."

<hr>

"That's when Mom fell off the pier," Matty says with a bright smile.

Margot's cheeks are bright red, her smile stretched as wide as I've ever seen it. "It wasn't my fault!"

"But it was," Matty replies. "Because you didn't reel in the line like you were supposed to."

"I'm with Matty on this," I reply. "You should have reeled it in."

Her gaze locks with mine, and something passes between us. What? I'm not sure. But my blood warms, and I catch myself gripping my knees beneath the table.

"I told you, Mom," Matty says as he stands and starts gathering plates.

"Honey, I'll get that," she insists, and starts to stand up.

"You will not. You cooked." He kisses her on the top of her head, then carries the stack of plates into the kitchen, leaving us sitting at the dining room table.

"He's been in a great mood today," Margot tells me. "Every day that passes, I see a bit more of the boy he was before Chad left." She stares at the door he'd just walked through, a soft smile on her face.

"He's a great kid," I tell her. "You should be proud."

"It's all God," she replies, turning back to me. "I can't take any credit."

"You can," I tell her. "Because He chose you to be Matty's mother knowing the type of man you would help him grow into."

Her eyes fill, but she quickly blinks the tears away.

Matty comes back in. "Dishwasher is loaded, pie leftovers are in the fridge, and I have homework to do. Thanks for an awesome game of chess," he tells me. "I look forward to beating you again soon."

I laugh and shake his offered hand. "I'm going to practice."

"Good. Because I'd like it to at least be somewhat of a challenge next time." Matty leans down and hugs his mom. "Love you, Mom."

"I love you, too, honey. I'll come check on you in a few."

"No rush. Homework time. See ya, Jax."

"See ya."

Matty leaves the room, but not without giving me a wide smile behind his mom's back. I have a feeling he thinks this is more than a friendly dinner, and a part of me truly wishes it were. I could see myself with them every night. The three of us as a family.

"I grabbed this today." Shoving those impossible thoughts aside, I reach into my back pocket and withdraw the cashier's check I'd grabbed at the bank on my way to the Finches' home earlier today.

She takes it, her cheeks flushing with color. "It's not too late to back out."

"I don't want to back out."

"I have paperwork for you to see. As well as an agreement I signed to pay you back. It wasn't drawn up by a lawyer or anything, though if you want one that has been, I can contact mine and have her—"

"Margot, it's fine. I told you, I'm not worried about it."

"This is a lot of money, Jaxson. How are you not worried about it?" Her eyes fill with tears. "How can you possibly be so okay just handing this over to me?"

I get up from the seat and move around the table, then squat down and take her hand in mine. "Because in the time I've known you, I've watched you raise a wonderful son, run a successful business, and take care of literally every single person around you. Including me. And for once, Margot, I want to take care of you. Even if it's just alleviating some of the stress you so readily carry on your shoulders."

The tears break free, and she throws her arms around my neck. I'm not expecting it, so I fall backward—taking her with me. By the time I hit the floor, my arms coming around her instinctively to keep her from hitting it alongside me, we're both laughing.

"I am so sorry!" She pushes up from the ground, though her slender body is still pressed against mine.

I swallow hard, wondering if it would truly be the

worst thing in the world to kiss her right now. To lean forward and press my lips to—my phone rings, the tone slicing through this moment between us.

Reaching into my pocket, I withdraw my cell and answer it, not bothering to look at the readout.

"Payne."

"We need you to get down to the office," Lance says. "Now. It's an emergency."

I'M PULLING INTO THE PARKING LOT OF THE LIGHTHOUSE TEN minutes later. I've no sooner put my truck in park than I see that something is clearly wrong. There are two sheriff's vehicles in the parking lot, as well as the vehicles of every member of Knight Security, and a blue sedan belonging to Bianca Theodore, a trauma surgeon from the Army who now works at a veterinarian's office here in town.

And then I see Pastor Redding's car, and my heart plummets.

What happened? Did the killer strike for keeps this time?

I know Margot is safe.

So my thoughts drift immediately to Lance's wife Eliza and their son.

To Elijah's wife, Andie.

To Michael's, Reyna.

Throwing my door open, I slam it behind me and race

up the steps and into the lighthouse. "What is it? What happened?" I demand.

All eyes turn to me, and Lance reaches down to lift an evidence bag bearing a three of hearts.

The walls close in around me and my heart hammers. Despite every impossibility that Morah is behind this, I know it's him. It *has* to be him.

"Who did he take?"

"Lanetti Ester."

CHAPTER 8

Margot

I haven't been able to think straight since Jaxson left a few hours ago. The feel of his body beneath mine, his arms around me—the memory has been swimming in my mind, playing on repeat until I'm so enamored by the idea of him and me that I can hardly think of anything else.

I set the book I've been trying to read aside.

There can't be anything between us. Especially not now that money is involved. I doubt he'd believe me if I told him I wanted a relationship even before he handed over that check, and dating a man who just gave me twenty thousand dollars feels—weird somehow.

Yet here I am, sitting in the foyer, waiting for him to return.

A flashback of me sitting in this same spot, waiting for Chad pops into my head, and I push to my feet. He'd come back, all right. Drunk and smelling of another woman's perfume.

Jaxson's not him.

Jaxson's not—well—he's not my anything.

He can do as he pleases.

So why does the fact that he practically ran out of here make me feel nauseous?

The front door opens, and I turn. Jaxson walks in and closes the door, locking it behind him, but he doesn't stop to talk to me. In fact, he barely makes eye contact with me as he heads for his apartment.

My thoughts go to his dad.

He'd told me that the man was ill. Did he pass? Was that the call?

"Wait, are you okay?" No response, so I follow. I've never seen him look so—tortured.

Jaxson opens his door and moves into his apartment, and I don't give him the chance to shut it before I'm pushing inside.

I repeat again, "Hey, are you okay?"

He shakes his head and starts pacing, hands on his hips. He looks tormented. Weighed down. And my desire to ease his agony is stifling. Without thinking too much about it, I step into his path and reach up to rest my hands on his shoulders.

The former Marine stops moving and takes a deep breath before looking down at me. The heaviness in his gaze, the way he watches me hungrily has me withdrawing my hands, though I remain where I am. "What is it?"

"Lanetti is missing."

My stomach plummets. "What? Missing? What do you mean?"

"I brought trouble here, Margot. And I don't know what to do about it."

"Jaxson." I take a deep breath to steady myself, then move in closer to him. "What trouble?"

"The last case I worked in LA. It was a serial killer. Took me five months to track him down, and in that time he killed seven young women."

Bile burns my throat at the mention of someone so evil. "But you caught him."

"I did. But he used a calling card, something to taunt us on the case and let us know it was him."

"What does that have to do with Lanetti?"

"Sheriff Vick found the killer's calling card at her house. And I found one at an attempted break-in yesterday."

I cover my mouth with my hands and process everything he's telling me. A killer on the loose in Hope Springs? Lanetti missing? I'm not even sure how to start wrapping my mind around it.

But I do know that the fact he's blaming himself is ludicrous. The only person to blame is the evil one carrying out these violent acts, but I can understand the weight of what he's carrying. "Was he released from jail? I'm assuming he went to prison."

"He did. And he's still there. Serving his life sentences. I don't know what's going on, but I intend to find out before anything happens to Lanetti." He shrugs out of his shoulder holster and hangs it on his chair, then removes his firearm and sets it on the table.

"Do you think Lanetti is alive?" While the girl hasn't been overly friendly with me lately, the last thing I want is anything bad happening to her. She's innocent. Sweet. Grew up in this town.

"I'm praying she is." He turns toward me. Something passes in his gaze. An emotion I can't quite pinpoint. "Margot."

"Yes?" Is he going to tell me he cares for me? That he feels whatever this is, too?

He runs a hand over the back of his neck. "I need you to promise me that you'll be careful. Please? You and Matty both."

That hope is dashed, but his worry over me warms my heart. "Of course. But—do you think whoever it is will come for us?"

"I think that if this is about me, they might. I can leave. Honestly, I probably should.'

"No. Please don't. I actually feel safer with you here."

"Margot. Whoever this is targeted Lanetti likely because of how often I'm at the diner. Probably because I was talking to her outside the bakery. I'm *living* here. What do you think will happen to you and Matty? I can stay at the lighthouse."

"No. If there's danger, you need to be here. Please,

Jaxson." Reaching out, I place a hand on his arm. It's more for me than him. If there's a killer in Hope Springs, I would much rather the detective be here. Even if whoever took Lanetti followed him here. "You've been staying here for a year now, if you leave now, whoever it is might still consider us a good way to get to you. And if you leave, there's no one here to keep us safe." I swallow hard as his gaze drops to my mouth, then back up to meet mine.

"I won't let anything happen to you or Matty."

"I know you won't."

Jaxson pulls away from me when his cell rings. As he pulls it out of his pocket, I get a quick glimpse at the name Rosalie flashing on the screen.

Who's Rosalie?

He tosses the phone onto his bed, and my cheeks heat. Is there someone in his life that I don't know about? Irrational jealousy is a thorn in my side.

"My ex-wife," he says.

"Oh. Sorry. I—" Did I say something out loud?

"You looked curious but like you didn't want to ask. Rosalie is my ex-wife. And of course she would be calling now. In the middle of the night. Because that's her timing."

"You mentioned she'd been calling."

"Incessantly."

"I've been getting weird calls, too, if it's any consolation." My statement is meant to be a half joke, to put him at ease, but the expression on his face is anything but amused.

"What do you mean?"

"Someone called and hung up without saying anything twice today. It's probably someone trying to make a reservation from a place with bad service. Happens occasionally."

"Do you know the number?"

"It came up unknown." I narrow my gaze on him. "What is it?"

"I'm going to have Elijah pull your phone records, okay?"

"Jaxson."

He fires off a text, then shoves his phone into his pocket. "It's just a precaution, Margot. I'm not risking it."

***

"Hey, honey." I smile despite the unease in my gut as I greet my son at his best friend's front door. He's been here working on his science project nearly all day, and while it's only a mile from here to the B&B and he'd planned on walking home, I couldn't bring myself to let him do that.

Not while Lanetti is missing and there's a possible killer on the loose.

Lanetti. Her mother is terrified for her daughter's well-being. I can't even imagine what the woman is going through. What would I do if something happened to Matty? Lose my mind. I would absolutely lose my mind.

"Mom, what are you doing here?"

"I figured I would come pick you up. Then we can grab some dinner at the diner before heading home."

He arches a brow. "What about the B&B?"

"Andie is watching the front desk for me." I grew up with Andie Montgomery—now Andie Breeth since she married Elijah, one of the men of Knight Security. Since she runs her own boutique that's only open three days a week, she occasionally steps in to help me run the front desk if I need a breather.

"Cool." Matty turns to Anthony. "See you later."

"Yeah, later." He closes the door after offering me a quick wave, and I wrap an arm around Matty's shoulders.

"How was your day?" I ask as soon as I've climbed behind the wheel of my car.

"Good. We got our hypothesis written and set the experiment up."

"That's awesome. What else did you do?"

"We played some Halo. Ate chips. Drank way too much root beer."

I laugh, then shake my head. "You are having nothing but vegetables for dinner, you hear me? Broccoli and carrots."

He rolls his eyes. "Yes, ma'am."

We fall into a comfortable silence, something that isn't unusual for us. We talk about nearly everything, or at least we do now. There was a time after Chad left that Matty was so far out of reach I'd been terrified he would do something that would land him in more trouble than I could get him out of.

Thankfully, he's been doing better since Jaxson came to stay with us. Not sure what the reasoning is, whether it's because he genuinely respects the detective or is just afraid he'll get caught more easily, but I'm grateful for the change regardless.

"You okay, Mom?"

"Yeah. Why wouldn't I be?"

"You just seem off."

"I'm okay. I just have a lot on my mind, that's all."

"Maybe a certain detective?"

Now it's my turn to roll my eyes. "Jaxson and I are just friends."

"Yeah, sure." He laughs. "It was cool of him to loan us the money."

Us. My boy won't even let me carry the weight of it alone. "It was. We're going to make sure we pay him back."

"If he'll let us. He seems even more stubborn than you."

I laugh and shake my head. "Maybe." My gaze drifts back to him. To the flecks of color in his hazel eyes. To the gorgeous grin he flashes when I catch him off guard.

"So what gives? Is it about Dad being back in town?"

I risk a glance at him, then pull into a spot in front of the diner. "You knew he was back in town?"

"Anthony's mom saw him."

My hands tighten on the steering wheel. "She told you that she saw him?"

"She told Ant and he told me. She told him not to, but we're best friends and have no secrets."

I sigh. I should have known Chad's presence would get

back to Matty. "I'm sorry, honey. I should have been the one to tell you."

"You should have been," he replies. "But I get it. I acted like a turd when he left. You probably were freaked out I'd revert to my turdish nature."

I arch a brow, unable to hide my smile. "Turdish nature?"

"Ant's words, not mine." He laughs, and seeing my boy smile in the midst of all my internal turmoil is like a rainbow streaking across a stormy sky. "Are you doing okay? Has he tried to get in contact with you?"

"He has." *God, how much do I tell him?* "He came to the B&B, and I met him at the diner last night." Was it really only last night? Why does it feel like it's been a month already?

"What did he want?"

I turn to face him, noting the sharpness of his nose and the strength in his jaw. He looks so much like his dad, but the kindness behind his eyes is something Chad never had. It just took me too long to realize it. "He wants a relation-ship with you." I leave off the financial issues, because we just got some of it under control, and I don't want to risk stressing him out further.

"Absolutely not."

"I won't let them force you to do anything you don't want to do."

"Then you can tell him that I never want to see him again." Matty's cheeks turn pink.

"It's not that simple, honey," I tell him truthfully. "Your dad is taking me to court for partial custody."

"But he can't do that. He didn't want me, remember? He signed away his rights to me. I don't even have his last name anymore."

"I know, baby, and I promise you that I won't let him get you. It's just going to be a fight for a while."

"Ugh. Why is he doing this? I hate him!"

"Matty." Reaching over, I take his hand as he wipes a tear from his cheek. "Baby, look at me."

He does.

"I already contacted Beckett. She's handling things, and we'll make sure he can't take anything else from us. But I want you to know that if you decide later on that you want a relationship with him, you can make that call."

"I never want to see him again."

"I know it seems that way right now, honey. But if it changes—"

"It won't." He withdraws his hand. "Can we go in now?"

"Sure thing. Grab us a table, I'll be along in just a minute."

Matty nods and gets out of the car, and I watch him like a hawk until he slips inside the diner.

Then, I take a deep breath, grip the steering wheel, and bow my head.

Lord, I know that You have a plan for all of us and that it is far greater than anything we could imagine for ourselves. But please, Lord, please help me be strong so I can fight for my boy.

Please help him heal the pain in his heart and see that he is worthy of love. That Chad's abandonment has nothing to do with him. Please, God. In Your holy name I pray, Amen.

———

By the time Matty is settled in bed and I've triple-checked all of the windows of my apartment, Andie has nearly finished shutting the B&B down for the night. She's just turning off the lights in the dining room as I'm coming down the hall.

"How's it going, momma?" she asks, then leans against the doorjamb.

"I'm exhausted," I admit. "Between Chad showing up with papers, Lanetti going missing, and trying to keep this place running, I'm burning the candle at both ends."

"Don't forget being an amazing mom," she says.

I laugh. "I'm not so sure about that most days."

"Well, I am. Come on. Let's have some tea." She wraps an arm around my shoulders and guides me into the kitchen, where she fills my electric kettle with water and turns it on.

"I should be making you tea."

"Absolutely not. You sit yourself down and let me handle it. My grandmother wouldn't hear of me letting an exhausted single mother make tea for me when I'm perfectly capable of doing it."

A familiar pang of grief over the loss of Andie's grandmother, Edna, hits me straight in the chest. "I miss your gran."

"You and me both." She sighs and continues filling two stainless steel tea ball infusers, then sets them in mugs and takes a seat at the small, circular table alongside me. "So, tell me. How are things with Jaxson?"

"What do you mean? There's nothing more than friendship there."

"Uh-huh. Sure. Then why does Elijah think something's going on?"

"He does?"

She wiggles her brows. "He thinks you two are dancing around each other like two lovebirds."

I can't help myself—I laugh. "There is no way that came out of Elijah's mouth." I may have only known him for a few years, but I cannot imagine him saying any such thing.

"Fine. I said it and he grunted in agreement." She leans back. "So, spill."

I open my mouth to respond, then close it. What am I supposed to say? Lie and say I feel nothing for the incredibly handsome, strong, protective, loyal detective? Tell the truth and spill the beans on the fact that I can't get him out of my head? That every time we make contact—a brush of the hand, a light touch—it feels like my skin is going to catch fire?

"Girl. You have it bad don't you?" Andie gapes at me. "Does Michael know?"

"No. I don't have it bad. He's just—he's cute." The

moment I say the word, my cheeks flush with embarrassment.

Andie laughs. "Cute? What are we, in middle school?"

"Please no. I can't go through the awkward braces phase again."

She snorts. "You and me both. But seriously. Spill. What's going on?"

"Nothing is going on. Look, I like Jaxson. He's handsome and kind and maybe there is a bit of a crush there, but that's all it is. I'm lonely. I went from having someone around all the time, to it only being Matty and me."

"Then why don't you talk to Jaxson? Be open with him and see if he feels the same?"

"Because things are too complicated. The fight with Chad is just getting started, and I have more baggage than I care to share." *And he loaned me twenty thousand dollars.*

She reaches over and covers my hand. "You know I have my own issues. Things I'm still working through. And Elijah has been there at my side every step of the way, just like I am for him. Just because Chad turned out to be a dirtbag doesn't mean you don't get a second chance."

"Doesn't it? I only wanted to get married once, Andie. One time."

"Sometimes things don't work out the way we planned," Andie replies, then gets to her feet as the kettle beeps. "And sometimes, when they fall back into place, they're better than we could have ever imagined."

CHAPTER 9

Jaxson

When I was young and living on the streets taking care of my little brother, I'd often pass by this large, impressive church near downtown LA. Its huge vaulted pillars, large ornate doorway, and colorful stained-glass windows made the church feel like something straight out of my imagination.

I remember being afraid of it, but feeling so drawn that on Sunday mornings, I'd walk my brother closer, then we'd sit on the bus bench across the street as families left the church after the service.

I'd wanted so badly to be one of them. To be someone who could belong in a place like that. And I had been so young that I didn't realize it's exactly where I belonged. That even though I felt terrified and alone, I wasn't.

Even though my dad bailed on me, my Father didn't.

It wasn't until I met Lance that I started really looking for my faith and trying to build my relationship with God.

Yet here I sit, trying to understand how He could allow something like this to happen. Because even though I know it's people who drive the terrible things that happen in the world, it's so hard to wrap my mind around the fact that Lanetti is out there somewhere, suffering.

"Lanetti is one of us," Pastor Redding says as he stands behind his podium. "She's a daughter of Hope Springs. A sister. A friend." He looks sympathetically at her mother who is sitting a few pews in front of me. "And as we close today, I want to remind everyone that when everything feels like it's falling apart around us, all we can do is turn to the Lord and fall to our knees. Because the greatest battles are fought through prayer." He's silent a few moments, then bows his head. "Let us pray. Heavenly Father, please be with us as we go into this week. Please remind us to always keep our eyes on You, and that even when things are at their bleakest, we need to reach to You for comfort. Please, God, be with Lanetti and her family. Please bring her home safely, Lord. In Your Heavenly name we pray, Amen." He looks up again and closes with, "Go in peace."

People begin to file out of pews, but I stay where I am, my mind going a million miles a minute. I got very little sleep last night because I'd been so focused on trying to figure out where Lanetti could have been taken.

Morah would have made contact by now. He would have left us with some puzzle that we'd have to solve in order to find her, even though his previous killings would tell us she was dead within hours of being taken.

I close my eyes, and bile rises in my gut. *Please, God, don't let her be dead.*

"How are you?" Lance slides onto the pew beside me and Eliza joins him, their daughter in her arms. The little girl is only a few weeks old and already stealing the hearts of everyone who sees her.

It hurts my heart a little, to know that I will likely never have a child of my own. I'd wanted kids—so badly—but Rosalie said they weren't in the cards for her.

Then she went and got pregnant and is having someone else's child. Likely another reason she wants to talk to me. So she can rub it in my face and take what's left of my dignity.

"Tired," I admit. "I was up all night reviewing what little facts we have. Any word from Sheriff Vick on the tip line?"

"Not so far." Lance looks nearly as exhausted as I am, though I imagine that's because of the little one currently sleeping in her mother's arms and not the case, though it could be both. "I spent a few hours last night and again this morning reviewing the security footage from our cameras throughout town. If we caught something by chance, I haven't found it yet."

"Hey, Jaxson."

I nearly jolt to my feet at the sound of Matty. He's dressed in slacks and a button-down blue shirt, his mother in a beautiful floral dress nearly the same shade. Her dark hair is curled loose around her face, and the sight of her steals my breath. "Hey, Matty. How's it going?"

"Good. Mom and I are heading to the diner, and I wanted to see if you would join us. Then maybe we can play some chess after? I'd love to show you another thing or two. You can come, too, Mr. and Mrs. Knight."

"I like to think you just got lucky," I retort, trying to keep my tone friendly despite the storm raging within me.

He grins, and it's such a beautifully rare thing to see him smile that I decide right here in this moment that I want to do whatever I need to do to keep this kid happy and on the straight and narrow.

"Let's do it," I say, then head out after him. "You two coming?" I ask Lance.

"We need to get Mable down for her nap," he says. "But next time for sure." He clasps Matty on the shoulder, then guides Eliza out of the church.

We're just about to follow them out when Chad steps through the crowd and right into our paths. The pungent stench of alcohol turns my stomach and triggers an anger I thought I'd long since buried.

Bradley Payne drank like this, and he'd nearly beaten me to death when I'd questioned him.

I look at Matty. The shift in his demeanor is instant. Gone is the sweet, happy boy who'd been standing in front of me mere seconds ago, replaced by a shell of a teenager. He's angrier than any one person—especially a kid— should be.

"Hi, son. It's good to see you. You look good." Chad reaches out to touch him, and Matty jerks away.

"This is not the time or place, Chad," Margot snaps, trying to keep her tone low.

"I beg to differ. You may have gotten the town in the divorce at first, Margot, but church is a public place, and I have just as much a right as you do to be here."

"Please go," Margot urges. "Matty doesn't want to see you."

"Your mother decide that for you?" Chad asks.

I push forward, placing myself right beside Matty. "You need to move, Chad. We're leaving, and you're in the way. You may be allowed to be in the church, but preventing us from leaving is something else entirely."

He glares at me, then takes a step forward, putting himself directly in my path. Given that he's a few inches shorter than me, I have to tilt my head to look down at him.

Rage burns through my veins, but the cop in me keeps it in check.

I would love to level this guy, especially given my current stress load, but it won't solve anything.

"You can't tell me what to do," he growls at me. "Keep trying, and you and I are going to have a problem."

"I'm not going to fight you, Chad. But you're making a fool of yourself right now."

Chad doesn't look away from me. "You're moving in on something that isn't yours. This is my family. My wife. My son."

"That's it!" Matty explodes, planting both hands on Chad's chest and shoving him back.

He's caught off guard and stumbles back into a church pew. By the time he recovers, his cheeks are crimson. "You disrespectful little—" He starts toward Matty, and I yank the kid behind me, stepping right in Chad's path.

All of the anger I've carried with me since I was a kid boils to the surface, and I have to clench my hands into fists at my sides and actively force myself not to use them. "Touch him. I *dare* you. There isn't a force in this world that will keep me from tearing you apart if you put your hands on that kid. I will *end you.*" I snarl the words, hoping Margot's ex-husband sees the threat of violence clearly enough.

Chad glares at me, then looks around me to Matty and Margot. "This isn't over."

"I think it is," Pastor Redding says as he comes to stand beside me. "You can leave now, Chad. Violence is not welcome in God's house. Certainly not against a child. You're more than welcome to return when you can respect the boundaries of those who come here to worship."

Chad continues staring up at me, then turns on his heel and leaves.

"I am so sorry," Margot says.

I turn to see her with her arms wrapped around Matty, who is visibly shaken. Without responding to her, I bend down to get on Matty's level. "No one gets to treat you or your mom that way, you understand? You just stood up to him like a man would, and you should be proud of that."

He sniffles, then uses the back of his hand to wipe his eyes. "I'm sorry for the scene, Pastor," he says.

"Don't be." Pastor Redding pats him on the back. "You're always safe when you're here. Remember that."

"I want to go home, Mom. Please."

"Of course." Margot offers me a tight smile.

"Let me walk you to your car. Make sure he isn't waiting for you at the B&B."

"Can I come in?"

I glance over my shoulder at Margot as she stands in the partially open doorway of my apartment. I'd left it cracked just in case she needed me. Though it seems silly now given I'm right upstairs and she has a B&B nearly full of people.

Matty ran to his room as soon as we got back, and seeing how upset he was made me want to go hunt his father down just so I can drag him here and make him apologize. Even if seeing his dad is what put him in the tailspin in the first place.

I just want to do something, anything to help.

I feel so absolutely helpless on all fronts right now.

My feelings for Margot.

Matty's pain.

Lanetti's disappearance.

I'm failing all the way around, and I desperately need to get this figured out so I can revisit what I'm feeling for the woman currently standing in the doorway of my apartment.

"Sure. Come on in."

She smiles and pushes in further, then offers me a mug of steaming coffee. "I thought you could use a jolt."

"Definitely wouldn't hurt. Where's yours?"

She laughs. "I've had more than my fair share of caffeine for the day." Her gaze lands on the pages scattered on top of my bed. Images taken, notes made, a timeline of all the cards I've found so far as well as Kleo's supposed hypoglycemia.

I can't help but feel like it's all tied together. Even though the facts are saying otherwise, and I've yet to find the ace of hearts card, my gut tells me it's all connected. And I've learned to listen to it above the noise.

"So, listen. About today."

I take a drink of my coffee, remaining silent as she begins to pace around the room, toying with her hands. She's so stunningly beautiful.

"You defended Matty, and I can't even begin to thank you."

"You don't need to thank me. Matty deserves better."

"I agree. And to have you come to his defense like that —even with as distraught as he was—you have to know that it meant a lot."

"I'm glad. Chad has no right to talk to either of you that way." *And if he'd put his hands on the boy, I would have dragged him outside and made him regret every moment of it.* Though I keep that part to myself because letting Margot know just how much rage I have bottled up isn't what she needs.

She needs stability. Safety. Not anger. This woman and her son have seen enough of that for lifetimes.

"He certainly seems to think he can." She shakes her head. "Anyway, I just wanted to thank you again. You didn't have to do that, and you stepped up in a big way."

"I won't ever let anyone speak to you or Matty that way."

She smiles, and the bell downstairs dings. Margot glances over her shoulder, and I hate that I know she's about to walk away from me. But before she does, she crosses over and stretches up to press her lips to my cheek.

I'm stunned.

Frozen in place.

My stomach twists into knots, and as she pulls away, I have to actively fight the desire to reach forward and crush her body against mine as I steal the kiss I've desperately wanted from the moment I first laid eyes on her.

But before I can respond, she's already gone, shutting my door gently behind her.

Margot

As I write a check for the final bill owed, I lean back in my chair and smile.

Monday morning came quickly, and even Matty seemed to be in better spirits this morning despite everything that happened with Chad. Of course, hearing from Beckett that she's taking the case in front of a judge to ask for it to be dropped entirely—and has high hopes that it will be—certainly helped.

Chad has no grounds to ask for partial custody when he signed away his rights.

Add to that his infidelity and the mountain of debt he left behind? According to her, he has literally no grounds, and the only reason he was able to get a lawyer to take it on in the first place was because he was sleeping with her.

I open a spreadsheet and make one final note about the deduction, then stare at the number left. It's what I owe Jaxson, and even though the number I owe is just as high now as it was before, knowing it's him I'm paying back versus multiple companies makes it easier to breathe.

The bell at my front desk dings, so I get to my feet and head into the foyer, a smile on my face. It fades as soon as I see the woman on the other side. Lanetti's mother looks beyond nervous as she fiddles with the strap of her purse.

"Patty, what can I do for you?"

Her swollen, red eyes narrow on me, but she doesn't speak right away. Instead, she takes a deep, steadying breath. "I would like to speak to you about my daughter."

"Of course. How are you holding up?"

"Not well," she replies. "As you can imagine."

"I can."

Her expression hardens. "Can you?"

"Not entirely, but if anything were to happen to Matty—"

"Yes, sweet Matty. If anything were to happen to him, I imagine the entire town would be in an uproar. But because it's my girl. Because—" Tears start streaming down her face.

"Patty, what's going on?" I come around the desk and wrap an arm around her shoulders, then guide her over towards the couch to sit down.

She sits, and I drop down beside her, keeping my arm around her. I've known Patty Ester a long time. And even though we have a significant age difference, we've always gotten along.

"I found Lanetti's journal and thought it might be helpful, so I gave it to Sheriff Vick. I should have read it first, but I was so happy to find something—anything." She chokes up.

"That's good, right? Did he find something?"

"There were a lot of things in there about the town. Things she observed working at the diner, and a few passages about how she wishes she lived in a big city. Then she wrote a lot about that detective that moved here—"

"Jaxson?" I interject.

"Yes. It's clear she had affections for him."

I don't respond, even though it was clear to anyone who had been around her whenever Jaxson was near that Lanetti had a crush on him.

"Then there were a few passages revolving around you."

"Me?" I sit back, surprised. "What about me?"

"She assumed you and the detective had something going, and she was jealous. Her last entry said that she wanted to get away from the town, somewhere she would never have to see the two of you." She chokes on her words.

"There's nothing going on between me and Jaxson." Not that it would matter if there was, but I don't add that because I don't see how it would be entirely helpful.

"He suggested that she might have run away. That it's a possibility."

Her response honestly catches me off guard. "Sheriff Vick thinks she ran away?"

She nods.

I recall the card found at her house. How would that make sense if she took off?

"He says it's a possibility. But I can't help but think they're looking in the wrong place. What if they miss something?"

"The sheriff isn't the only one looking for your daughter," I remind her. "Knight Security is, too. And I know for a fact that Jaxson doesn't think she ran away."

She closes her eyes tightly. "Did she say anything to you? Did you say something to her to make her leave? Is it possible she did run away?"

"Patty, you know I've always liked Lanetti. I never would have done anything to hurt her."

"Her writing is so angry. She was so mad when she wrote about you and Jaxson at the diner together. It was dated just last week. How did I not know she was so mad? I know she's an adult now, but we live together. How did I miss it?"

"Sometimes people are good at hiding what they don't want others to see. She probably didn't want you to know she was so upset."

"I miss my girl."

"I know you do." I wrap my arm around her again. "I am so sorry, Patty. I wish I could help."

"I just don't want to be alone, and I'm so alone. With Sean gone—" She sniffles, and I think back to her late husband who'd passed when Lanetti was in high school.

I recall Lanetti being broken up about it, but Patty had been a complete and total mess over his passing. She'd retreated into herself, becoming a shell of who she'd been.

"Now Lanetti's missing, and I don't know how I'm supposed to go on."

"We lean on God in times like these, Patty, it's all we can do."

"How can He let me suffer so much?"

"I don't know," I answer her truthfully. "But I do know that when everything is burning around you, the best thing you can do is pray. And I hope you know that this entire town is praying right alongside you."

WITH TWO FRESH TO-GO CUPS OF COFFEE IN HAND, I MAKE MY way up the front steps and into the lighthouse that serves as Knight Security's main office.

After I managed to calm Patty down, I'd called Andie to see if she could come in and watch the front so I could go tell Jaxson everything Patty had told me. I could have called him, but it just felt weird telling him over the phone.

So, I'd grabbed us both cups of coffee and headed over since he's on monitor duty today. According to Andie, he's the only one in the office right now as everyone else is out on an install.

The door is unlocked, so I step inside. Jaxson looks up from the computer he's sitting behind and smiles at me. But that smile fades almost instantly. "Is everything okay?" He pushes up.

"Yes, fine. I brought you coffee." I set it on his desk as he sits back down, then take a seat beside him.

"Thanks. I actually was just thinking about how badly I needed a caffeine boost, and this is much better than what I would have made for myself."

"Good." I set my purse down on the floor beside me. "Patty Ester, Lanetti's mom, came to see me at the B&B."

Jaxson's expression reflects his understanding that the conversation likely didn't go well. "Sheriff Vick talked to her already."

"How can he think she ran away? You found the card."

He sighs heavily and leans back. "At this point, he's not sure what to think. He didn't tell me what was in the journal, but that it implied heavily she was unhappy here."

"Patty told me what was in it."

He arches a brow.

"Lanetti had feelings for you, which you already suspected."

"More than suspected, but yeah." He runs his hands over his face. "She was angry that I didn't return them?"

"More than that, I'm afraid. According to Patty, Lanetti wrote pretty heavily about how angry she was at the relationship you and I seemed to have."

He stares back at me. "She thought we were dating?"

I nod. "She was mad and wrote about how she'd rather be anywhere but here and forced to see us together."

"Oh, man." He jots something down on a notepad sitting on the desk beside him. "I see why Vick thought she might have run away."

"But you don't think so."

"If we hadn't found the card, then I would," he replies. "The trouble is, there's no evidence to suggest Morah had anything to do with anything that's been going on, and even though I pulled all the old case files and had them sent over—" He shakes his head. "I know she didn't run away. I know this is all connected, I just can't figure out how. Normally by now, we'd have a call. Something."

"What do you mean?" When he doesn't respond, I reach over and place my hand on his arm. His gaze locks with mine, and the air charges around us. "Sometimes it helps to run things by another person, right?"

He swallows hard and breaks the connection when he pushes up from his chair. "In all the other cases, he left a riddle of some kind. Whether it was a note left at the crime scene or a phone call made after the abduction. And with Lanetti, there hasn't been one. No one has tried to make contact with me."

"Yet. It could still happen, right?"

"Sure. But every minute that passes makes it more unlikely we'll find her."

"Does Lance think she ran away?"

"No. Honestly, I don't think the sheriff believes it either. My guess is he told Patty that to try and give her some hope that her daughter was out there somewhere of her own volition." He drops back down into the chair. "I think she was grabbed because I was talking to her outside the bakery."

"It's not your fault, Jaxson."

"It feels like it is." His gaze meets mine again. I see his pain, and I want nothing more than to wrap my arms around him in an attempt to take at least some of it. "How are things going this morning? I could use some good news."

"Well, my lawyer is moving to have the case Chad filed dropped before I even have to go to court."

He arches a brow. "That's good news."

"It is. Maybe then he'll leave for good."

Jaxson's expression shifts again. "When did Chad get to town?"

"About a week ago? It was the day you picked up the paint."

"Which is the same day Kleo Finch's parents called in a missing person report." He walks over to the board. On it, I note he has my strange phone calls written down under a possible connection column. Seeing it, I stand and walk over to join him. "Were you getting these calls before he got into town?"

"No."

"And you said Lanetti and Chad got along?"

"Sure."

"Enough that he could get her to go somewhere with him?"

"Sure, but—" I try to follow his train of thought—and then it clicks. "Chad isn't a killer, Jaxson. Though he may be a lot of things."

"So far, we have no bodies."

"But the cards, you said that was the killer you put away."

"It was his calling card, sure."

"And how would Chad know that?"

"Deep research?" he asks. "He could have looked up my old cases and found the information somewhere. It wasn't made public during the trial, but it was definitely in the file. And we both know that if you know the right people, those aren't too hard to get your hands on once the case has been closed."

"But how could he have gotten it? And why? Chad is a lot of things, but it seems far-fetched that he'd be capable of this."

"I don't know, Margot, but he's the best lead we've got."

CHAPTER 11

Jaxson

My phone buzzes again, so I glance down to see yet another text from Bradley Payne. The man just won't quit. He's desperate to meet up so we can talk, though he promises that he won't show up again unannounced.

I've barely had time to process him given everything else going on, so I shove the phone back into my pocket and spare Michael a glance as he sits beside me. He looks almost giddy as we wait for Sheriff Vick to bring Chad into the conference room so we can talk to him.

While there's nothing to hold him on, I explained my theory to Vick, and he was more than happy to bring Margot's ex-husband in.

"Try not to look so excited," I tell Michael.

He grins. "I can't. I've been wanting to get this guy in an interview room for years now."

The door opens, and Chad walks in alongside Sheriff

Vick. The moment he sees us, his gaze narrows, expression turning furious. "What are they doing here?" he demands.

"They're working alongside us to locate Lanetti Ester, and we have a few questions for you since you were one of the last people to see her." The sheriff had asked to play this as though we were going to Chad for help rather than as a suspect.

I'd agreed. Sometimes it's easier to get someone to give themselves up when they aren't expecting it. "Mr. O'Connell," I greet, trying to keep things smooth.

He doesn't respond as he takes a seat beside the sheriff. As soon as I'd made the possible connection, I'd researched Chad O'Connell. The week before he showed up back in town, he'd booked a flight to Los Angeles, where he stayed for two days before returning to Boston. Which is apparently where he and his new girlfriend are living.

I'm waiting for Alaric to tie him to the visitor logs we were finally able to get a warrant for. But it's starting to fit together so perfectly that I can hardly stand not coming at him with everything I've got.

"You saw Lanetti at the diner last week, right?" I ask.

"Yes. As I told Sheriff Vick, I was eating there, and she sat down to have dinner with me."

Alex and Lilly had confirmed as much. "And the two of you left together?"

"I gave her a ride home."

"She didn't have her car?" Michael questions.

"No." He glares at me. "She'd asked for a ride home,

and I agreed. Where is this going?" he demands, looking from us to the sheriff.

Is he so volatile because he knows Margot's lawyer is working to throw out the case he presented against her? Or because he senses we're getting close?

"We're just trying to piece it all together," Michael replies, keeping his tone level. "So, can you tell us why you're back in town, Chad? Backstory can sometimes help," he adds with a dark smile.

"I'm assuming Margot told you why."

"She did, but I sense there's more to it," he replies.

"I miss my family. Is that a crime?"

"No," Michael replies. "But kidnapping is."

"Kidnapping—" Chad whirls on the sheriff. "Kidnapping, Vick, really?"

"We just need some answers, Chad," he replies.

"You've known me my entire life. Do you really think I would do anything like this?"

"No one thought you'd abandon your family either," Michael snaps.

Chad shoots out of his chair and rushes for Michael, who's already on his feet. I step between them, catching the right hook meant for my partner. Pain shoots up through my jaw, and I clench my hands into fists at my side.

"Knock it off!" Sheriff Vick yells.

I glare at Chad, knowing if he takes another swing, I'm not going to just take it this time. His glare shifts from me to Michael and he steps back.

"Coward," Chad snarls. "Had to have your boyfriend here step in for you."

Michael laughs because we both know the only reason I stepped in between them was to keep Michael from killing Chad right here in the station's conference room. "Anytime you wanna step into the ring, I'm game, O'Connell."

"I don't have time for this," he growls, backing further away.

"You good?" Sheriff Vick asks me.

"Barely felt it," I reply. "You're going to make time," I tell Chad. "Now, where were we?"

"You were busy accusing me of something I didn't do."

I ignore him. "Where were you the night Lanetti went missing?"

"At my parent's house," he snaps. "You can check with them."

"We will," I reply.

"Good. Fine." He stands.

"Why did you fly out to LA?"

"What?"

I cross my arms. "You flew to LA the week before you came here. Why?"

"I don't see how that's any of your business."

"It has to do with this case, which makes it my business."

He looks to the sheriff. "I want my lawyer," he snaps.

"We're not charging you with anything, Chad."

"Certainly seems like you are."

"Look, if you want your lawyer, I'll make the call. But it would really be easier if you'd just answer the question."

Chad's scowl deepens. "I was out there for a job interview."

It was hardly what I expected him to say.

"Then why are you coming after Margot for partial custody?" Michael demands.

"He's not." A theory turns in my mind and with it, anger burns my veins. "You were going to change it to a fight for full custody of Matty, weren't you? Why?"

"He's my son."

"You signed away your rights to him."

"Because Margot—" He cuts his thought short. "I wanted to take my son with me. Out of this town where everyone has an opinion about his father."

"Unbelievable." Michael shakes his head and turns away. "You're even bigger scum than I thought. How did you think that plan would work?"

I study Chad's expression. The way his gaze darts toward the door, how he toys with his hands on top of the table, and suddenly, the case he filed against Margot makes sense. "You knew it wouldn't work, didn't you? You knew that no judge in their right mind would award you full custody of your son. You were only hoping to scare Margot into paying you to go away like she did when you left town the first time."

"What?" Michael looks from me to Chad, then back to me. "What are saying?"

"You have no idea what you're talking about," Chad snaps.

"You were seriously trying to get more money out of her?" I ask, doing everything I can to keep my temper at bay.

"Chelsea thought that if I asked for just the money, it would look bad. We need the money. Margot got everything."

"So you had to put the custody fight on there, too. Because in comparison to losing her son or paying you off, you knew Margot would sell everything to protect Matty."

"Margot will land on her feet. She always does. And besides, she has your parents she could have gone to," he says to Michael, who looks about ready to shoot his sister's ex.

Michael opens his mouth to respond, then turns and storms out of the room, slamming the door behind him.

Chad flinches.

The longer I'm around him, the more I'm starting to see Chad O'Connell for what he is. A coward. A terrible person. An alcoholic. But not a kidnapper.

My hope that Alaric would find the prison records fades.

Because even as kidnapping Lanetti and using the cards to frame Morah would be a way to distract me, there's just no clear motive for it.

The case I'd built against him falls apart before my eyes, putting us right back to square one when it comes to

Lanetti's disappearance and the attempted break-in at Emigh's house.

"Sheriff, can I have just a few minutes with Mr. O'Connell?" I ask, glancing up at Sheriff Vick. He knows my history as a detective, the impeccable record I brought with me, so I'm hoping it's enough to buy me some alone time.

"Sure thing. I'll go grab some coffee." He stands.

"You're leaving me alone with him?" Chad demands.

"Nothing says I can't. Besides, as you well know, Jaxson was a detective with the LAPD. You'll be perfectly fine." He flashes a furious smile, then leaves, closing the door behind him.

Smiling, I lean forward. "The case against Margot isn't going to go anywhere, and you know it. So here's the deal. You're going to leave town, drop the case, and move on with your life. If Matty wants a relationship with you, he'll reach out."

Chad's cheeks turn crimson. "You don't get to tell me what to do, Payne."

"In this case, I do, because Margot and Matty are both far too good for you. And should you press forward, all that's going to happen is the case will get dismissed anyway, and then you look like even more of a fool for not doing the right thing and dropping it."

Chad doesn't respond, but his jaw clenches. "It's not right that she kept everything and I got nothing."

"You destroyed your family," I remind him. "That choice was on you and you alone."

"I want a fresh start."

"Taking Margot for all she has is not a fresh start. You want to start a new life? Get right with God. Ask for forgiveness. Make changes to yourself. Then maybe you'll realize just how much you messed up when you walked away from the best things that ever happened to you." I start to leave, then pause and turn back toward him. "And for the record, if I find out you didn't drop the case, or you come after Margot or Matty ever again, Michael will be the least of your problems."

CHAPTER 12

Margot

It seems ridiculous that I am yet again waiting for a man to show up. But here I am, sitting in the foyer of the B&B, pretending to be busy, while I wait for Jaxson to walk in the door. I know he talked to Chad today.

Or, at least, he'd been planning on it.

But he hasn't answered any of my calls or texts.

My stomach has been in knots most of the day, so the fact that we had two checkouts was a great distraction, but now the rooms are cleaned and ready for the next guests, leaving me exhausted but with no other busy work.

It's just after dinnertime, so the door isn't locked, but most of the guests have turned in for the evening.

Which means that I'm *technically* still working, right? In which case, standing here isn't so pathetic.

The door handle begins to turn, so I quickly shift my gaze down. That way, when he does come in, he doesn't see me staring after him. It's not until I hear the door close again that I look up. "Hey," I say with a smile.

Dressed in shorts, a tank top, and tennis shoes, Jaxson's muscled body is gleaming with sweat. It's unusual that he'd be out running this late, but based on his pink cheeks, I'd say that's exactly what he was doing. "Hey, I'm surprised you're still down here."

I shrug. "Had some work to do. Want some water? Lemonade? I made a fresh pitcher today."

"Sure." He seems off, uncomfortable even, which only spurs my nerves further.

After pouring some glasses, I set them on the small table in the B&B's private kitchen, then sit across from him. "Is everything okay?" I ask. "You don't usually run at night."

"I needed to burn off some steam. My mind can't seem to settle with everything going on."

"I get it. Lanetti missing is horrible. I can't seem to get my thoughts off of what she must be going through."

He nods but still doesn't touch his glass. "Michael and I interviewed Chad today."

I arch a brow. "You took my brother?"

The first crack of a smile graces his handsome face. "Yeah, I realized my mistake too late, but he handled things okay."

"What happened? Is he the one who—"

"No." Jaxson shakes his head. "I'm confident he had nothing to do with Lanetti's disappearance."

Relief helps me relax just a little. They're still no closer to finding her, but at least the man I'd been married to for thirteen years isn't responsible.

"Did he drop the case?"

"What? Chad? No. Why?"

"He should. Probably tomorrow. It was kind of late when we got out of the interview room."

"What do you mean? Why is he dropping it?"

Jaxson runs a hand over the back of his head. "I'm sorry for what he's put you through. You and Matty both deserve better. You know that, don't you?"

"Jaxson, what's going on?"

"Is Matty asleep?"

"Yes. What's going on?" Nerves churn my stomach.

"Chad was trying to get you to sell everything and buy him out. He never wanted custody of Matty, though he was planning to change the case he'd put together against you and try and take full custody under the guise of moving Matty out to LA."

I feel the color drain from my face moments before rage floods my system. "He was going to *what?*"

"He wanted you to sell this place and pay him off so he'd drop the custody charge. He didn't think it would ever go to court because he knew if it did, he would lose anyway."

I stare at Jaxson, completely dumbfounded by what he's telling me. "Does he really think so little of me? That I'm stupid enough to fall for that?"

"I can't see how he would ever think he could win that, but it was his plan. As outrageous as it was."

"How did Michael handle that confession? Oh, to be a fly on that wall." I stand and head over to the cabinet to pull some fresh cookies I'd made earlier from the jar.

I feel rather than see him move in behind me.

Turning toward him, I swallow hard, abandoning the cookies on the counter behind me.

"You deserve better," Jaxson says.

He's mere inches from me, his hazel gaze darting down to my lips. I draw my lower one into my mouth, attraction snapping between us like electricity.

"I'm starting to believe that," I tell him.

"Good."

The bell on the front door rings, shattering the connection like a bucket of cold water. "Sorry." I slip away from him and head for the front, finding a very pregnant woman on the other side of my standing desk.

"Hi!" she greets happily, offering me a wave.

"Hi, how can I help you?" I force a smile, though my insides are still like jelly after that heated moment in the kitchen. How does he make me feel that way without even a single touch?

"I hope so. I was hoping to get a room?"

"For how long?" I open up our scheduling software.

"Just tonight, if you have it available." She rubs her hand over her stomach.

"Actually, I do. The rooms are all booked tomorrow, but tonight is available." I smile at the look of bone-deep relief on her face.

"That's wonderful." She sets her bag down. "I'm

exhausted these days, and the idea of trying to track down somewhere else is not appealing in the least." The stunning, leggy brunette standing on the other side of my check-in desk looks about ready to have her baby any moment, though still manages to look effortlessly beautiful.

Her dark hair shines in the rays of sunlight streaking in from the window, and her brown eyes are such a bright caramel color I'm sure they must be contacts.

Even as it's ridiculous, I smooth out the front of my floral dress in an effort to make myself look even a bit more put together. "Well, I remember how tired I was with my son. But you look fantastic. When are you due?"

"Five weeks," she replies with a laugh. "And I have absolutely no idea how to get myself prepared."

"I remember those days. What brings you here to Hope Springs?"

"I'm headed to New York tomorrow morning for a conference, and I just couldn't bring myself to pass up the opportunity to knock Maine off of my bucket list." She beams at me.

"I completely understand. I just need a form of ID and payment." Smiling warmly, I wait as she digs into her purse. "Where are you coming in from?"

"Los Angeles," she replies, then slides her ID over to me. The moment I read the first name printed on her driver's license, my stomach turns into a pit.

"So, LA, huh?" Surely it's just a coincidence and it's not—

"What are you doing here?" Jaxson demands, coming out of the kitchen.

My stomach plummets, and all hopes that Rosalie is a common name in LA are blown out like a candle.

"Jaxson. What are you doing here? I was going to come find you tomorrow." She turns to face him, and I watch as his gaze drops to her pregnant belly and something flashes over his expression.

Pain.

"I live here," he growls. Gone are all traces of the man I'd seen in the kitchen mere minutes ago. "Let me ask again, what are you doing here, Rosalie?"

"I told you that I wanted to talk to you."

"And you thought showing up at the place I live is the best way to handle it?"

First his estranged father and now his ex-wife? I keep waiting for him to snap. To explode in anger and storm off, but Jaxson remains where he is, standing firmly in front of the kitchen door.

"First of all, I didn't know you were living in a B&B, just this town. But, Jaxson, I need to talk to you." She offers me an embarrassed smile. "Maybe we can do it some-where more private?"

"Everything I had to say to you I said once the divorce was final. You know—the one *you* asked for."

Her eyes fill and his expression softens. "Please, Jaxson. I promise you'll never hear from me again. I won't even stay. I'll leave tonight and head straight to New York. I just really want to talk to you."

I bear witness to the fight that plays out on his face. He's angry, that much is clear. The hurt is easy to see. Even not knowing fully what happened between them, I wouldn't blame him for turning her away.

So when he crosses over and lifts her bag off the floor, I find myself stunned. "Fine. We can talk in my apartment."

CHAPTER 13

Jaxson

I learned a long time ago that the enemy loves to kick you when you're down. Taunting you with your past like a weight around your ankles. But it still doesn't make it any easier to fight the battle when it feels like everything is closing in around you.

God, please help me. I need Your strength because I'm not strong enough to handle all of this alone. Amen. I finish the prayer as I unlock my door, then step aside so Rosalie can come in.

After shutting the door, I set her bag down and turn to face her. She looks good. I hate that she looks good.

Her hand rests on her swollen stomach, and it's like a punch to my gut.

How many arguments did we have because I'd wanted kids and she said she didn't? How many times did she tell me that I was just trying to stifle her career and make her nothing more than a military spouse whose only job was taking care of kids while I ran off and saved the world?

Her words, not mine.

I never expected any of that, though. I'd just wanted a family. And when I'd nearly died, my back shattered, unsure if I'd ever walk again, she'd left. Walked away like I was a broken toy she no longer wanted to play with.

Rosalie turns to me and smiles. "You look great, Jaxson."

"Don't."

"Don't what?"

"Feed me any kind words. Just tell me why you're here and what you want."

"Can I sit down?" she asks, gesturing toward the small table.

"Sure."

Rosalie takes a seat, and I join her because if I don't, I'm going to start pacing. "When I got the call from the hospital that you'd been shot—"

"It was a mistake. They never should have called you. I'd forgotten to update my emergency contact in the system."

"I know that." She smiles, but I can see the hurt on her face. "But it was a reminder that I still have things that I need to fix."

"We're done. There's nothing to fix."

"I know that, too," she replies. "But I—" She closes her eyes and takes a deep breath, then opens them again, and there are tears shimmering in the depths. "This is harder than I thought it would be. Whew. Okay. I got remarried a year ago."

"Good for you."

"He's a good man. A firefighter."

"Again, good for you."

"Anyway, he introduced me to God, and we've been going to a Bible study once a week."

"Okay."

"The way that I treated you after you nearly died—" She chokes on the words, and a tear slips down her cheek. "I was not a good person. I left you when you needed me most, and what I did was not okay."

"I don't need you to tell me that for me to understand."

"But *I* need you to know that I am sorry. That if I could go back and change the way I handled things, I would. I was young and stupid when we got married. I hadn't been ready to settle down. Then with your deployments and you being gone all the time, it weighed on me."

"So that justifies leaving me to die in a hospital bed?"

"No. Of course not." She shakes her head. "I waited for you to come home to alleviate my guilt. But I never should have left you. I just—it took me a long time to realize that I'd used you and our marriage to get away from my own family."

I wish I could say her confession is a surprise, but my own brother warned me that Rosalie was only using me. I was just too blinded by what I thought was love to see it.

"I was blinded by my immaturity," she says softly. "And I hurt you in ways I never meant to hurt you."

"What do you want from me, Rosalie? Want me to forgive you? Fine. Done. Want me to tell you it's okay and coddle you so you can feel good about the life you're living now? Sorry, I don't have that in me."

"Whether you forgive me or not is your choice, and I won't blame you if you don't. But I *needed* to explain it to you, Jaxson. I needed you to know that I am so sorry. That you deserved better. That I should have been there for you as your wife."

"Things happened the way they did, Rosalie, and there's no going back."

"I know that." She sniffles. "But when I got that call, it was like a sign that I was supposed to talk to you. And it's been weighing heavy on my heart ever since. I did love you, Jaxson. I want you to know that."

Her words settle over me, unlocking a bit of the brokenness I've carried since the day she left. It doesn't undo what she did, but maybe I wasn't quite as over it as I'd thought.

"Jaxson?"

I jump to my feet, still half asleep. Blinking rapidly, I stare down at Margot, who's standing in front of me, looking incredibly confused. "What? Are you—is everything okay?" Wiping the sleep from my eyes, I turn in a slow circle. It's still dark, with only a nightlight on.

"You're downstairs in the B&B kitchen. Are you okay?"

"I—" I rub my eyes again. "I let Rosalie use my apartment."

Her expression softens, going from worry to understanding. "And you came down to sleep in the kitchen? You could have taken one of the empty rooms. Or put her in one."

"I didn't want to make a mess."

"Jaxson." She speaks my name softly, then presses a slender hand to my chest. "You can use whatever you need."

I stare down at her hand, enjoying the warmth of her touch far more than I should be. "What time is it?"

"Four in the morning," she replies. "Why don't you come into my apartment. You can take the couch and get another few hours."

"I'm okay. I can just get up."

"Jaxson."

"No, seriously, it's okay."

She purses her lips as though preparing to argue, but then decides against it. "Then let me make us some coffee."

As she moves away from me, I rest my head in my hands, trying my best to wake myself up from the dead sleep I'd apparently been in. I'm not even entirely sure when I fell asleep, but it couldn't have been more than four hours ago since it wasn't until after midnight that I'd come downstairs.

Rosalie certainly had a lot to say, and I'm working my way up to the forgiveness I know I need to offer. But it's hard. Honestly, letting go of what she put me through feels impossible right now.

The scent of coffee fills my nose, and I raise my head as Margot sits across from me. She's wearing a pair of leggings and an off-the-shoulder cream sweatshirt, her hair in a messy bun atop her head. Her feet are bare, giving me a glimpse at pale pink toenails.

How can she be so effortlessly stunning first thing in the morning?

She turns to face me. "You okay?"

"I will be."

As soon as there's enough coffee to fill two mugs, she pauses the brewing and pours before replacing it again. She finishes prepping hers, then carries both of our coffees over to the table and sits down across from me. "Want to talk about it?"

"I never thought I'd see her again."

"You said she'd been calling."

"Sure, but for her to show up here—" I shake my head. "It caught me off guard."

"I can understand that. She's very pregnant."

"I'd always wanted kids." Saying it out loud makes the cut even deeper. "Badly."

"Why didn't you guys have kids? Sorry, I'm prying. If you don't want to talk about it, we don't have to."

"No, it's okay. Friends venting." I give her a smile as I take a sip of my coffee. "I was in the Marines at the time. Deployed near constantly, and she'd been trying to build a career in marketing. She told me that I was being selfish, that I wanted her to just sit at home with kids all the time." I shake my head. "But that wasn't it at all."

"Was she even open to discussing it?"

"No. Not once we were married. Before, she talked constantly about having kids. But once it was a possibility, she changed her mind. And I felt guilty for asking her to sacrifice her dreams for me, so I dropped it."

"Is that why you two split?"

I snort. "No. No, that was a few years later. You know I was injured overseas?"

She nods. "Michael said you nearly died."

"We were going in to rescue some civilians who'd been captured by terrorists. On the way there, though, our convoy was attacked, and the vehicle I was in was hit with a small arms missile. I shattered my spine, broke both legs, an arm, and was told I'd never walk again."

Margot gasps and covers her mouth with a hand.

"I met Lance in that hospital." I smile at the memory. It was the worst moment of my life, but Lance brought light to me that day. "He brought me an old Bible he'd been carrying when he nearly died. And he prayed over me. With me. Shortly after that, he introduced me to Michael and Elijah."

"Jaxson." Margot reaches across and covers my hand with hers.

"Anyway. When I got home, they weren't sure I'd ever walk again. They reconstructed my spine, but the doctors said it was unlikely I'd ever fully recover. As soon as I was out of the hospital and back at my apartment, Rosalie bailed."

"She did what?" Color floods Margot's cheeks. "She *left* you?"

I nod. "I woke up to a note she'd set beside the bed." Those moments come flooding back to me.

The pain of knowing she was gone.

The agony of being alone.

Of not knowing how I was going to survive.

"I was so angry. At myself. At her. At God. My phone was clear across the room, and I was still not walking, so I wasn't even sure how I was going to call for help. And then my gaze landed on the worn Bible by my bed, and I said a prayer for strength. Less than five minutes later, my brother showed up. He had a key, and when no one answered, he came in."

"I can't believe she left you." Tears roll down her cheeks. "Just lying in bed like that. Unable to take care of yourself."

"God provided for me," I tell her. "In that moment, when I felt that I had nothing left, I saw the Bible, and I turned to Him. I don't know that I ever would have fully given myself over if it weren't for that pivotal moment."

"Still." She shakes her head. "I don't understand how she could just leave you like that. Turn her back on you and—" Margot closes her eyes. When she opens them again, she appears to be slightly calmer. "You deserved better, Jaxson Payne."

"It's silly, but I still wanted to try and make things

work. After watching my parents' marriage fall apart, I only wanted to get married once. I met Rosalie my senior year of high school, right after I joined the Marines, actually, and we got married right after graduation. I thought she was the love of my life. I kept trying to call her after she left, even though my brother kept telling me it was pointless. Then when I got the divorce papers, I found out she'd been cheating on me and was already living with someone else."

"The father of her baby?"

"No." I shake my head. "According to her, she met a man who introduced her to God. They got married, and now they're starting their family."

"I know it's not the Christian thing to be so angry I want to scream at her, but I really, really do."

I smile, feeling a weight lift from my shoulders. "She came here to apologize to me."

"Seems like that's in the water," she jokes. "Your dad, too."

I smirk again. "You're not wrong there."

"How is that going, by the way? I'm here—if you ever need to talk."

"Thanks. He's been trying to get me to agree to a meet-up, but he's promised not to just show up again."

"What are you going to do?"

"I wish I knew," I tell her truthfully. "Until we find Lanetti, though, I'm not sure I can take on much more."

"So she just showed up?" Andie demands, shaking her head. "That's insane."

"She did. He handled it well, though." I look from Andie to Eliza sitting beside her, then to Reyna, Lilly, and Bianca, who are all seated around the booth in Hope Diner. We try to get together for dinner a few times a month, but with Eliza and Lilly both having new babies, it's been fewer and farther between our hangouts.

"It sounds like it." Bianca shakes her head. "I knew Jaxson had been through some stuff, but I didn't realize his wife had left him to die. That's horrible. Surgery like that—I'm impressed he's on his feet at all, let alone as active as he is."

Since Bianca was a prominent surgeon when she'd been in the Army, I'm not surprised she understood what I'd told her about Jaxson's accident. "I just feel so bad for him. Like, I just want to make him feel better."

"Make him dinner. Ask him on a date. That's how you can make things better," Andie jokes.

"We're just friends," I insist, though the twisting in my stomach at the mere thought of sharing a romantic dinner with him says otherwise.

"Girl, we know you have feelings for him," Reyna says.

"Seriously, it's apparent," Eliza adds.

"Just because you're all happy and in love doesn't mean I am, too."

"I'm not happy or in love," Bianca says. "And I can see it plain as day."

I roll my eyes and bump her with my shoulder. "Maybe we need to find you a man."

"No thanks. Good on that."

"How are things at the clinic?" Eliza questions.

Bianca, grateful for the subject change, jumps on it. "Not too bad. I prefer animals to people, so it's always relaxing."

"And Andie? How's the boutique?"

"Doing great. A big store in New York reached out to me about carrying some of my designs, so we have a meeting next month."

"What? Why didn't you say anything before!" Eliza exclaims.

Andie grins. "It didn't seem like the right time."

"Are you kidding me? We should be celebrating you! That's huge!"

Her cheeks turn pink. "I guess it is pretty cool."

"Pretty cool?" Reyna fist pumps. "That's *amazing*."

I smile as I listen to them carry on about possible ways of celebrating such a big win, though my thoughts drift almost instantly to Jaxson. I can see him, bruised and broken, lying in bed, waiting for the woman who should have been his partner to walk through the door.

How lost he must have felt.

How sad.

All while trying to find the strength to heal his body.

It makes me fall even harder for a man I have no business wanting.

"Hey, Margot. Where's your head?" Reyna asks.

"What? Oh, sorry." My cheeks heat. "I was just thinking about how horrible it must have been for him to be left behind like that."

"So your thoughts were on Jaxson." Eliza wiggles her brows.

"Yeah, I guess they were."

"And how often are they on the Marine?" Bianca asks.

"More than they should be. But we're just—"

"Friends," Lilly finishes. "Yeah, we get it. But my question is, do you *want* to just be friends? Or are you craving something more?"

My phone rings, thankfully putting an end to the awkward admission I was about to make. "Hello?"

"Hey, Mom." His tone is off, his voice different, and fear instantly turns my stomach into a pit.

"Matty, what is it?" I glance down at my phone. It's not even his number. "Where are you calling me from?"

"A friend of mine dropped his phone, and I can't find mine. Can you come get me?" he asks.

"Where are you? I thought you were at home." My throat constricts, and I slide out of the booth on legs that feel like jelly. My boy. Is he okay? Is he hurt? Did someone take him? My thoughts go to Lanetti, to the worst-case scenario.

"I snuck out to meet some friends, and they left me out at the beach. It's dark, Mom. I don't want to walk home."

Fear rips me apart. "I'm coming. Don't move. Can you send me your location? I only have the one on your phone."

"I can. But the battery is about to die. So I'll send it to you then stay here so you can find me."

"Okay. Please stay where you are. Keep away from the road." I push out of the booth.

"What is it?" Reyna demands.

"Matty snuck out and his friends left him. He's out by himself."

"Then come on, let's go get him." She stands.

"No, it's okay. I can do it."

"Margot, let me drive you." Reyna takes her purse. "Can we settle our bills later?" she asks Lilly.

"Of course. Don't even worry about it. Let me know if you guys need anything, okay?"

"Okay." I can't even think straight as I follow Reyna out to her car and climb into the passenger side. How could he sneak out like this? I thought we were past this. I thought things were finally better.

"Are you okay, momma?"

"No. I'm worried about him."

"We'll get to him. Where is he?"

I tap on the pin he sent through a text, then pull up the map and breathe a sigh of relief. "Just outside of town. Looks like ten minutes."

"See?" Reyna smiles. "We'll get him. Then you can be wringing his neck in twenty minutes for leaving in the first place."

We pull onto the main street and start driving while Reyna does her best to distract me, just like she did when we were teenagers. She talks about her school, asks me about the B&B, tells me about how she and my brother are talking about starting their family and then—headlights blind me and Reyna swerves.

"Hang on!" she screams as she jerks the wheel.

We go off the road, hitting a ditch, and my stomach lurches as we flip, landing down a hill upside down. My head slams into the window, and I scream.

The car stops moving, and everything is dead silent.

"Reyna?" I choke out.

She doesn't answer.

"Reyna!" I scream and struggle with my seat belt. It comes loose, and I fall to the roof of the car, landing on broken glass from what was left of the sunroof. I hiss through clenched teeth but try to crawl over to check her pulse.

Someone grabs my ankle.

I scream again.

They rip me back, and glass bites into my hands.

Scrambling for something—anything—I can use as a weapon, my hand closes around the handle of a glass break tool that fell from whatever cubby Reyna had been storing it in. They release my ankle just as I turn, swinging as hard as I can.

But there's no one there.

Headlights come to a stop behind me.

"Reyna!" Michael yells.

"In here!" I call out, hope flooding me.

My brother is here. He'll keep us safe.

Michael's face comes into view on the driver's side. He squats down, and tears blur his eyes. "Reyna, no, no." He checks her pulse.

She groans.

"Thank God," Michael breathes a sigh of relief. "I'm going to get you down, okay?"

"Sure thing, gorgeous," she groans. "What happened?"

"We'll figure it out." He wraps his arms around her and cuts her seat belt with his pocket knife, then carefully pulls her from the car.

Since whoever grabbed me dragged me most of the way out, I manage to make it all the way out of the car before Michael is around to my side, setting Reyna down and coming to me.

"Are you okay? Where are you hurt?" He looks me over.

"I'm sorry. I don't know what happened. Someone ran us off the road and—Matty! He's out here somewhere. He needs help." I try to get up, but Michael pushes me back down.

"Easy. Matty is fine," Michael says. "He and Jaxson were playing chess all night. They should be here any minute—"

Sirens wail in the distance, and another set of headlights pulls up beside Michael.

"That doesn't make sense. He called me."

"Reyna texted me as soon as he did, so I called Jaxson for backup. He said Matty was sitting right across from him all night. I don't know who called you, but it wasn't him."

More dread coils in my gut, and my body begins to shake, the adrenaline wearing off. With it, excruciating pain in my hands, knees, and the side of my head returns.

"Mom!" Matty screams.

"She's over here!" Michael calls out.

Seeing my boy racing toward me, his eyes wide with panic, soothes my soul. He's okay.

My son is okay.

Which means I will be, too. He kneels beside me and I reach for him, needing to wrap my arms around my boy. He's gentle as he hugs me back, then pulls away, tears in his eyes.

"Are you okay, mom?"

"I will be," I try to smile, but I know the pain must be visible on my face.

Jaxson drops to his knees beside Matty. "Where are you

hurt? Any large wounds?" He looks me over, and I show him my hands.

"Baby, can you go see Aunt Reyna? Check on her please?"

He hesitates a moment, looking between me and Jaxson, but then nods. "Sure, Mom. I can do that." He smiles at me, then gets to his feet and heads over toward Michael and Reyna.

"What is it?" Jaxson starts looking me over in more detail, clearly worried I have a life-threatening injury I didn't want Matty to know about.

"Someone tried to drag me from the car."

"What?" His tone changes instantly, going from worried to angry.

I meet his gaze, doing my best to focus on him and not the pain. "I think someone was trying to kill me."

CHAPTER 15

Jaxson

"There are no plates," Elijah tells me. "But this person followed Reyna and Margot out of the diner parking lot."

"Anything on the phone?" I ask him.

"Nope. It was a burner and has since been turned off. We can't locate it, but the last ping was in that parking lot."

"And the pin they sent?"

"Easy to do. Anyone can send a pin anywhere without being in that location. It was a trap."

The front door of the lighthouse opens, and Lance strolls in alongside a furious-looking Michael.

"Chad has an airtight alibi," he growls.

"How airtight?" I've seen criminals have seemingly strong alibis, only to have them broken the second I get them across a table.

"He was sitting in a jail cell after being picked up for drinking and driving," Lance tells me.

"How are they?" I'd left them at the hospital so I could try and make headway on who was responsible for the call and the accident, but I've been desperate to get back to Margot ever since I left.

"Reyna has a concussion and some bruising, but is otherwise okay. Margot has a concussion and lacerations on her hands and abdomen, courtesy of whoever tried to rip her out of the car."

"Matty?"

"He's good. He's staying the night with my parents so Margot will hopefully take things slow." Michael looks beyond furious, and I'm certainly right there with him. He could have lost his wife and sister in one accident, and we can't seem to figure out how or why.

"I was out at the scene of the accident this morning," Lance tells us. "Looking for a card."

"You think this is tied to Lanetti?"

"I didn't find one," he tells me. "But that doesn't mean it's not. It just seems far too suspicious that Lanetti is still missing, we have no leads whatsoever, and now someone targets Margot."

"I should have moved out. The second I thought this could be tied to me." Furious at myself, I begin to pace.

"No. You're right where you need to be. If you hadn't been there, someone could have grabbed Matty, too." Michael steps in front of me.

"No one came after Matty, though."

"Because you were there with him. If someone is

targeting my sister on Chad's behalf, grabbing Matty would be the way to go."

It was my thought, too, and why Chad was my first suspect. "And if this is tied to Lanetti?"

"We'll get it figured out. But you've been up all night." Lance clasps a hand on my shoulder. "Head back to the B&B, get some sleep, and we'll keep you updated."

"I can't sleep until we get some answers."

Alaric even called earlier to let me know that he'd found nothing notable but he would keep digging. However, I know him well enough to read his tone, and he doesn't think there's a connection.

As improbable as it is, there's someone else out there using Morah's calling card to taunt me. But why? Who?

"You need sleep," Michael says. "So do I. We'll link up later, okay?"

"Sure." But I don't feel good about leaving.

"Margot needs you," Michael tells me. "Go check on her and make sure she's safe. Please? It will help me rest."

"Okay."

"Thanks."

"Yeah." I turn back to Lance. "Call me the second you have something?"

"I will. Silas is out on an install, but he's going to stop by the scene of the accident and look, too. See if we find anything the police may have missed."

With a nod, I turn and leave the lighthouse, Michael beside me.

We step out into the sunlight, and Michael stops on the porch. "We're friends."

"Yeah. We are."

"Then I want you to know that if your interest in Margot is more than friends, I'm okay with it."

"What are you—what do you mean?"

"I saw the way you looked at her last night," he tells me.

"What do you mean?"

"Like you were willing to tear apart the entire world if it meant keeping her safe."

EXHAUSTED, I STEP INTO THE B&B.

Margot is standing behind the front desk, and the sight of her catches me off guard. Her face is bruised, one of her eyes encircled in black, the white of it bloodshot. There's a bandage at her hairline, and both of her hands have white gauze wrapped around the palms, leaving her fingers free.

"What are you doing?" I demand. "You should be resting."

"I'm fine," she insists.

"Margot—"

"I needed to do something," she insists. "My mom kept Matty tonight so I would rest. But I don't know how to rest. How can I rest, Jaxson? Someone tried to kill me. What did I ever do? I don't—"

"Margot," I interrupt, closing the distance between us. I

reach out and cup her unbruised cheek, and she stops speaking.

"I'm scared."

"I know. But you need to rest. We're going to find whoever did this."

"Reyna could have died, too."

"But she didn't."

"But she could have." She closes her eyes, and a tear slips free. "What if this is because of Chad? What if somehow—"

"It's not him," I tell her. "He was in jail last night. Sleeping off an overindulgence of alcohol."

She relaxes slightly. "Is it bad that I'm relieved it wasn't him?"

"No." And because I can't help myself, I pull her against me and wrap my arms around her. Margot envelops me back and we stand in the lobby holding onto each other for longer than friends typically would.

Holding her feels as familiar as drawing breath. "I almost lost you last night. I don't know what I would have done if—" I pull away.

"I'm okay, though. Michael scared off whoever it was, and we live to fight another day."

Footsteps on the stairs carry down happy chatter, so I step aside as Mr. and Mrs. Avery from room two stop in front of the desk.

"Margot! What happened to you?" Mrs. Avery asks, the grandmother of seven immediately coming around the desk to get a closer look at her hostess.

"I had a car accident." Margot smiles. "But I'm okay."

"Thank God. Are you sure? Do you need anything? Honey, you should not be on your feet."

"That's what I've been trying to tell her," I say.

"Listen to that man," she scolds Margot, who shoots a smile my way.

"I will. Soon. How has your stay been? Is there anything you need?"

"We're just fine," Mr. Avery says. "You go get some rest. We're headed to the diner, then to do some antiquing."

"Oh, you should stop by—"

"We have a plan," Mrs. Avery interrupts holding up a piece of paper. "You go rest. Now. I insist."

"Okay. Fair enough. But please come knock on my door if you need anything," she says.

"We will." Mrs. Avery offers me a final wave before looping her arm through her husband's and heading out the door.

"Well, you heard her. So let's go get you some rest." Forcing her to leave her work behind, I guide her toward her apartment, then hold open the door for her.

She stops just inside the door and turns to me. "Are you going upstairs?"

Something in her tone catches me off guard. "I can stay on the couch if you need me to."

"Yes, please. I don't—I don't want to be alone."

"Then I'll be right here." In demonstration, I plop down on her couch. "Yell if you need me, okay?"

She nods. "Thanks, Jaxson."

"I'll always be here for you, Margot. For you and Matty. No matter what."

———

MY PHONE RINGS, THE SHILL TONE RIPPING ME FROM SLEEP. "Payne," I answer, tone gravelly. It's dark, nearly pitch black in the living room of Margot's apartment.

"Andie and I just pulled up to the B&B, can you let us in?" Elijah asks.

"Sure thing. Is everything okay?"

"We found Lanetti."

"I'm coming." I end the call and rush to the front of the B&B, then open the door for them. He hands me a paper cup of coffee as he passes by. I lead them to Margot's open apartment, then flip on a floor lamp. "Is she alive?" I ask, dreading the answer but desperate for it at the same time.

"She is," he says. "But she's pretty bruised up and is asking for you."

I set my coffee aside and pull on my boots.

"How's Margot?" Andie asks as she shrugs out of her jacket.

"I checked on her about an hour ago, and she was doing okay." Truthfully, I'd only nodded off about thirty minutes ago, since I'd been checking on Margot every hour.

"I'll check on her soon. Are you okay?" Andie asks me.

"I'm not the one who almost died," I tell her.

She rolls her eyes. "You men and being afraid of your feelings."

"Come on, you can hammer him later. We need to get to the hospital." Elijah kisses Andie, then heads for the door.

"Have her call me when she wakes up?"

"Will do," Andie replies, then settles down on the couch with a book.

Elijah and I get into his truck, and I sip my coffee. "Where was she found?"

"She wandered into the hospital," he replies. "Has a broken rib and some nasty bruises."

My heart aches for her. "Was she assaulted?"

"We don't know," he replies, jaw tight. "She won't talk to anyone but you."

"Why me?"

"Not sure, she won't say."

The drive to the hospital is thankfully a short one, and we're pulling into the parking lot ten minutes later. I down the rest of my coffee and jump out, then head toward the front doors beside Elijah.

Did she get a good look at who took her?

Did they let her go or did she escape?

So many questions hammer through my mind as I follow Elijah down the hall. Sheriff Vick is standing outside a room, talking to one of his deputies. When he sees us, he dismisses the man and runs a hand over his graying hair.

"How is she?" I ask.

"Alive. But she's not really speaking. Just asking for you."

"I'll let you know what she says." I push into the room. Lanetti is sitting on her bed, her face pale and bruised. When she sees me, though, she breaks into tears and sits up.

"Jaxson. You're here."

"I am."

"He told me you wouldn't come for me. That I'd die there."

"Who told you?"

She shakes her head. "I didn't see him. He always had a mask on. But he told me that you didn't care about me. That you were selfish. I knew he was wrong." The tears slide down her cheeks rapidly, and I reach out to take her hand.

She stills beneath my touch.

"How did you escape?"

Her expression darkens. "He was holding me in an old shed outside of town. I'd been tied in a corner, and he would lock the door from the outside every time he left. This time, though, he forgot, and I ran the second I knew I was alone." Her eyes fill. "I was so scared. But I knew I had to get away."

"You did great," I assure her with a smile. "Truly, you were strong, Lanetti."

She beams at me. "Thank you, Jaxson. Seriously. It means the world to hear you say that."

"Have you told Sheriff Vick anything? You need to tell

him everything you've told me, and if there are any other details you remember. Then we can catch this guy."

She nods. "I'll tell him everything."

The door opens, and Lanetti's mother rushes in. The change in the girl is subtle, but enough that I pick up on it.

"Lanetti!" her mother cries out as she falls against the side of the bed, wrapping her arms around her daughter.

I withdraw my hand, and Lanetti smiles at me, then hugs her mother. "I'm okay, Mom," she says.

"Of course you are. Because you're strong. What happened?"

"I'll let the sheriff know you're ready to talk to him, okay?"

"Will you come back?"

"I'll visit you again."

She breathes a sigh of relief. "Thanks, Jaxson. Truly."

"Thank you for escaping."

I leave and shut the door quietly behind me, trying to figure out just how to explain the knot in my gut that's saying the worst is yet to come.

Whoever went after Margot is the same one who took Lanetti.

I know it.

I feel it.

I'm the link between these two women.

So how do I prove it?

CHAPTER 16

Margot

Jaxson has been gone most of the day, but hearing Lanetti is alive and going to make a full recovery is enough to plaster a smile on my face even though we're still no closer to figuring out who tried to grab me from the accident and why.

But with Silas sitting in my foyer, acting as my own personal guard, I don't feel at risk. He's hardly spoken at all, though his adorable four-year-old niece, Eloise, is currently playing chess with Matty. Well, he's trying to teach her and letting her win.

Seeing them sitting there together and witnessing how kind my son is makes me long for another child.

"Yay! I won! I won, Uncle Si!" She rushes over to Silas, who lights up like a Christmas tree when he sees her excitement.

"That's great, Nugget. I knew you could do it." He high-fives her, and she does a little dance.

"Matty said that I'm a natural." She looks back at Matty with a wide smile, and he nods.

"It's true. A prodigy."

Eloise beams at Matty, then rushes over to him. "Can we play again?"

"Only if you take it easy on me," he replies.

"No promises," she says. "Because if I take it easy, how will you learn?"

Silas smiles, then shifts his attention back to the computer in front of him.

"Want some coffee?" I ask him.

"That would be great. Thank you."

"Creamer?"

"No, thanks. Just black."

"You got it. I'll be right out." With a smile, I head into the kitchen and start prepping the coffee. I don't know much about the former Navy SEAL, other than the fact that out of all the Knight Security guys, he had the roughest time overseas.

Michael won't ever go into details, and I don't press.

But Silas is quiet, reserved, and keeps to himself. Except when Eloise is in the room. It's clear how much he loves the little girl he's been raising since her parents died.

As soon as I'm done with the coffee, I head into the foyer again and offer him a mug, then sit on one of the high-back chairs across from him. "Eloise is adorable."

"She's perfect," he replies.

"It must be hard, raising her all alone."

"You would know a thing or two about being a single parent," he replies.

"Sure, but it's different. Matty was older when Chad left. You've been raising her since she was an infant, right?"

He nods.

"That takes a strong person, and you're doing a fantastic job. Not that you need me to tell you that."

The closest thing I've seen to a smile when Eloise isn't around graces his face. "Still nice to hear it sometimes."

"That's true."

He takes a drink of his coffee, clearly uncomfortable with the personal conversation. That is, if his fidgeting is any indication. "You've done a great job with your son. He's a good kid."

"He is. I give God all the credit for that one, though. He guided us both through Chad leaving and helped keep me sane when I wanted to lie down and cry."

Silas doesn't respond, and I get the feeling he's not entirely sure about his own faith. "I haven't seen you at church."

"I don't go," he replies, then turns back to his computer.

"Thanks for bringing her here, and for staying."

"Thank you for the coffee." He offers me a half smile, so I get up and head into the kitchen to start prepping for dinner. Should I be cooking? Probably not.

But I'm desperate for lasagna and something that will keep me busy. Aside from fresh towels, which Matty ran up to room three, and a lightbulb replacement in room four, which Matty also handled, no one has really needed anything.

It's been quiet. And quiet allows my mind to wander.

The bell over the front door rings, and I glance over as Jaxson comes inside.

Just seeing him makes my heart flutter and my stomach twist into nervous knots. I can still feel his arms around me from last night, still feel the gentle caress of his fingers against my cheek when he'd come in to check on me because he thought I was asleep.

Oh, to have the love of a man like that.

What would that be like?

He and Silas fall into a deep conversation, and Silas nods, then says something quietly in response. What are they talking about? Me? Lanetti? An update in the case?

The two men shake hands.

"Eloise, we have to go, Nugget."

"Ahh, Uncle Si! I haven't won, though!"

"We'll play again," Matty promises.

"Okay." She sticks her bottom lip out in a pout, but hugs Matty, then bounces over to her uncle. "Bye, Mrs. Anderson."

"Bye, sweetie. We'll see you soon, okay? Thanks again, Silas."

He nods, then takes the little girl's hand and heads out the front door.

Jaxson watches them leave, then turns to me. He looks exhausted. Dead on his feet.

"Oh, Mom?" Matty says.

"Yeah?"

"Uncle Michael said he's gonna come pick me up tonight if that's okay? He got a new update to Halo and I really wanna try it out. Please, please, please?"

I smile. He's been hovering over me all day, so to see him acting like a teen again makes my heart happy. "That's fine. What time?"

"Like seven?"

"Okay. You better have something green with dinner."

"Jello can be green."

I arch a brow.

"Fine. I'll have broccoli. Aunt Reyna's been making him eat better, anyway. I'm going to go text him. Hey, Jax!"

"Hey, kid."

Matty leaves the room, bounding into the apartment and closing the door.

The air between Jaxson and me feels heavier somehow, though I'm not sure what's changed. Was it last night? What almost happened? Or something more? "So since Michael and Reyna are taking Matty for the night, I don't suppose you'd be up for some lasagna, huh? I have a craving that will not be sated."

Jaxson smiles, but it doesn't reach his eyes. "That would be great."

"How's Lanetti?"

"She's doing okay, surprisingly. Girl is resilient."

"It's amazing she's alive."

"It is," he agrees. "Anyway, I'm going to go grab a shower and maybe nap for a bit. You okay?"

"Yeah. I can call if there's an issue, but it's been quiet around here. It would be foolish of someone to walk into a fully booked B&B and try to take me." It's meant to ease his obvious nerves, but all it does is cause his brow to crease. "Seriously, Jaxson. It's okay. I promise to yell if I need anything."

After a moment of hesitation, he nods and heads back up the stairs.

"Hey, Jaxson?"

"Yeah?" He turns back toward me.

"I'm really glad you're here."

"I am too."

After pulling the garlic bread out of the oven, I set it on the counter, then look over the spread before me. It's six forty-two, and everything is ready except me.

Lasagna, garlic bread, a Caesar salad with homemade dressing, and a freshly baked tiramisu, courtesy of Kyra Redding, cover one side of the kitchen counter, making my entire apartment smell like a classy Italian restaurant.

I press a hand to my stomach. Why am I nervous? I've eaten with Jaxson more times than I can count. Matty wasn't there for a few of those either, so why does this feel so different?

Because I feel different.

Moving as fast as I can without running, I slip into my bedroom, then pull my hair down from its bun and run a brush through the dark strands, stopping only long enough to study the bruises covering half of my face.

Ugh. I look like a hot mess.

But this is as good as it's going to get tonight. So, with that in mind, I slip out of my cooking shoes and into a pair of brown flats that match the centers of the sunflowers on my dress.

I shut the door to my bedroom. "Matty, your uncle will be here any minu—"

"Already here," Michael announces as he and Reyna breeze into my apartment. She has a bruise on the side of her head, but otherwise looks in good spirits. It puts my mind at ease, because every time I close my eyes, I see her upside down in that car.

My brother takes one look at me, then at the food on the counter and the pristinely set table, and narrows his gaze. "What is happening here?"

"I—nothing. I'm eating."

"With who?" He arches a brow.

"It's none of your business," Reyna insists.

Matty comes down the hall with his backpack. "Man, this smells delicious. Jaxson is one lucky dude, Mom. You outdid yourself."

My cheeks heat, making my face feel like it's fifty degrees hotter than the rest of my face.

"*Jaxson?* You did all of this for Jaxson?" Michael gapes

at me, feigned betrayal in his dark gaze. "How long has this been going on?"

"It's not going on," I insist. "This is the first time—well, not the first time I've cooked for him—but the first time like this." I'm rambling. Mortified. Unsure. My stomach churns, so I press a hand to it.

"Michael, stop acting like this," Reyna says, lightly smacking him on the arm.

"Like what?"

"You're teasing her and it's not fair," she replies.

"But—"

"He stood up for me, so as far as I'm concerned, he's good enough to date Mom."

"That's all it takes, huh?" Michael musses his hair, and Matty leans into him. The camaraderie between them warms my heart. "Look, I want you happy, Margot. I'm just messing with you. I just wish you would have told me you were interested in him like this."

"I don't know that I am—or I didn't know that I was —" I close my eyes and take a deep breath. "Listen, I invited him over for dinner since Matty was going to be with you, so I could thank him for everything he's done for us. That's all."

"Uh-huh." Michael grins, and the amusement on his face tells me we're far from finished discussing this.

"Look, can you go, please? He'll be here soon, and I need to finish a few things." I start ushering them toward the door.

"You look beautiful," Reyna tells me. "Call if you need anything?"

"I will. Thanks." I smile at my brother's wife, then guide them out of the B&B and shut the door quickly. I have no idea if Jaxson is still upstairs or not, and the last thing I want to do is bring him down sooner than I need to.

I want everything to be perfect.

I need everything to be perfect.

I've just shut the door to my private apartment when I hear a slight whistling sound. *Strange.* Thinking Matty might have left something playing on his computer, I head down the hall toward his room. But as I get closer to the bathroom at the end of the hall, the noise gets louder and stops sounding like whistling and more like— "Oh no!" Water spews out from beneath the sink, pouring onto the ground.

I drop to my knees and rip open the cabinet, only to get sprayed with a face full of water. "No, not today! Ugh! Why?" I cover the pipe with my hand, and water spews through my fingertips. Frantically, I scan the immediate area for anything that I can use to temporarily hold off the water until I can get a wrench from the garage.

My gaze lands on an olive-green towel on the ground. *Yes!* Thank you, Matty, and your terrible cleaning skills. With one hand on the pipe, I kick out of my shoes and stretch out my leg, gripping the towel with my toes.

As soon as I have it in reach, I release the pipe just long enough to wrap it with the towel. Breathing heavily, I sit for just a moment, but right as I'm starting to get up, water begins pouring through the towel.

"No, no, no!"

"What's happening here?"

I glance back at Jaxson, who stands in the doorway looking like he just stepped off the cover of a magazine—all while I look like a wet rat.

Why?

"I don't know. The pipe just started spraying water. I was going to go turn the main off temporarily, then grab a wrench and try to fix it." Since Chad took off, I haven't had a lot of overhead, so I save money by trying to fix things myself.

It's amazing what you can accomplish with a how-to video and a frugal attitude.

"I'll go turn off the water and grab the tools." He starts to roll up the sleeves of his button-down.

"No, I can do it. Please, you're wearing such nice clothes." I tighten the towel and get to my feet. Then slip on the water. I go down—hard—until Jaxson catches me against his chest. Desire burns in my belly, and I turn my face up to him, feeling my cheeks heat. "And now you're soaking wet."

"Worth it," he replies without hesitation, then clears his throat and heads for the door. "I'll grab the tools. Dinner smells delicious, by the way." After flashing me a grin, he turns and leaves.

As soon as I know he's gone, I risk a look at myself in the mirror.

My hair is drenched, all remnants of loose curls gone, and the dress I was wearing is plastered against me like a second skin. *Fantastic.* So now I'm bruised and soaking wet.

The water stops spewing, letting me know that Jaxson has turned off the main for my apartment—which is thankfully separate from the rest of the B&B. Shoving my disappointment for the way this evening is turning out down, I grab some towels from the linen closet and start mopping up water from the floor.

A few minutes later, he returns with his sleeves rolled up and a toolbox in hand. "I can handle this if you want to get changed. I imagine that's not all that comfortable."

"Understatement," I say with a half smile. "Thanks. I'm sorry about this. I really didn't want to work tonight."

"No worries at all." He flashes me a grin. "I'm actually decent with plumbing. And worst case, we can call Lance."

"You are a lifesaver, thanks." I quickly make my way out of Matty's bathroom, and into my bathroom, then strip out of my clothes and hang them over my shower curtain rod to dry.

Knowing the evening is what it is now, I choose to wear a pair of flannel pajama bottoms and a T-shirt with the words *Hope Springs Music Fest.* I may not look like a million bucks, but I'm comfortable, and that counts for something.

I'm just heading back down the hall as Jaxson is stepping out of the bathroom with his toolbox. "All good. One of the pipes was loose, so I tightened it. You shouldn't have any more issues."

"Came loose? Does that just happen?"

"It can," he says. "They're older pipes. But everything tightened just fine, so I don't think anything is broken."

I breathe a sigh of relief. "Well, I really appreciate it."

He sets his toolbox down, then steps up to the sink to wash his hands. "This all smells amazing."

"We should have already been eating. I think some of it might be getting cold." I stare at it in frustration. I worked *hours* on dinner. Is it really going to be spoiled because of some loose pipes?

"I think it smells amazing, and I know it's going to be delicious." He dries his hands, then turns to face me. "What can I do to help?"

"Nothing. Please sit." I gesture to the small round table in the center of the kitchen, then start plating dinner as he takes a seat.

Easy, Margot. It's just dinner with a friend. You can do this. You've done it before.

"So, other than the indoor waterpark, how was the rest of your day?" Jaxson questions.

I laugh. "It was good." Turning with plates in hand, I set them down, then grab each of us glasses of water before taking my seat. "Are you up for leading the prayer?"

"Sure." He reaches out with one of his hands, and I slip mine in without hesitation. The feel of his palm against mine warms my blood, calming the storm in me without him even trying. I close my eyes, hoping to keep my feelings from displaying all over my face.

"Heavenly Father, we are forever grateful for Your mercy and grace. We thank You for this food before us and the company we share together. We would have nothing in this life without You, and even if we don't always understand why things happen the way they do, we thank You for always being there and we trust in Your plan because it is far greater than our own. Thank You for keeping Margot and Reyna safe the other night, and for bringing Lanetti home. Amen."

"Amen." I withdraw my hand and put a napkin in my lap. "You should know, you're Matty's hero."

"Oh?" he asks, then takes a drink of water before loading up his fork with some lasagna.

"After what you did the other day at church when Chad came after him, and the fact that you used to catch bad guys for a living? Absolutely."

"I'm no hero."

"To him you are. Ever since that day at the church when you stepped in. He's been so angry with Chad, and after that blowup, I'm not sure what Chad would have done if you weren't there to stop it." I swallow hard, trying to smother the anger that's resurfacing. Chad would have physically hurt Matty. Of that, I'm sure. And then my son would wear those emotional scars for the rest of his life.

"Do you think he would have hurt him?" Jaxson asks after swallowing his bite. "Was he ever violent before?"

I hesitate. I've never told anyone about Chad hitting

me. I thought it was because I was embarrassed, because I didn't want to be looked at like a victim. But truthfully? I was protecting him. Because I know my brother, and I know what he would do if he found out that Chad ever put hands on me.

I'm so tired of protecting him. "He hit me once."

Jaxson's gaze turns murderous, and he slowly lowers his fork. "When?"

"The day I kicked him out. I'd ignored the cheating. The violent outbursts where he'd scream at me or throw things. But when he put his hands on me, all I saw was Matty getting hit. Matty witnessing it. I knew I couldn't let him experience that, so I told Chad if he didn't leave, I was calling Michael." I laugh nervously, then put some food on my fork even though the vulnerability I feel right now as I pour my words out to Jaxson has made me anything but hungry. "Chad might not be afraid of much, but he's terrified of my big brother."

Jaxson reaches across the table and covers my hand with his. "I am so sorry, Margot."

"I didn't want to say anything before because—"

"Michael," Jaxson finishes.

"Yeah." I smile at him, surprised at how much relief I feel just sharing this with someone. "I never want my brother to suffer because of something that I caused."

He withdraws his hand and takes a bite of food as the words hang between us. Then he takes a drink of water and says, "You think it's your fault he hit you?"

"No. Not that. But I married Chad. Even though my

parents asked me not to. Michael was already gone by then, and they told me that I could stay with them. That I didn't have to get married just because I'd gotten pregnant." I swallow hard, feeling the shame resurfacing. I hadn't wanted to sleep with Chad that night, but I'd been so afraid he'd walk away from me if I didn't that I gave in.

I listened when he promised me forever.

Cried silently as he used my body.

Then felt even more shame when the pregnancy test came back positive.

"We've all done things we regret, but you got a great deal on that one because you got Matty."

I smile at him now, then quickly wipe my eyes as tears threaten to fall. "You are absolutely correct. I can't even say I regret it because I love my son with everything that I am. He's my whole world. And even though things with Chad turned out the way they did, I am grateful that God blessed me with my son."

Jaxson takes a bite of his salad. "I am too. Kid is great company."

I doubt he realizes just how much his words mean to me, and I can't bring myself to speak it out loud without tearing up again. God has always been there for me. Even during the darkest moments of my life, when I felt like I was walking the road alone, I knew He was there. And that's what's helped me get through.

The knowledge that my sins have been washed clean by the love and sacrifice of Jesus. That God has a plan and has been with me every single step of the way.

"I told you all about my marriage going up in flames. About Rosalie's cheating."

"And her abandoning you," I add, still furious at the woman for what she'd done. Letting her walk out the door without giving her a piece of my mind was harder than I thought it would be.

But saying anything to her now wouldn't fix the past. And there's a part of me that's glad she turned her back on him.

Because now he's here...with me. Even if we are just friends.

Still, my heart aches for him. For the man who nearly died serving his country, then came home only to be shoved aside by the woman who vowed to love him forever. Who does that? What type of person would treat the man they love that way?

"It is all part of God's plan—Lance helped me see that. He came out after she left and stayed with me as I recovered, even though he was barely out of the hospital himself. It's his faith, and his guiding me to my own, that kept me alive. And thanks to God, I not only walked again, but I'm doing things every day the doctors claimed would be impossible."

"You said your brother was there, too?"

He nods. "But he was in college at the time, so he couldn't be there all the time. Lance was. His parents even flew out to help, and I'd never met them before."

"That's so kind."

"It was. And for someone like me who'd never had a

functional family, it felt—warm. Like home. This is delicious, by the way."

I return his smile and take a bit of my own food. "It really is. Plumbing emergency and all."

Jaxson's grin spreads, and my stomach fills with butterflies. He's so handsome. So kind. Why couldn't I have met him before Chad?

But then I wouldn't have Matty. And I wouldn't trade my son for anything.

I can, however, be grateful that God brought Jaxson to me now.

Even if it's for no reason other than friendship.

CHAPTER 17

Jaxson

The amount of anger I feel knowing Chad ever put his hands on Margot far surpasses everything I have ever felt.

I want to hunt him down.

Make him hurt.

Even as I know vengeance is not mine.

So I take a deep breath and drive the conversation in another direction, all while silently vowing to always protect this woman and her son. I steal a glance at her now, looking absolutely gorgeous despite the bruises on her face and the stress she's under.

How does she manage to look so put together when I feel like I'm falling apart?

"So, you know a lot about me and my family," Margot says, then takes a bite of her bread. Does she know how stunning she looks? Even sitting here in sweats and a baggy T-shirt, she looks just as gorgeous as she did in that sunflower dress, covered in water, flustered and frustrated. "Can you tell me about yours?"

Her question is like a bucket of cold water. "It's not a great story," I reply honestly. "My mom never really wanted my brother and I, so after my drunken father bailed on us, she drove us to a homeless shelter and left us."

Margot's expression turns horrified. "She did *what?* Are you serious? That's horrible!"

"It was," I agree. "I managed to keep my brother and I out of the system by working odd jobs and stealing food when we had no money to afford it. We ate leftover scraps from restaurant kitchens and slept wherever we could find a place."

"Jaxson."

The way she says my name soothes a bit of the pain that has followed me all of my life. That feeling of being unwanted, the feeling that Rosalie only cemented by leaving me. For a long time, I didn't understand why I was so unlovable. What was so wrong with me. I can't even count the number of times I laid in a dark alley, holding onto my brother to keep him warm, while silently sobbing. "We survived. My brother is married now with a baby on the way. He has a good, steady job, and managed to get into college. It all worked out."

"But at what sacrifice?" She reaches across the table and covers my hand the same way I covered hers. "I am so sorry you went through that."

I swallow hard, then turn my hand to hold hers. It just

feels so right. Like this woman was made for me, and I for her. Like I was born to love her. To protect her. To cherish her. "It all turned out okay. And it took me a long time to realize that I wasn't alone. Even when I thought I was."

"You have always been perfectly loved," she replies.

"Which was a great thing to realize for a man who felt unlovable."

"You're not unlovable," she says quickly, her gaze holding mine. "You just didn't find the right person."

"Neither did you," I reply.

I could lean around the table and kiss her. It's small enough that it would take very little effort to touch my lips to hers. And I want to so badly. I'm desperate to know what her mouth would feel like on mine.

Is this the woman? The one I was always supposed to find?

An alarm shrieks, pulling us apart. I jump to my feet, then reach behind me and close my hand to the firearm at my back. "What is that?"

"Fire alarm." Her eyes widen, and she sprints out into the B&B.

Pajama-clad, sleepy-eyed people are already rushing down the stairs.

"Everyone outside, please! Be safe, move carefully!" she orders as she dials 9-1-1 on the front desk phone. "Oh, what is happening now?"

I open the door and help everyone file out, all while keeping my attention on making sure Margot remains safe.

"How many are outside?" she asks.

"Six," I tell her.

"Six." Her eyes widen. "There's still a couple upstairs. They're elderly, have hearing aids. They may not have woken up." She turns and heads for the stairs, but I grip her arm.

"I'll get them. Go outside and make sure everyone is fine."

"Jaxson—"

"Go." I head upstairs, and by the time I get to the top, I see smoke billowing out from the door of one of the rooms. Since I don't know what room they're in, I slam my boot into the door, splintering it open.

Smoke fills my lungs, and I cover my mouth with my arm as my eyes burn. Flames climb up the far wall, but the bed looks made, so I rush further down the hall to the only other closed door.

Knowing that if they didn't hear the alarm, they won't hear me knocking, I kick the door open, then stumble inside. Smoke follows me in, and I rush forward as a groggy elderly man sits up and moves between me and his wife.

I point behind me. "There's a fire!" I yell.

He reaches up to his ear and presses something.

"Fire!" I yell again.

His eyes widen, and he rushes out of bed and grabs his wife's robe.

"What's happening?" she asks after turning her hearing aid on.

"There's a fire, Midge, we have to go."

She stands, then sways on her feet.

I don't hesitate as I scoop her up, knowing that it won't be long before the fire spreads out of the room. Especially since I kicked the door open in my search for them. "I'll carry you down. Leave your things, the fire department is on their way. Cover your mouth and nose with something."

She uses the sleeve of her robe, and he grabs a throw blanket, then follows me out into the hall. The smoke is so thick it burns my eyes and throat. Since I'm carrying her, I can't cover my nose, so I do my best to hold my breath as I rush down the stairs, her husband behind me.

The moment we're out in the fresh air, I draw in a heavy breath and set her down.

"Thank you. Thank you," the husband says as he wraps an arm around her.

I nod, then cough as I try to take another deep breath.

Margot rushes to my side. "Are you okay?"

I nod again, trying to stifle my coughing. But as I straighten, I see a shadow move around the back of the house. "Stay here. Stay with everyone."

"What? Where are you going?"

I don't answer, just reach behind and grip my firearm, then rush around the side of the house as fast as I can move, given the smoke I inhaled.

The shadow keeps running. "Wait! Stop!" I keep running after whoever it is, knowing in my gut they had something to do with this fire. Flames like that don't just happen.

The person leaps over a fence, then sprints across the street and disappears into the tree line. I jump over, determined to catch them, and then—someone lays on a horn and tires screech. I leap back just in time to avoid being smashed by a passing car.

They continue driving, and I start toward the trees as soon as they've passed, though I know without a doubt the person I was chasing got away.

This time.

"ACCELERANT WAS USED," FIRE CHIEF PETER PAULSON SAYS as he crosses over to where Margot and I are standing just outside the B&B. Pastor Redding came a few hours ago and picked up all of the guests, and he, Doc, Lance, and Mrs. McGinley took in all four couples, allowing them to stay in their spare bedrooms.

Thankfully, no one was hurt.

"So it was arson." I cross my arms. Since I shared that someone ran from the scene with Margot, she's not surprised either.

"That's what I'm leaning toward. Any idea who could have done it?"

"I don't have cameras inside the B&B for the privacy of my guests, and no one was staying in that room." She looks about one bad news delivery from falling over, so I wrap an arm around her shoulders to steady her.

I do it without thinking, and I'm grateful when she leans into me rather than pulling away.

"The window was open, and since you said you just opened the door—" Paulson trails off.

"I didn't touch the window," I reply.

"It was closed," Margot confirms. "When I went in there and cleaned this afternoon after checkout, I made sure it was closed and locked. I always do."

"Someone must have gotten in, then climbed out that way after starting the fire. Any idea who it could be?"

"Chad is the first one who comes to mind," she growls. "But I'd be surprised if he were that stupid."

"You'd be surprised what people will do when they feel cornered." Peter writes something on his notepad. "We all went to school together, and I remember what a hothead he was."

"But burning down the B&B?" She shakes her head. "That seems like a lot."

"You were run off the road by a strange car, and now your B&B is hit? Chad has the most to gain over hurting you. We'll look into him, and I'll be sure to pass this information on to Sherriff Vick." He looks at me. "Can you give me a description of the person you saw running away?"

"Sure. It was dark, though, so I didn't get as good of a look as I would have hoped. They were fast, managed to jump over the fence without hesitation. Whoever it was wore a black hoodie, a mask, and dark pants. But that's all I've got. I'm sorry. Elijah is checking security footage now, seeing if we caught him on the exterior cameras."

"Great. You'll let me know?" he asks.

"Sure thing."

"Awesome. Give it a couple more hours before you go inside," he tells Margot. "There's substantial damage to the upstairs, and we need to make sure it's sound before you go in."

"Substantial damage?" Margot chokes on the words. "How substantial? Will I be able to reopen soon?"

Peter hesitates. Just long enough that I can imagine he's trying to pull the punch as much as he can. "It's bad, Margot. But we'll get it figured out, okay?" Peter gently taps her on the shoulder, then turns and leaves.

"Substantial damage," she chokes out. "Jaxson, I was *barely* making it before. I owe you money. What am I going to do? This is my only income."

I turn her to face me. "We'll get it figured out, okay? Don't worry about me. I'm okay. I don't need the money."

"It's your money."

She's spiraling. I run my thumbs over her cheeks. "Why don't we head over to Michael and Reyna's? They said to come over when we're done here, and they'll have some food ready. Let's get you something to eat, then we can start figuring out the rest."

She begins to cry and covers her face with both hands as her shoulders shake. "I'm so sorry, Jaxson. I—"

"Don't apologize." Wrapping both arms around her, I draw her in against my chest and hold her tightly as she cries.

My cell rings, and I ignore it. But then it rings a second

time, and Margot pulls away. "Answer it, please. I'll be okay." She forces a smile, her eyes red.

I withdraw my cell, and not recognizing the number, press it to my ear. "Payne."

"Jaxson?" The woman on the other line sniffles. "Is that you?"

"Lanetti?"

Margot's eyes go wide.

"He found me again."

"Where are you?" I demand.

"You said you would keep me safe," she sobs.

"Tell me where you are!" I roar into the phone.

She cries out as though she's been struck. "He—he said I could call you." Her voice cracks. "He said to tell you something."

"Where are you? Who said to tell me something?"

"Roses are red, violets are blue, wherever I go, you're coming too. By the seashore. By the seaside. I'll be forgotten, swept away by the tide." She chokes on a sob. "Jaxson, please—" The call ends, and I stare down at my phone, fear and anger churning in my gut.

He's toying with me.

I'd be willing to bet he let her go to give us all a false sense of security.

A win so we'd play his game harder.

And now he's giving me the chance to find Lanetti— even when we both know she'll likely be dead long before I do.

CHAPTER 18

Margot

"Repeat the riddle," Lance says.

"'Roses are red, violets are blue, wherever I go, you're coming too. By the seashore, by the seaside, I'll be forgotten, swept away by the tide.'" Jaxson is pacing back and forth, trying his best to keep his tone level, but I can see his fear.

It's written all over his face. All over all of our faces.

I'm sitting in the lighthouse while Lance is standing before a dry-erase board, writing down the riddle Lanetti relayed to Jaxson. Elijah has headphones on and is still combing through the B&B's exterior security footage, while Silas sits on a desk, staring at the riddle.

Jaxson keeps pacing.

He'd wanted to take me to Michael's first, drop me off then come here, but with how shaken he was, I insisted on driving us here. My brother and Reyna are dropping Matty off with my parents, then coming straight over here as soon as he's settled.

"Wherever I go, you're coming too. Is that referring to you finding her?" I ask.

"That would be my bet," Lance replies. "How did this guy work before?"

"It's not the same person," Jaxson says, stopping and placing both hands on the back of a chair. "My former partner confirmed that Morah's still in prison and no one has visited him since he was convicted."

"So a copycat." Silas continues staring straight ahead. "That means he could be a wildcard."

"He already proved that by letting Lanetti go, then grabbing her again." Jaxson straightens and crosses his arms.

"You think he let her go on purpose?"

Jaxson nods. "It was a game. A way to show us what he's capable of."

"I don't see anything we can use," Elijah says as he removes his headphones. He looks up, his gaze traveling over everyone in the room. "Sorry, I didn't hear anything else. What happened?"

"We're about to dive headfirst into one of the most difficult cases of my career. You said there's nothing we can use?"

He shakes his head. "A couple stills of the guy as he was slipping out of the B&B. He did climb out of the window."

"How did he get in?"

"Looks like your apartment," he tells me.

My blood chills. "What?"

"Because he came in when the alarm was disabled, we didn't get a proximity alert. It looks like whoever it was entered through your bedroom window."

"My bedroom? He was in my bedroom?" The room around me begins to spin as panic sets in. "I feel sick." Bile burns in my throat.

Jaxson crosses over and stands beside me, then presses a hand to my upper back where he starts rubbing slow circles. "You and Matty are safe," he reminds me. "That's what matters."

My mind is reeling, going over the events of the evening while trying to figure out just how someone managed to get in through my bedroom window. I *always* check to make sure it's locked. Literally every single night before I go to bed. Which means they had to have come in at a time earlier in the day and unlocked it. All without me knowing. *Matty.* Matty had been home. They could have hurt him.

The room spins faster and faster.

I look up at Jaxson. "The pipes. What if someone loosened them to distract me so they could get upstairs?"

Jaxson's gaze darkens.

"What pipes?" Lance asks.

"The pipes in Matty's bathroom were leaking. I was distracted while I tried to get the water to stop pouring out. What if they used that to sneak upstairs?"

"But I came from upstairs, and I didn't see anyone."

"It's entirely possible that they managed to get up before you saw them, though. It was at least five minutes before you got downstairs. It had to be." I try to recall feeling like anything was off, but I'd been so occupied with my nerves over the night as well as the pipes that I probably would've missed an entire drumline if they'd played through the B&B. "And whoever it is must have gotten into my apartment through the front. They had to have. I don't see how they got in through my bedroom window when I lock it every single night."

"We didn't see anyone on the cameras," Elijah insists. "Just your registered guests, and nothing popped as out of the ordinary with any of them. We ran backgrounds," he adds.

I can't even get into how violated that would likely make my guests feel if they knew about it, because right now my top priority is trying to make sure Matty is secure.

"Is it possible Matty unlocked the window?" Lance asks.

"No, I—" I groan and cover my face. "It was me. I did open the window before church. It was so nice out, and I wanted to get some fresh air into the apartment. I must have forgotten to lock it."

"It's not your fault."

"It is my fault," I snap at Jaxson. "Whoever set my B&B on fire got in because I forgot to lock my window. They had direct access to my son because of my carelessness." My eyes fill, and I suck in a breath. How stupid could I be?

The door opens, and Michael steps in, Reyna at his

side. My brother's dark gaze, so like my own, finds me, and I rush forward, feeling like a terrified little girl again who'd had a nightmare and went to her big brother for help.

He wraps his arms around me, and I hold on to him, breathing in his familiar scent.

Jaxson makes me feel safe.

But my big brother will always feel like home.

"It's okay, sis. Matty is with Mom and Dad, and we'll catch this guy, okay? Both of them," he adds, and I know that he's speaking about whoever took Lanetti.

Sniffling, I pull away, then take a deep breath and steady my emotions. "Okay."

"Catch me up on what we've got," Michael says, then leans back against the desk as Reyna moves to my side and wraps an arm around my waist.

"Hey, sweetie, can I come in?" My mom cracks the door to my childhood bedroom, then peeks inside.

"Sure thing." I set my pen aside and turn to face her in the desk chair that's been mine since my freshman year of high school.

My mom walks into the room, then takes a seat on the edge of my bed. "Matty and Dad are outside working in the shop."

I smile, so happy that they're bonding. It wasn't too long ago that my dad, a former cop now bound to a wheelchair, would do nothing but sit in front of the television, depressed and wishing he'd died rather than been injured. "That's good."

"Yeah. It's nice to see them together. Matty looks a lot like your father did when he was younger. Same as Michael."

"Our genes run strong," I reply.

My mom chuckles. "How are you holding up?"

"Not great. I barely had enough money to keep the doors open as it was, and now with the fire—I'm just not sure I can afford to reopen." I fight back the tears threatening to spill. Crying will do me no good. I know that, but I still cried my eyes out in the shower earlier. I haven't even begun to consider how I'm going to pay Jaxson back too.

All in all, I am grateful no one was hurt in the fire, but I'm not sure how I'm going to climb out of this one.

"God will see you through, baby girl. He always will."

"Maybe this B&B isn't what I'm supposed to be doing." I run my hands over my face.

"What do you mean?"

"It's just—it's been an uphill battle, Mom. It ruined my marriage—"

"No. It didn't ruin your marriage," my mom interrupts. "Chad ruined your marriage because he couldn't be faithful." The anger on her face is potent, which is honestly amusing given the fact that my mom is one of the most even-tempered people I've ever met.

"It wasn't until the B&B that we started having problems."

"This life tests us all. He failed. You didn't. The B&B had nothing to do with it." She runs her hands over the skirt of her dress, smoothing out the light blue fabric.

"Either way, I just don't see how I reopen. I have to reimburse everyone who's been displaced and handle the fact that their personal belongings either have water and smoke damage or were destroyed altogether. Then I'll have to pay the deductible and any additional out of pocket expenses the insurance won't cover, somehow pay the bills while it's in repair—" I close my eyes as the walls start to close in on me again.

My mom's hand covers mine, so I open my eyes to see that she's now kneeling in front of me. "It'll all work out, baby. Don't lose sight of your dreams."

"What if it doesn't? I have nothing else, Mom. I have no husband to help cover bills, which means I'll have to get a full-time job, but I don't have any actual skills. I went from school straight to being a mom." Fear shreds me apart. What will I do? How will Matty get into college? I'll likely need every penny I've saved for him just to get us a place to live.

"You hush right now, Margot Anderson. You are the smartest, most talented woman I have ever had the pleasure of knowing, and I will not hear you talk poorly on yourself just because you've hit a speed bump. You hear me?"

"A road bump? My entire business—and home, by the way—nearly burned completely to the ground."

"That doesn't mean you get to say terrible things about yourself, young lady."

I let out a laugh. Leave it to my mom to put things into perspective. The woman has never met an obstacle that took her down. "You're right."

"I know I am. You and Matty will stay here until your B&B is repaired, and then you'll be right back on your feet. Your dad and I can help with the bills."

"No, Mom. You guys are not going to help with that."

"Yes, we are. In fact, your father already called the bank this morning and paid your mortgage on the place for the next six months."

"Six months?" I choke on the words. "What? Why?"

"Because you're our daughter, Margot, and there's not a thing we won't do for you." She stands and takes a seat back on the bed.

"You guys can't afford that, Mom. Seriously. I'll figure it out."

"You don't have to do it all on your own. And yes, we can. We've been squirreling money away for decades. Take the help, honey." She smiles softly at me.

"That was for retirement. Not this."

"Honey, trust me that things will be okay." She squeezes my hand. "And if you can't trust my words, trust in God. He's never let you down, and He's certainly not going to stop now." She arches a brow. "Why don't you tell me about how things are going with that gorgeous detective?"

"What?" The conversation change, has me confused.

"Don't treat me like a fool, Margot. I see the way he looks at you. And more importantly, the way you look at him."

"We're just friends." My cheeks heat, though, because even with everything going on, my thoughts drift to our near-kiss. "I do like him, though. I just don't see how it would work."

"Which part?"

"Matty needs me. He needs stability."

"And you don't think Jaxson could provide that?" Her tone tells me that she does.

"I do, I just don't want to risk starting something and having him get attached. Besides, Jaxson is one of Michael's best friends."

"Which makes me like him even more. Your brother is an excellent judge of character. He never did like Chad."

"Fair enough." I laugh. "Still, Jaxson may not even be interested in taking us on in that way. It's one thing to date, it's another to take on a child, too."

"The man has been living at your B&B in a tiny apartment when we both know he could have bought an actual house."

"Mom."

"Am I wrong?" She arches a brow again, and I shake my head.

"You're not wrong. But he's been able to save money

staying with me, so I imagine that was some of the draw." Again, I leave out his financial help because if I tell her, she's going to read way more into it than there is.

"I very much doubt that." She stands. "Now, I have to go cook, but I wanted to forewarn you that I have every intention of inviting him over for dinner since he's currently staying with your brother and Reyna."

The smile that graces my face comes out of nowhere, as do the butterflies that flutter to life in my stomach.

My mother grins. "That's what I thought."

CHAPTER 19

Jaxson

"*Roses are red, violets are blue, wherever I go, you're coming too. By the seashore, by the seaside, I'll be forgotten, swept away by the tide.*"

The riddle is on repeat in my head as I continue staring at the words Lance wrote on the office whiteboard. Like a word problem, I start crossing off the information that I believe is clouding the true message.

Roses are red, violets are blue. That one is easy enough, it's a simple beginning to tie the rest of it together. I draw a line through it.

Wherever I go, you're coming too. That could simply refer to the fact that I'm trying to find her. Or referencing the fact that this person followed me from LA. I underline it with a green marker, then move onto the third part.

By the seashore, but the seaside, I'll be forgotten, swept away by the tide.

Swept away by the tide.

Is she being held somewhere near the ocean?

The door opens and Michael strolls in. He offers me a paper cup full of coffee from Kyra's bakery, then turns to face the board. "Any ideas?"

"None. And I've been staring at it for hours. It just doesn't make any sense."

"Is this the same format as the other riddles?" he asks.

"No. They were all different, but this one is lacking something the others had. He loved to put the information right in front of my face, that way when I saw it, it was a flashing neon sign to remind me how I failed."

"You don't think this one has it?"

"Possibly. But it's too vague." I circle the last part. "This is the portion I think is trying to point us somewhere. But there are hundreds of miles of shore and nothing leading us to any particular part."

"We'll figure it out. Elijah is running all kinds of programs to try and decipher."

"We're running out of time." I set my untouched coffee aside, then turn and grip the back of my office chair. "She's going to die, Michael. And for all we know, the stuff with Margot's B&B is all tied to this, too. What if—" I can't say it, the possibility far too much to deal with. If anything happens to Lanetti, I'll be devastated.

But Margot? Matty? It will kill me.

"My sister and Matty are safe," he reminds me. "My parents aren't going to let anyone near them. Dad may be in a wheelchair, but he's a great cop and an incredibly accurate shot."

"I'm afraid."

"I know you are. We all are. Have you talked any more to your old partner?"

"Alaric said that he's digging into old case files to see if there's a possibility that we missed a familial connection. A lot of times when it's a copycat, it's someone who's close to the killer."

"You trust him?"

"With my life," I reply without hesitation. "Alaric is as good as they come."

"Good." Michael claps me on the back. "Then let's take a break and go eat."

"What? I can't go eat. I have to figure this out."

"You won't be any good to anyone if you starve. My mom invited us over for dinner, so let's go get something to eat, then we can come back with fresh eyes."

I swallow hard, staring at the board. It feels like I'm betraying Lanetti if I leave, but I know as well as anyone that sometimes a change of scenery can trigger something that breaks a case. "All right."

"Great." He lifts my coffee and hands it back to me. "Drink. You're going to need all the caffeine you can get."

"Why?"

"My dad knows you're into my sister."

I stop dead in my tracks. "What?"

Michael grins. "I might have told him you were putting the moves on Margot."

The blood drains from my face. "What? Why? Why would you do that?"

That smile spreads. "So you *are* putting the moves on my sister?"

I stare at him, unsure how to answer. What's the procedure for sharing a near-kiss with the sister of one of your best friends?

"Relax, Jax. I know you're into Margot. I picked up Matty before your date, remember?"

"Date—that was just dinner."

Michael arches a brow. "Don't lie to me, dude. We both know it was more. It's cool. If it's me you're worried about, don't be. I know you're a good man and you won't treat her poorly."

"Never."

"Then we have nothing to worry about." He opens the door. "Now, onto dinner and a family grill session we go."

The drive over is quiet, giving me the chance to continually break down what the riddle could possibly mean. It's always a location, but Sheriff Vick has had deputies out on the shoreline all day, driving ATVs and using drones to canvas the area, and as of the phone call I had with him a few minutes ago, they've found nothing.

Not a single lead to follow.

Lanetti is still missing, and her kidnapper is in the wind.

Parking on the curb behind Michael's truck, I take one final deep breath before climbing out of the truck. Matty is sitting on the front porch.

"You shouldn't be out here," I tell him.

"Mom said it was okay since you were right behind

Uncle Michael. I've only been out here a few minutes." His tone is off, almost worrisome.

"Are you doing okay?" I take a seat beside him.

"Do you think my dad lit the B&B on fire because of what I said to him at the church?"

"Absolutely not," I reply without hesitation. "If he did light the fire, he didn't do it because of you."

"My mom doesn't know if she'll be able to reopen."

The knots in my stomach grow, and my chest tightens. "We will figure it out, Matty."

"I don't know. I just—my dad has caused her so much pain. I try to pretend that I don't know, that I didn't see him—" His voice cracks, and a tear slips down his cheek.

Unsure what else to do, I wrap an arm around his shoulders. "What did you see?"

Matty is quiet a moment. "He hit her."

My stomach plummets. Margot hadn't ever wanted Matty to know what his father had done. It would break her heart to know that he'd seen the whole thing. "You saw it?"

He nods. "I saw him hit her. I heard her cry out." More tears slip free. "But I'd been so afraid of him that I hid. I should have protected her. It was my job." Seeing the weight this kid carries reminds me an awful lot of the one that had been on my shoulders.

And it breaks my heart.

"Matty, listen to me."

He looks up at me, meeting my gaze. I see so much pain reflected in his gaze that it guts me.

"It wasn't your job to protect her. It was your dad's, and instead, he's the one who hurt her. That's not on you."

"I hate him, Jaxson. I hate him so much." He angrily wipes tears away.

"Did you know that my dad walked out on us when my brother and I were little?"

"Really?"

I nod, hoping that pulling the focus off of him will ease a bit of his pain. "Afterward, my mom abandoned us at a homeless shelter and never came back. When I knew we were on our own, I took my younger brother, and we lived on the streets, surviving as we could."

Matty looks absolutely horrified, but it's no longer pain in his eyes—it's anger. "That's awful."

"It was. But we got through it. My dad has since tried to make contact with me again—through my brother—but I want nothing to do with him either."

"He wants to talk to you like my dad wants to talk to me?"

"Yes. The thing is, we can forgive them for what they've done to us, but still not allow them to continue to cause us pain."

"My mom took me to see Pastor Redding earlier, and he told me that I needed to work on letting go of the anger and forgiving him. But I don't know how to do that. I'm so mad."

We sit in companionable silence for a moment, both of us weighing what it means to forgive like we want to be forgiven. It's heavy, and something much easier said than done.

I sigh. "Well, I'll tell you what, if you figure it out, let me know, will ya?"

He lets out a light laugh. "You do the same?"

"Deal." I remove my arm from around his shoulders and offer him my hand.

He shakes it, then we turn to look back out over the quiet neighborhood. "I'm worried about my mom."

"She's the strongest woman I've ever met," I tell him. "You don't need to worry about her."

"You look after us too, right? I mean, I know that you're not going to be living at the B&B anymore—"

"Who said that?"

He stares at me like I'm supposed to know why he came to that conclusion. "The place burned to a crisp!"

"We'll get it back. Then I fully intend on moving back in. If your mom will let me." Truth be told, I'd live in a tent in the backyard just to be close to them.

"Really?" His entire expression lights up, and I get a heavy dose of instant regret because I'm worried I've crossed a line and promised something I shouldn't have.

"I—"

The door opens, and Margot steps out onto the porch with a smile that doesn't quite reach her eyes. She's breathtaking in a violet sundress, her hair loose around her face. "Hey, Matty, your grandmother is asking for help with the mashed potatoes. Think you can lend her a hand?"

"For sure." He jumps up, then drops back down and

wraps his arms around me in a quick hug that manages to catch me by surprise and completely fill my heart all at the same time. "Thanks for the talk, Jaxson. You're the best."

"Anytime, kid." I pat him on the back, and he heads inside.

"Care for a walk?"

"Sure." Nerves dancing in my gut, I follow her down a small path that leads through the houses down to the beach. It's rockier here, meant more for strolling than sand-castles, but that doesn't stop Margot from removing her sandals. "Is everything okay?" I ask after we've been walking in silence for a few minutes.

"Thank you."

"For what?"

She stops walking, so I move in front and face her. "You comforted him."

"Matty? Of course. Why wouldn't I have?"

"I heard what he told you. That he saw—" She closes her eyes and swallows hard. "I didn't think he did."

"It's not your fault any more than it was his responsibility to protect you, Margot. You both deserved—deserve—so much better than that. Matty is a great kid, and you—" I stop speaking, completely unsure if I'm crossing a line here, but then instantly realizing that I honestly don't care. "You are strong. Beautiful. Kind. And you've captivated me from the moment I first laid eyes on you."

Her lips part, her gaze locked on mine. "I care about you," she says softly. "And so does my son. He's my priority, Jaxson. I have to know that you won't hurt him."

"Never," he replies. "I will never hurt either of you."

Margot takes a step closer, and I reach out, cupping her cheek. I rub my thumb over her soft skin, and she leans into my touch. Every single moment I spend with her, I find myself even more captivated than in the last.

I thought I'd loved before.

But even that love pales in comparison to the affection I feel for this woman. "I've been dreaming about kissing you since we met."

She tilts her face up and opens those gorgeous almond eyes. "Then do something about it, Detective."

I smile, then lean in. We're a breath away when my phone rings. If I weren't in the middle of a case where a girl is missing, I might have ignored it. But I am, so I don't. "I'm sorry," I mutter.

She laughs. "It's fine. We seem to have terrible timing."

"We're going to change that," I reply, then note the unknown flashing across the screen. "Hello?"

"I give the girl a riddle to tell you and you're playing date night on the beach?" The voice is disguised using some kind of device, so it's robotic and I can't tell whether it's male or female.

I rip Margot behind me, putting her between the ocean and me as I scan the shoreline. "Why don't you just break it down for me? The riddle you gave me was too complicated."

"It was not. You've solved harder. A girl's life is on the line, Payne, and you're playing house with a harlot and her son."

Anger burns in my veins, but I swallow it down. Right now, I need to stay levelheaded. Focused on getting him to reveal something—anything. "Then give me something else to go off of. Because I've been staring at that riddle since you had Lanetti tell it to me." Frantically, I continue scanning the shoreline, looking for any sign that someone is out here with us. How does he see us?

"Here's one for you. Hickory dickory dock, you've broken the clock. Time is up, the girl will drown, hickory dickory dock." The call ends, so I shove the phone into my pocket and pull Margot up the beach. We make it ten steps when I hear the faint click of a pressure plate beneath my boot.

If I hadn't been in combat zones, I might not have even noticed it. But I have been. And the realization that I may not walk away from this settles over me.

"Stop moving!" I yell, and she freezes. "Did you feel anything beneath your feet?"

"No. Just sand."

Given that she's barefoot, she would have felt it before I did. My phone rings again. Carefully, I reach into my pocket with the hand not holding Margot's and pull it out, then press the button and put it to my ear, knowing without looking who will be on the other end of the line.

"I wouldn't move if I were you," the voice says. "Or it's going to get messy."

"You did this."

"I gambled on your obsession with the harlot. You'd want to get her alone. I planned for it."

"How did you know it would be us? Anyone could have wandered down here."

"I suppose I just got lucky. Though I'd hoped it would be you watching her die. I suppose I'll have to watch the show and see what happens next. Tick, tock, Payne." The line ends.

"Stay where you are. Don't move." I pull up Michael's contact and tap the screen.

"Where'd you go?" he asks.

"I need you to call Sheriff Vick and get a bomb squad down to the beach."

"What happened?"

"I stepped on a land mine, and I'm not sure if Margot did, too."

"On it. Don't move." He ends the call. I can't risk glancing back at Margot, but I gently squeeze the hand that I'm still holding.

"A land mine?" she chokes out.

"It was a trap for you," I tell her, "So I'd say I'm pretty grateful it was me who stepped on it and not you or anyone else."

"Jaxson—"

"Stay calm, okay? It's going to be fine. Not my first land mine."

She chokes on a sob. "That doesn't make it any better."

"Just breathe."

Just ahead, on the path we'd been coming down, Michael and Reyna race down the stairs. Michael has his phone to his ear, but he stops before stepping off the final stair, and I know it's because he's worried there are more.

"We came down that way," I tell him. "But I wouldn't risk it."

"Sheriff Vick is on his way. They don't have much in the way of a bomb squad, but he made a call and a team is headed here. He's bringing metal detectors, so we should be able to get a good idea of where they are."

If they're made of metal. I don't need him to finish the thought to understand just how much trouble we're in. Depending on how this was made, we could be dealing with a crude plastic explosive that the detectors won't pick up.

One wrong step from someone and—boom.

CHAPTER 20

Margot

How did everything get so messed up? How did I come out here to share a moment with a man I'm falling for and end up standing on a land mine? Or *possibly* standing on one. I don't know. I can't even focus. Jaxson's still holding my hand as the bomb squad from a few towns over checks the sand beneath my feet.

They haven't found another explosive device yet, but that doesn't mean anything. It's entirely possible there's another one hidden somewhere. It makes me sick to think about it. How did this person know it would be us walking through here? How did they manage to place it in the *exact* spot we would be walking, given how much shoreline there is? A child could have stepped on it.

An innocent party who came down here for a quick stroll.

"You're clean," the officer tells me.

Jaxson releases my hand. "Get off the beach."

"I'm not leaving you."

"You need to be there for Matty."

My gaze finds my son's terrified one as he stands beside my dad just above the steps leading down to me. "I need you to be okay."

"I'll be fine. Who knows, maybe I'm not on one either."

But we both know that's not true. He wouldn't have stopped moving if he hadn't felt it. Right?

"Please, ma'am. We need to continue checking the area, and we can't even consider defusing it if you're in the area. We need this space clear."

Tears burning in my eyes, I nod, then leave Jaxson behind as I walk the carefully marked path up the stairs.

"Mom!" Matty runs to me, wrapping his arms around me in a crushing hug. My mom envelops the both of us, then Michael joins in. My father reaches out and takes my hand, so I squeeze his in return.

"I'm okay, honey. It's okay." But is it? Jaxson's still standing on a land mine. What if—no. I shove the fear out of my mind. He's in God's hands. And God will bring him through.

"Is Jaxson going to be okay?" Matty asks.

I turn to face the scene that might as well be straight out of a thriller show. The bomb squad tech in his thick suit kneels at Jaxson's feet and slowly brushes some sand away from his foot. A few seconds later, he stops, then lifts his head and says something to Jaxson.

The former detective lifts his head to the sky, but I'm

not close enough to make out his expression. Is he praying? Begging for mercy?

Please, God, don't let him die. Please don't let him die.

Dread coils in my belly as the bomb tech raises his hand, signaling something to the other officers on the beach. They exchange looks.

"Oh no. He's on one, isn't he?" I ask Michael.

My brother doesn't say anything, but he doesn't need to because his expression says it all. He reaches over and takes my hand, squeezing it gently. Reyna is on his other side, while Lance, Elijah, and Silas are all lined up beside her.

Both Lance and Elijah have their heads bowed in prayer, while Silas stares straight ahead, his jaw set. I can only imagine that they must be reliving some horror from their time overseas. Some tragedy they bore witness to or suffered through.

A car screeches to a stop behind us, and I glance over as a woman wearing blue scrubs jumps out and races toward us, her eyes wide in fear. She looks at me, then crosses over to Silas and stands silently at his side.

Bianca. She saved all of their lives on more than one occasion, according to my brother, and relocated here almost a year ago. She doesn't speak as she joins us, so I don't either. I stand, hand in hand with Matty and Michael as the bomb tech kneels at his feet again.

Even though we're a safe distance away, I can feel Jaxson's gaze locked on me, so I stare straight at him, imagining what would have happened had his phone never rang. It helps to distract from what might be the very last time I see him.

The minutes turn into what feels like hours, before Jaxson finally moves. Slowly, he lifts his foot, and for a moment, I can hear nothing but the pounding of my own heart.

"We're clear!" the tech yells. The crowd around me cheers, and I let loose the breath I was holding. Michael releases my hand, and Matty wraps his arms around me, crushing me to him.

The adrenaline leaves my body in a rush, and I begin to shake, unable to keep myself stable. Jaxson remains on the beach a moment, then the tech guides him up toward the stairs, likely to avoid any other incidents.

After what feels like forever, Jaxson is making his way up the stairs to join us.

Lance is the first to greet him. He wraps his arms around him and mutters something I can't quite make out. Elijah is next. Silas offers him a nod before turning and heading for his truck.

Bianca throws her arms around his neck in a crushing hug. "Don't you know that you can't die on us yet, Payne?"

He smiles but doesn't respond. Body stiff, I can all but see the stress sitting on his broad shoulders.

"You good?" Michael asks him before offering him a hug.

"Yeah. Bomb tech said it was a dud," he replies, looking from Michael to me.

"A dud?" I ask. "I don't understand."

"It was a pressure plate, but there were no explosives."

"Then why make the call? Why scare us?"

Jaxson's gaze settles on mine. "It kept us from getting back to work on finding Lanetti."

"THERE." MY DAD FINISHES WRITING BOTH OF THE RIDDLES ON a whiteboard he had Michael dig out of his storage shed. Apparently, it was used when he was coaching football. Now it contains a riddle crafted by a killer.

How times have changed.

The bomb squad found over a dozen dead pressure plates all along the shoreline. The man must have gotten out there and placed a bunch, only hoping we'd happen to stumble onto one.

It was good planning, I'll give him that.

But even refocused, they haven't gotten any closer to figuring the riddles out, so my father—a former detective —suggested they get more eyes on it. Sheriff Vick is standing in the corner, his thumbs in his gun belt, as he studies the words.

"'Roses are red, violets are blue, wherever I go, you're coming too. By the seashore, by the seaside, I'll be forgotten, swept away by the tide.'" Jaxson reads it for his former partner, Alaric, who is currently on speaker phone.

"The second one?"

"'Hickory dickory dock, you've broken the clock. Time

is up, the girl will drown, hickory dickory dock,'" Jaxson says.

"It fits the formula," Alaric says. "The warden insists that he's had no visitors."

"Mail?" Jaxson asks.

"Nothing there. Apparently he doesn't get letters. I'm driving out to talk to his sister in the morning. She's his only living relative, though they were estranged."

"I remember she didn't even show up for his trial," Jaxson says. "Thanks for doing this, Alaric. I appreciate it."

"Anytime. I wrote these down, so let me play with them a bit and see if I can come up with anything."

"Appreciate it."

"Talk soon," he replies.

Jaxson ends the call, then crosses his arms and stares at the whiteboard. We've hardly spoken since the beach, and his mood has been volatile at best. Not that I blame him. I'd be furious too.

I am furious.

"We can eliminate the 'roses are red, violets are blue,'" Lance says. "And the 'hickory dickory dock.' Since those are likely just rhyming mechanisms."

Jaxson leans forward and underlines everything but those two lines. "'Wherever I go, you're coming too.' That's likely just him pointing out that I'm going to find her."

"'By the seashore, by the seaside, I'll be forgotten swept away with the tide,'" my dad repeats.

"She's being held somewhere near the ocean. The

drowning line confirms that. The tide gives us a count-down clock," Jaxson says.

"Sure, but Sheriff Vick ran drones and bots all up and down the beach, and we haven't found anything." Elijah checks his watch. "And we have less than an hour before the tide comes in."

"What am I missing?" Jaxson snaps, anger radiating off of him.

"We'll get it figured out." Lance looks back at the sheriff. "You still have guys out there?"

He nods. "They're walking up and down the beach. So far, they haven't found anything." The man looks exhausted. It's not typical Hope Springs action to have a missing person and a killer on the loose, so I imagine it's wearing on him more than it would the average seasoned detective.

I look at Jaxson. This is personal for him.

"Are there any caves nearby? Coves that get submerged?" Lance asks. "Anywhere someone could be tucked away?"

"We checked them," Sheriff Vick replies.

"What about that old barn near the Klines' place?" my dad asks. When no one immediately answers, he turns to look at me. Even with everything going on, my cheeks flush with color. He only knows about that place because he busted a high school party I'd snuck out to that was held out there. Of course, we'd been forced to retreat up to the shoreline as soon as the tide came in.

"I thought that thing was long gone," Michael says.

"I haven't thought about that place in years," Sheriff Vick replies. "It's possible that it's been destroyed."

"It's somewhere to start." Hope burns in Jaxson's gaze. "Where is the barn?"

I clear my throat. "Patrick Kline owned some property right off of Sunny Shells Cove. He had an old barn up there that he'd rent out for weddings, but it would flood anytime the tide came in, and eventually, the wood started to rot. When he passed, his kids never did anything with it, so it was used as a make-out spot for teens."

Jaxson whirls on the sheriff. "Did you check there?"

"It's private property," he replies. "We need a warrant."

"Then get one." Jaxson grabs his jacket and heads for the door. I start to follow, feeling beyond helpless, but then decide it's better to stay out of the way. So even as I want to wish him luck, as I want to tell him to be safe, I simply wrap my arms around myself and remain where I am as Lance and Elijah follow him out.

Michael offers me a soft smile, then kisses Reyna, who's been silent this whole time, and slips out after them.

"How are you doing?" my sister-in-law asks as she wraps her arm around my shoulders.

"Fine." But when I look at her, she gives me a smile that tells me she knows I'm not. I note the look she exchanges with Andie.

"Come on. Let's have some girl talk." She guides me down the hall and into the bedroom I grew up in. After closing the door behind Andie, the three of us sit on my bed, which still boasts the same fox quilt my mother made for me when I was young.

"So?" Andie urges.

"I told you guys that I'm fine."

"Margot, I've known you nearly my entire life. We all know you're not. So spill."

"Lanetti is missing, my B&B was nearly burned to the ground, and I'm falling for a man I have no business falling for." The words spill from my mouth without a filter.

"I already knew about the first two and I suspected the third. What I don't understand, though, is why you think you have no business falling for him?" Andie asks.

"He's one of Michael's best friends."

"And you're mine," Reyna replies. "Yet you didn't seem to mind when I married your brother."

"That's different."

"How so?" She crosses her arms.

"You didn't have a son to consider."

"And if I had?"

"I don't know." I cover my face with both hands and take a deep breath. "It's complicated."

"Sure it is."

"We're not questioning that," Andie says. "You both have baggage. He works with your brother, lives at your B&B, and you do have a son to consider. But Jaxson is a good man, Margot. He would never hurt either of you."

"Not on purpose." I lie back on my mattress. "He could

have died today, and all I could think about was that I didn't get the chance to really tell him how I'm feeling."

"I'd be willing to bet he knows because he's feeling the exact same way," Andie replies.

My thoughts drift back to the moment on the beach. Right before his phone rang and reality crashed down on top of us like waves eating away at the shoreline. "He told me that he would never hurt us," I confess.

"See!" Reyna and Andie both yell, then Reyna gently smacks my arm.

I know their perky moods are meant to distract all of us from what's happening right now. It's entirely possible they're walking into a trap. That Michael, Jaxson, and Elijah—along with all of the other men of Knight Security—may not make it home.

And with that in mind, I force a smile because I know they likely need the distraction too. "He told me that I've captivated him from the moment he first laid eyes on me."

"Swoon," Reyna replies.

"And then he told me that he'd been dreaming about kissing me."

Andie's eyes widen. "Did he? Tell me he did."

"No," I reply. "He didn't get the chance." I close my eyes as tears threaten to spill, reality smothering me once more.

"He will get the chance," Reyna tells me. "They'll find her and come home." She sits up and reaches down to take my hand, then takes Andie's in her other. "Please, God, keep them safe. Please help them find Lanetti and bring everyone home. In Jesus' name, Amen."

"Amen."

CHAPTER 21

Jaxson

"I don't see anything," Elijah says as he guides his drone over the top of the barn. We're all dressed in full tactical gear, ready for a fight should one come our way. And after the stunt this guy pulled on the beach, I'd say we're up for one. The barn is still standing, but there are holes along the sides, though we're not close enough to see into the structure.

"Want me to get closer?" he asks Lance.

"Go ahead. We need to know what we're walking into." He glances over at me. "Any word from Sheriff Vick?"

I check my phone, not at all surprised when I don't see a text from him. Getting a warrant for something like this is not going to be easy. Asking to access private property with nothing but a hunch? That certainly wouldn't fly in LA, and I'm willing to bet it's the same here. "No. But I'm not waiting for a warrant. I say we go in."

The wind whips at us, and the sound of waves crashing into the shore is a backdrop to the pounding of my pulse. Adrenaline courses through my veins as I try to remain focused on what's coming next.

My phone buzzes, so I pull it back out of my pocket and read the text.

Margot: Be careful. We still need to get our timing down.

I know her text is meant to ease my nerves, to bring me back to reality, and it does that. But it also brings the image of her standing on the beach as the breeze toys with her hair, face tilted up toward mine, front and center.

The intensity in her gaze as she stared up at me.

Me: I hear practice makes perfect.

Before I can get too distracted, I shove the phone back into my pocket.

"You in position?" Lance asks Silas through our shared comm units.

"I am. And I don't see any movement either," he replies, his voice coming through clear in my ear.

Normally, it's me who would be at a distance with a rifle, watching over my team on the ground. It's what I did in the Marines. What I'm best at. But given how personal this is, I *need* to be on the ground. Right there in the middle of whatever goes down.

So Silas is watching over us from a vantage point that will hopefully grant him a clear shot should anything go down. We could be walking right into a trap. Or we could find nothing.

"Good. Everyone else agree with going in prior to a warrant?" Lance asks.

"There are benefits to not being a cop, boss man," Michael says as he withdraws his firearm. "I say we go in."

"I got something," Elijah says.

My stomach lurches, and we shift our attention to the monitor in his hands.

"What is that?" Michael asks.

The light catches a glint of metal hanging on an old nail on the side of the barn. Elijah moves the drone in close enough that we can see it's a necklace. *Cherry blossom.* "That's Lanetti's." I withdraw my weapon. "She was wearing it outside the diner right before she first got taken. She's in there." Hope floods my system, mixing with the adrenaline and a heavy dose of fear.

What if we're too late?

Images of Lanetti's body, swollen from the water, assault my mind, and I have to actively force them out in order to refocus.

We're not too late.

We will find her.

God, please let us find her in time.

"I texted the sheriff, let him know we have a sign that she's in there and we're going in." Lance levels his gaze on me. "Ready?"

"Yes."

He holds his weapon at the ready. "Then let's go get her."

My heart hammers as we make our way down the embankment, with Lance leading us, me right behind him. I don't have to look back to know that Elijah is behind me and Michael's following him.

We move like a single unit, nearly silent—our years of training working like muscle memory. The wall of the barn is hard beneath my back, despite the aged wood. I follow Lance's lead, taking slow, careful steps forward.

We reach the rusted nail where the psycho hung Lanetti's necklace. I eye it furiously as we pass.

If anything happened to her—

Lance moves quickly to the other side of the door, then nods to me. I come around and slam my boot into the front, weapon raised as we rush inside. It doesn't take but a few seconds to realize that it's empty. Decades of the tide have brought in sand from the shoreline, and as I walk, what's left of the floorboards creak beneath my boots.

"Where is she?" I demand, turning to Lance. "Her necklace was right outside. I saw it. I know it's hers." I'm spiraling, as I spin in a circle. I was so sure. I felt it. She has to be—something scrapes, and we all whirl to face the far corner.

It's empty, but the scraping sound fills our ears again.

As carefully as I would be if I were defusing a bomb, I inch forward, keeping my firearm raised. Lance, Michael, and Elijah all flank me, and when we reach the corner, I peer down into a small crack in the floorboards.

And meet a pair of terrified eyes.

"Got her!" I yell, then quickly holster my weapon and

drop to my knees. Gripping the floorboard in my gloved hands, I yank the board free and toss it to the side. Lanetti's eyes are wide and afraid, tears streaking down her cheeks.

There's duct tape over her mouth and the water from the rising tide has nearly filled the worn space beneath the barn.

Another half hour and she would have drowned.

"I got you," I say as I reach in, and with Lance's help, we pull her up to the surface.

Her body trembles as I hold on to her, trying to bring her some semblance of comfort.

"I'll make the call," Michael offers, smiling warmly at her as he moves out of the barn.

"Hey, Lanetti, I'm going to remove the duct tape, okay?"

She nods at Lance, and he reaches up and tears the tape from her face. "I was so scared. I thought I was going to die!" She leans into me again, burying her face in my chest.

"You're okay now. We found you," I tell her. Her hair is soaked at the ends. All of her clothing from the waist down is drenched from the cold seawater. Carefully, I undo the wire wrapped around her wrists, and she hisses when it bites into her skin. "Sorry," I mutter.

"It's okay. You're here. You found me." She throws her now free arms around me and begins to sob, her shoulders shaking. "He was going to kill me. I know he was. Thank you. Thank you for finding me."

It's near midnight before I'm walking up the steps to the Anderson's home. I'd texted Margot to let her know I was on my way, so instead of knocking on the door and risking waking her entire family, I remain just off the porch, waiting for her to step outside.

Exhaustion plagues me, seeping into my bones and dragging my mood down.

Yes, Lanetti is safe.

Guarded.

But we still haven't caught the man responsible, and I'm starting to wonder if we will. Once again, Lanetti has no idea who had her. She'd been drugged and woke up beneath the barn this time, and he'd grabbed her while she'd been walking to the diner, in a spot where there are no security cameras.

This guy is a ghost.

The front door opens, and Margot slips out into the dim porch light. Just seeing her eases some of the weight I'm carrying. Truthfully, I hadn't realized how much I'd come to rely on seeing her every day until I wasn't.

Her hair is up in a messy bun, and black-rimmed glasses sit on her face. She's wearing an oversized cream sweatshirt and black shorts. She steals my breath.

"Hey," she greets in a loud whisper as she takes a seat on the middle step, then sets the Bible she's carrying in her lap.

"Hey." I take a seat beside her. "Doing some light reading?"

She laughs softly. "I'm struggling a bit these days, so I'm trying to remind myself that even when things get hard, we still need to give it to Him."

"I get that feeling."

"What's going on? How's Lanetti?"

"She's good. In good spirits. No major injuries, but they wanted to keep her overnight for observation. We're installing a security system at her house in the morning, and per her mother's request, I'll be shadowing her whenever she leaves."

"Bodyguard time," she replies with a smile.

"Apparently."

"You don't seem too happy."

"I feel like I'm missing something." I look at her and smile, a bit embarrassed. "You know, I used to be good at my job."

"You *are* great at your job," she replies. "Sometimes mysteries just take time to solve."

"Time we don't have."

"We have Lanetti back."

"But how long until he takes her again? Or goes after someone else?" I keep my gaze trained in the distance.

"I don't know," she says softly. "But I do know that worrying won't add even a single moment to your life."

"Luke 12:25. Nice." I bump her gently with my shoulder, and she beams at me.

"It's the one I've been repeating to myself as I try and figure out just what I'm going to do now that my home and business are in shambles."

"We'll figure it out."

"We'll?" she asks, arching a brow.

Heat creeps up my neck. "You know. I'm here for you. Whatever you need."

"You've already loaned me money you shouldn't have," she replies with a sigh. "You've done enough."

"No. When it comes to you, I worry I'll always come up short."

"Why would you say such a thing?"

Since I feel like I've already put it all out there anyway, and given the seemingly near-death experience we both had on the beach, I figure I can't really mess things up any more than they already are. So I turn to face her. "You deserve so much better than me. It's important to me that you know that." I run a hand over the back of my neck. "Because even though I recognize it, I'm desperate for a shot at whatever this is." I gesture between us, knowing the words I'm speaking are not nearly as eloquent as I'd originally planned.

Candlelight. Fresh flowers. A nice restaurant. That's where I should be sharing my growing feelings.

Not her parents' front porch.

But Margot reaches forward and runs her hand over the scruff of my short beard. "We can agree to disagree on your thoughts about what I do and don't deserve because you're the only one I want, Jaxson. I've just been waiting for us to fix our timing."

Relief floods my chest, and I feel like I can breathe again.

"I think I can make up for bad timing." Slipping a hand around the back of her neck, I pull her forward, press my lips to hers, and everything changes.

CHAPTER 22
Margot

Color floods my world, dancing around me in flashes of lights despite the darkness, as all of my worries and every ounce of stress fade away the moment his lips touch mine.

The kiss is world-tilting. Life-changing. And the desire that floods me, searing me from the inside out, is far greater than anything I've ever felt before.

Too soon, he pulls away.

"I was tired of having bad timing," he jokes, his crooked smile melting me all over again.

I laugh. "Me too."

Silence envelops us, though I can hear his worry-filled thoughts as though they were screaming at me. Hoping the closeness will bring him at least some comfort, I lean into him. His arm comes around my waist, and he presses a kiss to the top of my head.

We might as well have been together for years, rather than it being mere moments from our first kiss. But that's how things have always been with Jaxson. Since the moment I met him, he was familiar. As though I were made for him and he for me.

"How is Matty doing?" he asks. "I know today must have scared him."

"It did, but he's doing okay."

"He's strong."

"That he is," I reply. "How are you doing?" I sit up. "You said you were worried about Lanetti and this case, but that's hardly the only thing you have going on." When he doesn't say anything, I continue, "Rosalie showing up? Your dad trying to force a reunion?"

Jaxson laughs, though there's little humor in it. "I'd momentarily forgotten about both of them." He shakes his head. "As far as Rosalie goes, I haven't heard anything from her—which makes me beyond grateful. My dad and brother keep harassing me, but neither have shown up here."

"Your brother?"

He nods. "Brad has decided to forgive our father and wants him in our lives. He's been pushing me to move past everything that happened."

"Have you?" I question. Forgiveness is something I struggle with, too. Even as I know not forgiving is a weight that will drown you if you're not careful.

"I'm not angry anymore. But forgiving and letting someone back in your life are two different things."

"It's hard. To move past everything."

"It is. And now that he's dying—" Jaxson trails off, and the first glimpse of pain over his father's prognosis settles onto his expression. "I can't understand why I'm upset that he's going to be gone soon. I shouldn't be, right? I mean, it's not like he cared whether we lived or died."

"Have you considered hearing him out?"

He turns to me. "So he can make excuses?"

"Maybe he won't make excuses," I reply. "If he's truly trying to make amends, then maybe the prognosis is just what pushed him to do it now. It's possible he's been wanting to reach out to you for a while."

Jaxson shifts his attention away from me for a moment. "Maybe."

My gaze lands on the scar along the side of his face. One I've seen many times but never had the courage to ask about. Without thinking, I reach up and run my fingers along the jagged line.

"I got jumped outside of a bar," Jaxson replies. "I didn't drink—still don't, thanks to watching my parents struggle with alcoholism, but I'd gone to meet my brother. I'd just gotten out of the hospital and finished my last physical therapy session, and four guys jumped me as soon as I got out of my truck."

"What? Why?" I can all but feel the color drain from my face.

"My Marine sticker on the back of my truck," he replies. "I guess they were looking for a fight and I happened to be in the right place. Because I was still weak,

I couldn't hold them off, and one broke a bottle, then gave me this." He touches the scar on the side of his face. "Tyler showed up right after and we were able to fight our way out of it."

"That's horrible!" I cannot tear my gaze away from him. For one man to suffer so much—nearly dying overseas, his wife leaving him, nearly dying stateside—and then still cling to his faith?

"It wasn't pleasant, that's for sure," he replies with a smile.

"How are you so positive about it?"

"I survived," he replies. "I was new in my faith when it happened, and still learning, but even as I was facing them down, I had this unbelievable feeling of peace. Like, I just needed to hang on to my hope because everything was going to be just fine."

"You are amazing, Jaxson Payne."

"Nah. I wouldn't say that. I've done plenty I'm not proud of."

"What we've done in our pasts doesn't matter," I remind him. "Because we are cleansed by the blood of Christ. His death brought us salvation."

"I know that," he replies. "But I still struggle with the shame."

Reaching over, I thread my fingers through his, then pull his hand over to my Bible. We sit like this for a few minutes, hands joined on top of the worn leather cover.

"What made you leave LA?"

"Honestly? I'm not sure." He turns to me. "I loved my job, even when things got hard. I felt like I was making a difference, like I was helping people."

"You were. You still are."

He smiles at me. "When Lance came out to interview Eliza's ex-husband, I hadn't seen him in years. But after he left, I started feeling like I was missing something. Like maybe my future wasn't in LA. I ignored it at first, brushing it off as just needing a vacation, but the more time went by, the stronger it got. When he asked me to fly out to help, I did so without hesitation. My friend needed me, but I always expected to go home. And then I got here, and I don't know, I guess it just felt like this is where I belonged."

Warmth spreads through me as he looks over at me, our gazes holding. Truth is, I've felt like he belonged in my life from the moment we met.

And every second we've spent together has just cemented that for me.

But even with that, I'm still afraid of what falling in love with this man could do to me. I didn't feel even half of this for Chad, and he still broke my heart when things went the way they did. How am I so quick to give this kind of power over to someone else? Someone who undoubtedly has even more power over me?

"I'm a bit afraid," I admit. "Of this. Of what we're becoming together."

Jaxson chuckles. "Then that makes two of us."

Somehow, knowing I'm not alone in my fear makes me feel even better. "Yeah?"

"Rosalie destroyed me," he admits. "My confidence, my self-worth, she took it and crumpled it up, then tossed it in the trash. Getting into another relationship just never seemed like a good idea."

"Chad did the same to me," I admit. "I felt so unworthy, like I wasn't worth him sticking around."

"You know now, of course, that it wasn't you, right?"

I nod. "Mostly. I still have moments of doubt."

"When those moments hit, come find me. I'll show you just how wrong they are."

Turning my face toward him, I smile. When he leans in this time, the kiss is tender, a caress of our lips that I feel straight down into my toes. I long to reach for him, to bury my fingers in his thick, dark hair, but I pull back.

Jaxson lets out a breath. "I wish I would have kissed you months ago."

"That makes two of us."

***

"Hello?" I finish pouring my third cup of coffee for the day, then take a seat at the table where I've been going through my financials, looking for any way to reopen my doors by Christmas.

"I call with great news." Beckett's happy tone on the other side is like balm against the nerves that stirred when I saw her name on the screen.

"I could use some good news."

"Well, Chad dropped the case this morning."

"Really?" Relief removes a bunch of strain that had been on my shoulders. "You're serious?"

"I'm not sure what got into him, likely knowing he was going to lose, but yeah. And he sent over a formal apology, which I forwarded to your email."

"That's amazing."

"It really is. So, what are you going to do now?"

"Hopefully reopen the doors to my business."

"What do you mean? What happened?"

"Someone lit it on fire."

She's silent for a moment, and I know it's because she's letting my words sink in. Beckett grew up here in Hope Springs until her family moved to Boston when she was in the seventh grade. We spent a lot of time helping out over at the B&B when it was owned by the couple I bought it from.

"Arson?" she asks.

"Yeah. There's been a lot happening here in Hope Springs that you've missed. You know Lanetti Ester?"

"I do."

"She was abducted. They found her under the Klines' old barn."

"Are you serious! Is she okay?"

"She's fine now, but they still haven't found who took her."

"What does that have to do with your B&B?"

"Honestly? I'm not sure. But the detective who's been

staying there—"

"Mr. Tall, mysterious, and buff? Yeah, I know of him."

I laugh. "He believes it's somehow related to him."

"So wild. Apparently I need to make the trip out there so we can catch up on something other than your awful ex-husband."

"Well, I'd offer you a place to stay, but as of now, I'm not sure how I can get my doors opened again."

"What do you need?"

"A time machine so I can go back in time and prevent the place from burning down?"

Beckett laughs softly. "'Here on earth you will face many trials and sorrows. But take heart, because I have overcome the world.'" John 16:33. I go there whenever I'm struggling beneath the weight of it all." She sighs into the phone.

Beckett and her husband were only married two years before he passed away when the private plane he'd been flying suffered catastrophic engine failure. On top of that, during their marriage, she'd dealt with fertility issues, and when he died, I know it felt like another blow to her already tattered heart.

Kyra and I had driven out there to sit with her, pray with her, and be her sounding board when she'd been angry at the Father for taking her husband away. Helping her through that loss was one of the hardest things I'd ever done. Matty had only been about a year old, but I remember watching her hold him and praying hard that she'd be granted the chance to be a mother.

Someday.

"I'm trying to keep my head above water, but I admit that it's been more difficult. When Chad left, I had Matty and the B&B to keep me occupied. But now, with the B&B gone—"

"How bad is the damage?"

"Could be worse," I admit. "I'm meeting a contractor out there later today so he can give me an estimate on reopening my doors."

"Who are you meeting with?"

"One of Lance's friends out of your neck of the woods. Guy named Everett Dorsey?"

She laughs. "I know all about him. Guy was on the cover of every eligible bachelor magazine before he settled down and got married. I feel like I heard the sighs of all the women sad that he was off the market."

I smile. "Well, hopefully he's good at his job, too. He redid the lighthouse after it burned down."

"I heard about that. Mrs. McGinley told my mom, and she told me. So insane."

"It really was."

"Call me after you talk to the contractor. I want to know what he says."

"I will." And because I haven't had the chance to tell anyone, I can't help myself. "Also, you know said handsome former detective?"

She laughs. "I do."

"We're sorta dating."

"Wait, what! Seriously? What is sorta? Like, you're not sure you like him? Or you've been on a date?"

"We haven't been on an official date yet, but—I don't know. He makes me feel—everything. Is that a thing?"

"It really is," she replies, her tone taking on a sadness that makes my heart ache for her. "Pauly and I had a connection like that. Hang on to it, girl, because it is not easily found."

"We kissed last night, and it was—I felt more in that moment than I had in my entire marriage to Chad. And that's a really bad thing to say."

"No, it's not. I get it. Besides, Chad was—I don't even know how to put it kindly. Difficult from the first moment you guys started dating. You were just too young to see it. We all were, or I would have warned you."

"That's a fair point."

"Well, I better get going. I have a deposition starting in an hour, and I need to prepare. Call me when you're done though, okay?"

"Will do. Thanks, Beckett."

After hanging up the phone, I pour my coffee into a travel mug, then carry it out to my car. My parents took Matty to the beach for a picnic and some fishing, so the house is abnormally quiet. And, if I have to stare at one more spreadsheet, I might go insane.

I need to do something.

Anything.

Even if it's just picking up some of the trash at the B&B while I wait for the contractor to show up. I've just started my car when my cell dings. Jaxson's name brings a smile to my face as I open his text. Since he's been on bodyguard duty today, I haven't heard much from him, but we have plans to meet up for dinner at the diner.

Jaxson: I cannot stop thinking about you.

Me: Same. You've been on my mind all day.

Jaxson: Dinnertime can't come soon enough. Oh, also, you should know, Michael knows that we're seeing each other now and has decided it's time to give me the "What are my intentions" talk, so I might be a bit late.

I roll my eyes.

Me: Just remind him that he married my best friend and I didn't say anything about it. I can date one of his and he doesn't get a say.

Jaxson: LOL. I'll give it a try.

Me: How is today going?

When he doesn't immediately respond, I go ahead and turn up the music, then start the drive. As the weight of everything I have to do starts to crush down on me, I turn the drive into a mini worship session, blasting my Christian music as loud as I can.

I belt out *Strong* by Anne Wilson, nearly tearing up in the process. Life really has been hard. The blows just keep coming, and even as I know that Jesus overcame the world, just as it says in John 16, it's still hard to keep my eyes focused on Him when all I want to do is curl in a ball and cry.

The B&B looks depressing when I pull up and see the empty parking lot. With a sigh, I climb out and make my way up to the front door, unlocking it and pushing inside. Aside from water damage and the thick stench of smoke, the lobby is relatively untouched.

At least until you look to the left and get sight of the charbroiled stairway.

What once was gleaming mahogany is now singed black wood.

It makes my heart ache just looking at it.

The floor creaks behind me, so I turn. Chad is standing in the doorway, and seeing him there instantly brings a wave of fear over me. Is Knight Security still monitoring the exterior cameras? Will someone hear me if I scream?

"Hey, Margot." He remains in the doorway, not coming any closer to me.

"What do you want, Chad?"

"I'm going to be leaving town for a bit, heading to an alcoholic rehab facility, and I just wanted to leave this." He holds up an envelope. "Then I saw that you were here, so I figured I'd just face you."

Crossing my arms, I don't take the bait. "What is that?"

"An apology."

"My lawyer said you sent one to her already. She forwarded it to me."

"This is in addition to that. Everything I've done to you is wrong, and I know that. I think I knew it even in the midst of it, but I—" He trails off and rubs a hand over the back of his neck. "This is harder than I thought. I broke things off with Chelsea."

"Am I supposed to be happy for you?"

"No, it really doesn't matter. I just—I don't even recognize myself anymore. Something Jaxson said to me in the interrogation room has stuck."

"What was that?"

He shoves the hand not holding the letter into his pocket. "He said 'you destroyed your family. That choice was on you and you alone.' And then reminded me that if I wanted to start a new life, I needed to get right with God and ask for forgiveness." His eyes fill. "You were the best thing that ever happened to me, and I ruined it."

This is not a side of Chad I've ever seen before, and it throws me off. Sure, he's gaslit me before, but this feels different. And the way he's looking at me is different. "I don't want to go back to when we were together."

"I know. I'm not asking for a second chance with us. I only—I want to do what's right by you and Matty, so there's a check in here, too. It's not much, but it's everything I had in my savings account that I didn't need for this program. I'll be staying with my parents when it's over, so I hope it'll be okay if I'm in town."

"Sure." I clear my throat as emotion claws at me. "You're really going to get help?"

He nods. "Matty deserves better. The alcohol changed me. The way I saw things, the way I saw myself, I know I can't break the addiction alone. I spoke with Pastor Redding this morning, and he's going to come sit with me once a week so we can work past the blocks I have when it comes to my faith, and hopefully, with God's help, I'll be able to be the father I should have been from the beginning."

I smile even as tears fill my eyes. There's a glimpse of the teenager I'd fallen so hard for, a small shred of hope beneath the weight of despair he's carried ever since those two pink lines showed up on that pregnancy test. Even before then, really. "That's great, Chad."

He smiles. "I hope that—" A gunshot rings out, and Chad stops speaking, his eyes going wide.

I don't even have time to scream before blood is pooling on the front of his shirt, and he stumbles forward.

I rush for him. "Chad!"

Standing behind him is someone in a mask, their gun held straight out.

"Run," Chad urges. He tries to stay standing but falls, I manage to slow his fall, cradling him as best I can as we sink to the floor.

"There are cameras," I tell the person as they move further inside. "They're monitored."

"Get up." The voice is disguised with some kind of device, making the person sound even more menacing. They aim the weapon at Chad again. "Or I'll finish him now."

I get to my feet. "Okay. Please, no."

"Get out and get into my car."

"Margot, don't." Chad grips my ankle. He tries to get up again, but falls down. He's pale, too pale, his eyes rolling back into his head.

Blood pools on the floor beneath him, and I know he

doesn't have long. So I kneel and remove his hand from my ankle. "Get Jaxson," I whisper, then stand and pull away. The masked man grips my arm, and I feel the pressure of a weapon against my back.

"You try to fight and I put a bullet in you now, understand?"

"Yes," I choke out.

"Good girl."

CHAPTER 23

Jaxson

For what is probably the tenth time in the last five minutes, I look down at my phone. Margot still hasn't texted me back. Which, given the workload she told me about earlier today, I'm not overly surprised about. She wanted to spend the morning going over the B&B's financials, trying to come up with a plan for after Lance's buddy Everett gives her a quote.

I've already decided that I'm going to help. Even if she won't accept money, I plan to lend a hand on labor so she can at least save something.

"You look like a man with a lot on his mind." Lanetti sets a mug of coffee in front of me, then takes a seat on her couch and smiles.

"Somewhat."

"More about your date tonight?" she asks. Her tone isn't joyful, though, and based on the look she gave me when I was talking to Michael on the phone earlier, I decided to keep Margot out of our conversations.

It's clear Lanetti has feelings for me, and I'm not entirely sure how to explain to her that I'm not interested in her that way. At least not without hurting her feelings.

"Somewhat," I reply.

"No need to be nervous, any woman would be lucky to have dinner with you."

"Thanks." I try not to look too uncomfortable as I check my phone yet again. *Why hasn't she texted back?*

"Do you like to fish?" Lanetti asks.

"Sometimes," I reply. "Though admittedly it's more about the quiet than the actual fishing."

She laughs. "Well, my mom kept my dad's old fishing boat. It's not impressive, but maybe we can go sometime."

"Maybe." I turn my attention to the notes I've scrawled on a yellow legal pad. It's a base timeline, as well as things we found at the crime scenes.

"What do those mean?" she asks, gesturing to the playing cards I've doodled along the edges.

"Back when I worked homicide in LA, we had a case where a man was abducting women, then leaving a playing card at each of the scenes."

"That is awful."

"It was."

"And it's somehow tied to this? Or are you just trying to show off your amazing drawing skills?" Her smile widens.

"We found one where you were first abducted, and one at an attempted break-in at one of our client's houses."

Her smile fades. "That's a scary thought. You think it's the same person?"

"No, I put him behind bars."

"Of course you did," she replies. Her tone isn't mocking or playful, but serious. She leans forward and places her hand over mine. "You're an excellent detective, Jaxson. I know you'll figure it out and keep me safe in the meantime."

Slowly, I remove my hand. Maybe it is time to fumble my way through that conversation.

"Listen, Lanetti—" My phone rings, the shrill tone cutting me off. "Payne."

"Get to the hospital," Michael snaps.

Every muscle in my body goes rigid, and my stomach is little more than a pit. "What happened?"

"Chad's been shot, Margot is missing. There was a card left at the B&B. A three of hearts."

My own heart breaks.

"Bianca is coming to watch Lanetti," he adds. "Get here now." Michael ends the call.

There are absolutely no words to explain the bone-deep fear that settles over me. The way my ears drown out all sound as I picture Margot's beautiful face in the dim light of her parents' porch.

As I recall the way she'd smiled up at me.

Someone knocks on the door, and I jump.

"What is it?" Lanetti asks, not moving. "Is everything okay?"

"No." I stand and cross over to the front door, then check the peephole before pulling it open. Bianca is on the other side, wearing dark jeans, motorcycle boots, and a leather jacket, her dark hair in a braid.

"You good?" she asks.

"No. But I will be."

"What's going on?"

I turn to Lanetti. "Margot is missing. This is Bianca Theodore. She's going to stay here with you."

"What? No. I need you, Jaxson."

"Margot is missing," I repeat, the words not feeling real even as they leave my lips. "I have to go."

"She may be missing, but I'm not. What if he comes for me?"

"Then I've got you, girl," Bianca replies. "I'm an excellent shot, and I know what I'm doing." She walks in and takes off her jacket.

"Okay, well—have some coffee, Jaxson didn't touch it." Lanetti crosses over to me and wraps her arms around me. "Be safe, Jaxson Payne. I still want to go fishing."

I MAKE IT TO THE HOSPITAL IN RECORD TIME.

By the time I've gotten into the waiting room, Pastor Redding, Michael, Lance, Silas, and Elijah are all waiting for me.

"Where's Matty?" He's my first concern. Was he there when Chad was shot? Was he taken, too?"

"With my parents," Michael replies. "He's been there all day. They have him at the house, and Sheriff Vick sent a deputy over."

There's at least a sliver of good news then. "How long has she been gone?"

"Security footage shows her leaving twenty minutes ago with someone dressed all in black. They were wearing a mask, so we couldn't get a good look at their face."

"Why wasn't someone watching the monitors? Why didn't anyone intervene?" I demand.

"Whoa." Lance holds up his hands. "There was no alarm that went off, and the fire damaged the exterior and lobby cameras."

"I can't—she can't be missing." I try to suck in a breath, try to do anything to rationalize. "Why was Chad there? Did he have something to do with this? Partnership gone wrong?"

Michael shakes his head. "As much as I wish I could pin this on him, he was there to apologize." He reaches into his pocket and withdraws an envelope. "Found this. It's an apology note and a check for three thousand dollars."

I stare at it. "It could be a lie. He could be trying to throw us off."

Elijah crosses his arms. "I don't think so, brother."

"Do we have *anything*? Any lead to follow?"

"Not so far. We have to wait for contact—"

"This is Margot!" I yell. "There's no waiting! We have to move!"

Michael crosses over and plants both hands on my shoulders. "Breathe," he says. "I want to find my sister, too, but if we act rashly, we're bound to make mistakes."

I know he's right.

I'm trying to remain calm.

But Margot is *everything* to me. What if I lose her?

My cell rings, so I reach into my pocket and withdraw it, halfway expecting to see an unknown number. Instead, my former partner's name flashes on the screen. "She's missing," I say into the phone.

"Who's missing?"

"Margot. He took her."

"Oh no." Alaric is quiet a moment. "I got nothing from the sister. I really don't think it's him, man."

"It has to be. Somehow." I try to take a breath, but I can't focus on anything but how terrified Margot must be. Is she hurt? Is she even alive?

"Look, I'm booking a flight. I'll be there in a few hours."

"You don't have to do that."

"I know I don't. But you're like a brother to me, Jaxson, and I know you have your new family out there with those security guys, but my feelings for you will never change. I'll let you know what time my plane lands, and I'll meet you at your office."

Normally I'd insist he not come out. But he's the only

other person who worked that case with me. The only one who knows Morah like I do. "Thanks, man."

"Anytime. You'd do the same."

"You know I would." I end the call, then turn to Lance. "My former partner is flying out. He knows Morah, too, and he's going to help."

"Good." Lance runs a hand through his hair. The head of Knight Security was a Captain in the Army, a Ranger, and is one of the few people I trust with my life. "I want to say a prayer, then we need to get to work. Elijah, you're on security. Pull the footage from every camera you can."

"Warrant?"

"Just do it," Lance replies.

Elijah nods. "You got it, boss."

He turns to Silas. "You get with your cousins. See if one of them can fly out and help us locate her."

"On it." Since he never prays with us as a group, Silas turns his back and walks away, already prepping to make the call. I'm honestly a bit relieved that he's going to do so. Silas's cousins opened a Tracer business and can track anything with a pulse. They find people that have been missing for decades. Sometimes dead…sometimes alive.

Please be alive, Margot.

"Michael, you and Jaxson head over to the B&B and see if anything was missed. Scrape the place."

"You got it," we both respond at the same time.

Lance nods, then bows his head, we all do the same. "Lord, we ask that You watch over Margot. That You keep her shielded, and that You guide us to her so that we may bring her home. Heavenly Father, we pray that You will help us remain strong and that You will be with Matty during this stressful time. Please watch over Chad and guide Doc as he does what he can to save him. In Your holy name, Amen."

Twelve hours.

It's been half a day since Margot was taken, and we still aren't any closer to finding her. I sit on a church pew, staring at the cross that hangs behind the altar, my heart heavy, my fear crushing me. The sun has started to come up, basking the world in rays of gold, but I can't stomach the beauty of it when I know that Margot is suffering.

I put my trust in God a long time ago. I know that no matter what I face in this life, He has promised a Kingdom where there will be no more suffering. No more pain, or tears, or loss. And I am trying so hard to cling to that when everything around me is falling apart.

"I thought I might find you here." My former partner and his wife arrived in town late last night, and he's been working tirelessly alongside us, searching for anything we might have missed. "Even after all these years, I still can't fathom how I survived not believing God was there."

He'd been a nonbeliever until his now wife introduced him to Christ and he found his faith in the midst of the fear he'd lost her. Even though he didn't fully understand, Alaric leaned on God in those moments because he felt the Holy Spirit guiding him.

"Once you truly open your heart, you realize just how much you need Him."

"Amen to that, brother." He's silent a moment. "Do you remember when Wrenley was missing?"

"That's not something you easily forget," I reply.

"Fair enough." He chuckles. "We found her, though, didn't we?"

"We did."

"Because God guided us to her."

"I don't feel pulled in any direction right now," I reply. "I just feel lost."

Alaric nods in understanding. "God is still there, brother. Even if you can't feel Him."

"I love her."

"I knew that before I even got on that plane."

"Fair enough," I repeat his earlier words. Alaric knows me better than I know myself. We might as well be brothers for all the time we spent together when we were partners. "I don't know how I'll survive without her."

"You won't have to find out, because we're going to bring her home."

"You sound so sure."

"Because I feel it. Margot is going to be fine, Jaxson. That call will come in, and we'll find her."

"And if we don't?" I ask, voicing the deepest fear I'm

carrying right now. What if we never find her? Or what if we're too late? How will I tell Matty that I lost his mother? That she's gone?

"We will," he replies. "And if not? If the worst happens? Then God will carry us through what comes next."

CHAPTER 24

Margot

My stomach lurches as the boat moves yet again. I'd been drugged as soon as we were in the car, so by the time I woke, I was already in the hull of a boat. Fear consumes me, but I try to beat it back because I know it won't help me now.

Only God can bring me out of this.

I'm tied to a chair, my mouth gagged with a scarf. My feet are secured to the legs of the chair, my arms behind my back. I have no idea how long I've been here, but when I first woke, it was dark outside. Now, light streams in through a small window on the side, though it's partially boarded up so I can't see anything.

There is no one down here, and I keep frantically watching the door, waiting for someone to walk through it and explain to me what's going on. Has my abductor already called Jaxson? Given him a riddle?

Is Matty scared?

Did Chad survive?

Tears fill my eyes, and I close them, forcing myself to take a deep breath.

"The Lord is with me, so I will have no fear. What can mere people do to me?" I repeat the verse from Psalm 118 over and over again in my head, hoping that doing so will ease some of the terror.

But all I can think about is leaving Matty behind. I don't even have a will. What if they send him back to Chad and he spirals again? What if—

The story about Daniel in the lion's den comes flooding back to me.

It was Matty's favorite story when he was younger.

The lions could not harm David because of his faith in God. Because he believed, with his entire soul, that God would bring him through the trials he was facing.

Not a scratch was found on him, for he had trusted in his God. I repeat the verse from Daniel, over and over again.

I trust in my God.

I trust in His plan for me.

And I believe, with everything I am, that my time on this earth is not done.

God, please be with me. Please help me stay strong. I know that You are here with me. That You have never left me alone. Thank You, God, for your promises. Amen.

The door creaks, and I open my eyes.

My abductor is wearing all black, their face shielded with a ski mask. They don't speak to me as they come through the door, walking over toward where I am and checking the ties.

Daniel and the lions. I can do this.

I try to speak, but the words come out garbled. Thankfully, the person removes the gag.

"Why are you doing this? Who are you?"

They don't speak to me as they withdraw a phone and tap the screen.

"Where is she?" Jaxson demands over the speakerphone.

"Alive. For now. But based on your previous performance, I wouldn't imagine she'll stay that way for long." Just like at the B&B, the voice is disguised.

"I'm here! Jaxson!" A hand cracks across my face, and I groan, my mouth filling with copper tang. *Daniel and the lions. I can do this.*

"I am going to find her," Jaxson growls. "And when I do, you will receive no mercy at my hand."

"That's not very becoming for a man of God," the man replies.

"Tell me where she is."

"I think I'll let you figure this one out for yourself, Detective. Have fun fishing."

The door opens again and a second masked figure walks in. Bile rises in my throat when I see the vial and syringe in their hands.

"Jaxson!" I scream. "They have a—" The person ends the call and tosses the phone to the side. "No. Please no. Don't do this!"

"You're a distraction for the detective, and I need him focused."

Daniel and the lions. I can do this. "You don't have to do this. You can let me go."

"No, we can't. We have plans, Margot, and they don't include you." The second person fills a syringe, then offers it to the first person. They start toward me, and I take a deep breath, once again turning to my God.

Father, please give me strength. I have to survive for Matty. Please let me go home to him.

As soon as the person is close enough, I slam my head into theirs. Pain rings in my ears, but instead of focusing on it, I throw my chair back, hoping that the fall will break it. Unfortunately, it doesn't, but I still try to fight the hold, doing everything I can to loosen at least one of the ropes.

My heart pounds.

The first person stands and rips the mask from their face.

Nothing would have prepared me for the shock as I find myself looking back at someone I've known my entire life. "Patty?"

"You shouldn't have done that," the second person snarls, then rips their mask off. "You weren't supposed to let her see your face, Mom!" Lanetti rushes forward and lifts my chair up off of the ground.

"I don't understand. You were kidnapped," I say as I try to piece everything together.

"I only needed Jaxson to *think* I'd been kidnapped," she snaps. "So he'd turn to me, where he *belongs*. Instead, you kept getting in the way." She moves around in front of me. "It's always 'Margot this, Margot that.' Ugh, it's exhausting!" Bending over, she lifts the syringe her mom dropped. "You would think he would've noticed me, but no, he was always only looking at you."

"This is about Jaxson?"

"Are you really this slow? No wonder Chad left you."

"He—you shot Chad!" I say to Patty.

"He had it coming."

"You taught us math in high school. You were our teacher!"

"Which is how I know he deserved it."

"But the cards. The B&B. The fire. It was all you?" I ask.

Lanetti smiles at me, but the girl who used to babysit my son, who served me coffee at the diner, is nowhere to be seen. "The card thing was clever, wasn't it? It took some deep digging into Jaxson's background to find that. Of course, I hadn't been looking for that in particular, just something I could use to get him to notice me, and when I read about the cards, I thought it was brilliant. After all, he stole my heart, so using them to capture his seemed fitting."

"The girl wasn't supposed to survive, though. I'm just glad they didn't find the card."

"What? What girl?"

She arches a brow. "No need to worry, we got the dose right this time. Just needed a little more." She steps forward.

"We need to handle this," Patty says. "We can't risk getting caught."

"Well, we can't risk her surviving and getting away now, either." Lanetti moves closer to me, then comes around behind me. "So, how should we do this? Straight to the jugular?" Something pinches against my skin, and I close my eyes, whimpering as fear takes a bite out of my soul.

Is this really it?

"Please don't," I tell them both. "Please don't take me away from Matty."

"Matty will be fine. We both know your parents will take him in. Probably better off, too. If you couldn't keep Chad around, what makes you think you can keep Jaxson? We wouldn't want little Matty growing up with an unhealthy outlook on relationships, now would we? Besides, Jaxson and I will watch over him."

"You can come back from this, Lanetti. It's not too late."

"It is too late," she replies. "Because I want Jaxson and you're in the way. None of them could see it either. None of them know just how perfect he is for me."

"Okay, we can talk about this later. Maybe at the diner. Over some food."

Lanetti snorts. "Why, so I can serve you dinner while you two play googly eyes over the table? He's mine!" she yells. "You had your chance, this is mine!"

"Lanetti," Patty scolds. "Do it so we can leave."

"You never let me have any fun."

Footsteps above us silence both women. "Down—" I

can't finish because Lanetti wraps an arm around my throat and squeezes, pressing the needle against the side of my throat. "Shut up or I'll do it now."

Please, God, let that be help. Please don't let me die down here. Tears stream down my cheeks as I struggle to breathe against the hold on my throat.

More footsteps just outside the door.

Patty raises her gun.

And fires.

A man groans, and the door splinters open. Three men dressed in tactical gear rush in, their weapons aimed.

Jaxson.

Michael.

Silas.

And behind them, Elijah is down, a hand pressed to his side. *No!*

"Let her go, Lanetti," Jaxson says.

"I'm doing this for us, Jaxson. Don't you see it? With Margot around, we can't be together. Not really."

"We can talk as soon as you put that needle down," Jaxson says. "Come on, you're not a killer."

"I could have been. If that brat Kleo Finch had gone down and stayed down like she was supposed to. And I can do it now too. I'm not afraid. Then you'll see. You'll see."

"Lanetti."

"Drop your weapons," Patty orders.

"Not a chance," Michael snaps.

"Then—"

A gunshot sounds, and Patty yells in pain as she falls to the side. I slam my head back into Lanetti's face and she screams, jabbing the needle into the side of my throat.

Everything moves in slow motion, and I stiffen. Did she push the contents of the syringe into my veins? Am I going to die? Even now that Jaxson has found me?

Daniel and the lions. I can do this. It's going to be okay. Jaxson is here.

Michael lunges for Lanetti, taking her to the ground as Silas tends to Patty. Jaxson comes straight for me, setting his weapon down beside him as he kneels at my feet.

"Hey, stay still, okay? You're going to be okay."

"I don't know what's in it," I tell him. "She was going to kill me, though." I'm barely keeping it together, barely managing to keep myself from trembling as he reaches up and tugs the needle from my neck.

"She didn't inject you, okay? It was just a stick."

I nod, tears streaming down my cheeks, because I know that speaking right now is not going to lead to anything but me losing it altogether.

Jaxson uses a knife he'd tucked into his tactical boots to cut the ropes binding my legs and arms. As soon as I'm free, I fall forward, both arms going around his neck. I bury my face against his chest, my entire body trembling from the adrenaline.

"See! It's always about Margot! It should be me!" Lanetti roars.

"Keep all questions and concerns to yourself until the

end of your prison sentence," Michael snaps as he marches Lanetti out of the room.

Silas reaches down and lifts Patty, carrying her out, and soon it's just Jaxson and me.

He pulls away and cups my face, leaning his forehead against mine. "Thank You, God. I thought I'd lost you, Margot," he says.

"I wasn't sure I was making it out of here, either. I kept thinking about Daniel and the lions though," I choke out. I'm rambling as my body begins to tremble. "Jaxson, I—how did you know? How did you know where we were?"

"Lanetti told me her dad had a fishing boat she wanted to take me out on. Then, when your abductor called, they told me to have fun fishing. We raced back to the house and discovered that Bianca had been drugged and Lanetti was gone."

"I'm so glad you found me," I choke. "Thank you for finding me."

"I will always find you. Do you hear me? I love you, Margot Anderson. With everything that I am and everything that I will be, I am yours. And this might not be the best time to tell you, present circumstances and all, but there is no one else I want to be with. It's you. I think it's always been you."

He kisses me, not waiting for a response. But if he had waited, I would have told him the same things. That I love him with everything I am. With all of my heart and soul. He's my person. My promise of love in this world.

"I love you, too, Jaxson," I reply, leaning my forehead against his. "I love you, too."

"HOW ARE YOU FEELING?" JAXSON ASKS AS HE SITS UP FROM the couch he's been sleeping on for the past two hours. We're still in the hospital since Doc wanted to watch me overnight just in case. And even though I sent Matty home with my parents, Jaxson insisted on staying around.

"Hopeful."

"Yeah?" he asks.

"Yeah. It's funny, but it took being abducted for me to realize that everything is going to be okay. I'll find a way to open the B&B again, and it's going to be better than ever."

Jaxson gets up and crosses over, then leans down to press a kiss to my forehead. "You amaze me, Margot."

I beam up at him, unable to even put into words how he makes me feel. Like my heart can't help but beat fast and slow all at the same time.

Someone knocks on the door.

"Come in," I call out.

It opens, and a man walks in wearing jeans and a leather jacket, his hair longer on top and shorter on the sides. I've never seen him before, nor do I recognize the redhead walking in alongside him, her belly swollen.

"Hey, heard she was up," the man says.

"And you thought you'd come interrogate us?" Jaxson

hugs the man and the woman, then turns to me. "Margot, this is my former partner, Alaric, and his wife, Wrenley."

"Hi, it's so nice to meet you both." I sit up a little straighter and offer a smile. "You're here all the way from LA?"

Alaric nods. "Flew out when Jax told us you were missing. There's not much we wouldn't do for the man. After all, it wasn't too long ago he was helping me track down my lovely wife." Alaric smiles and wraps an arm around his wife.

She beams up at him.It's adorable. Utterly and completely heart-melting.

"How far along are you?" I ask her.

"Four months," she replies. "But I look like I'm going to give birth tomorrow. This is our third."

"Congratulations, that's amazing." I glance over at Jaxson. Will he want more kids? Should we talk about that? *Getting ahead of myself.*

"Thanks. We met your son before, he's a great kid."

Pride swells within me. "He is a pretty great guy."

"He is. Anyway, we just wanted to pop in to meet you. We'll be heading out tomorrow, but I told Jaxson that I'd love for the three of you to come visit us in LA. Whenever you're up for it."

"You're leaving so soon?"

"Wrenley runs a women and children's shelter," Jaxson tells me. "They have their big annual event coming up soon, so she said she needs to get prepared."

"That's so wonderful. It must feel so good to help others like that."

"It's a blessing, to be sure." Wrenley steps forward and squeezes my hand. "Take care of Jaxson for us? He's not as strong as he pretends." She winks at Jaxson, who rolls his eyes.

"I will," I promise.

They embrace then step out, but before I can say anything, Chad is wheeled into the room. His chest is bandaged, his face pale. But he's alive. And even though they'd told me he was, seeing him makes me feel a bit better.

"I needed to see that you were okay," Chad says. "I just —I was scared for you."

"Thank you for trying to stop them from taking me."

"I didn't do enough."

"You tried," I tell him. "And that's enough to me."

"You don't need to thank me." He smiles softly, then turns to Jaxson and holds out a hand. "Thank you for taking care of Margot and Matty."

Jaxson hesitates a moment, then takes Chad's hand. "I'll always take care of them."

"I'm counting on it," he replies. "Margot's always deserved better than me. I'm glad she found it."

CHAPTER 25

Jaxson

Waves crashing against the shore will always be a soothing sound to me. Something about the way they ebb and flow, smoothing out the sand as they slip away.

Which is precisely why I chose the shoreline for this particular meeting. I'd gotten here earlier than the agreed-upon time, hoping that I could calm some of my nerves before Bradley Payne arrives.

It's been a whirlwind of a month, picking up the pieces of Lanetti and Patty's betrayal. It shook the town to know that two of their own were capable of such horrific things. Kidnapping Margot, drugging Kleo, Lanetti faking her own kidnapping… It'll provide topics of conversation for months to come.

But I can't be focused on that right now.

Because I'm trying to move forward, too.

Things with Margot are great, and construction at the

B&B is well underway. Everett was able to offer a steep discount on labor and materials, granting Margot the ability to open the doors by Christmas, which is what she was hoping for.

She's even planning a big Christmas party for the town as a fun reopening event.

Matty's started visiting Chad once a week in rehab, and I can see on the kid's face how happy he is that his dad is making an effort. I figured if he could forgive his father, it was well past time I forgave my own.

"You look pensive."

I turn to face my father. This time, I'm not blinded by anger, so I can see the hollowness of his gaze and the gauntness of his face. It's so strange to see him like this, when he's lived in my head all these years as a healthy and intimidating man pushing forty. "It's been a wild month," I reply.

"I heard." He shoves his hands into his pockets and stares out at the ocean. "Your brother filled me in on everything that went on. Your girl, she's doing okay?"

"Margot's good," I tell him. "She's strong."

He smiles but doesn't look at me. "That's good, that's really good."

Silence settles between us.

Bradley clears his throat and turns to face me, so I offer him my full attention. "Saying I'm sorry feels pathetic, but I really am, Jaxson. I'm so sorry for everything that happened. For all of the pain I caused you and your brother. He told me about some of it. Of the things you did to survive."

"I'm past it now."

"I know you are. You've always been stronger than me. Even when you were young, you'd handle things better than me. When I started drinking, it was just my way of dealing with the unhappiness burning inside of me. I know now it was the enemy, trying to break apart my family—and succeeding."

"You're getting help now."

"I got sober," he replies. "You should know, I looked your mother up to try and make amends with her, too."

"And?"

"She died a few months after I left."

A knot in my chest tightens, and I press a fist against it. "That's a shame." I could have looked her up once I got on the force. I could have looked both of them up, but I'd made it a point to keep that door closed.

"It is," he agrees. "She overdosed. I keep thinking back. What if I'd just been stronger? If I'd done things differently, we could have been so much better." Tears stream down his cheeks, and his voice wavers. "I messed up, Jaxson. You boys leaned on me, and I failed you."

My throat burns with unshed tears. "We survived."

"But it should have been easier."

"I'm not sure it should have been," I tell him. "Does it suck? Sure. Was I angry? For a long time. But I am where I am, and I'm the person I am today because of the trials I suffered through. God brought me out of them, and He made me a stronger man for them."

"He really did," Bradley replies. "You do so much good, Jaxson."

I swallow hard, trying to smother the emotion clawing up my throat. "You said you're sick?"

He nods. "Doctors give me a few months, but to be honest, I'm feeling like it's only days now. I'm tired." There's no fear on his face, no anger, just acceptance. And I wonder if he realizes that his reaction to what's coming makes him stronger than he seems to give himself credit for.

"You're doing right by trying to get things in order."

He sighs. "I sure messed up this life. I could make excuses. My parents were never around, I never knew what it meant to be a father, but at the end of the day, they're just excuses. And I grew tired of making them."

His words are heavy, and they settle upon my shoulders like a weight.

"Jesus forgives us," I tell him. "If you believe in Him."

"I do. For a long time, I struggled with my faith, but I can honestly say that's one thing I am certain of these days." He smiles at me, and a knot I hadn't realized was there loosens in my chest. "I never stopped thinking about you boys," he says. "Tried to find you, but your mother had sold the house, and no one had seen her."

"You looked for us?"

"For years," he replies. "It wasn't until you adopted your brother that you popped up in the system and I realized you'd stayed in LA. And by then, I was so ashamed of what I'd done, I drowned that shame in alcohol and hoped it would kill me. I guess I got my wish." Before I can respond, he turns to me. "I came and saw you in the hospital."

"What?"

"When you came back stateside. You were in a coma, but I came to see you." His voice breaks. "You were already a man, but all I could see was my little boy." He chokes on a sob. "Tubes and wires, bruises and bandages. I wanted nothing more than to change spots with you. To be the one in that bed."

I stare at him, trying to process everything he's saying. "I didn't know you were there."

"I left before you woke. But I checked in from time to time. And then one day, I came, and you had been discharged and sent home."

My heart thaws toward him, and suddenly the weight of forgiveness is not nearly as heavy as it had been. "For what it's worth, I forgive you."

He turns to me again, hope burning in his eyes. "You do?"

"I do."

His eyes fill. "Can I?" He holds out his arms, and I embrace him, pulling his slight form in for the first hug I think my father and I have ever shared. Even before, when I'd been young, I can't remember ever hugging my dad.

Even when I'd been scared or hurt as a boy, he'd push me aside. Tell me to man up.

I thought I'd moved on. That I'd fully processed everything I went through as a child, but now I'm understanding that I wasn't quite as far past it as I thought. Because this—this embrace—it feels an awful lot like healing.

Tears slip down my cheeks as we pull away. "Are you staying in town?"

"I checked out of my hotel this morning. I've been staying with Tyler. He offered to take me in until—you know."

"I'll be flying out to see you both," I tell him. "I promise."

He smiles. "I look forward to that. Both my boys in one place. I don't deserve it."

"None of us deserve the forgiveness we receive," I tell him. "But Jesus loved us so much, He died for it."

"Hey, stranger." Margot slips her hand into mine and leans against my shoulder to stare out over the ocean. "I thought I'd find you down here."

I look down at her and smile. Her hair is in a thick braid down her back, and she's wearing a white T-shirt and baggy blue pants. Her toes are painted a bright coral that matches the tips of her fingers.

She's light.

Hope.

Love.

"You are so beautiful."

Her cheeks flush with color. "Why, thank you, Detective. You know, if I didn't know any better, I'd say you were trying to woo me."

"Always."

"How did things go with your dad?"

"It was harder than I thought it would be to say goodbye to him."

"So it went well?"

I nod. "He apologized. Told me that he wasn't making excuses because he knows he messed up." My throat tightens again as I picture him crying beside a hospital bed when I'd been so out of it I had no idea I wasn't alone. "He came to see me at the hospital. When I was in a coma."

"Really?" Her eyes fill. It's one of the things I love about her. Margot feels everything. She's empathetic and understanding, kind and forgiving. Even after everything Chad put her through, she's been driving Matty to see him, even taking the man care packages so he doesn't feel forgotten while he's in rehab.

"Yeah."

"How are you doing with all of it?"

"I'm good. Honestly. I feel better than I have in—I don't even know how long." I press a kiss to the top of her head.

"I'm so glad."

"Me, too. I thought I'd forgiven him and moved on, but it wasn't until I said the words that I felt that weight lift."

"I'm so glad you gave him a chance. That you forgave

him so you both can move forward. Did he tell you anything about his prognosis?"

"The doctors give him a few months. He's staying with my brother, so I think I'll be heading out there for a bit to try and help. If you're okay with it."

"Absolutely. Why wouldn't I be?"

"I was also thinking maybe the three of us could fly out? I can introduce you to my brother as my fiancée."

"Sure that would be—wait, what?" She pulls away from me, staring up at me like I'm speaking another language.

Nerves settle in my stomach like lead, but I reach into my pocket and withdraw the ring I'd bought the day after we'd rescued Margot. I'd known then that I wanted to spend the rest of my life with her.

That I never wanted to go another day without her.

And after asking both Margot's father and Matty for permission, I decided not to put it off any longer. So I drop down to one knee. She covers her mouth with both hands, eyes filling.

"Margot Anderson, I never thought I would be on my knee again. I never thought I'd ever love anyone enough to want to take this next step, but you are the air I breathe, baby. You are my life. My love. My soulmate. I love you so much. Please make me the happiest man on this earth and marry me?"

She nods, unable to find the words.

"Yeah?"

"Yes!" she yells and tackles me to the sand, mouth

waiting for mine. I wrap my arms around her and capture her lips with mine.

Cheering fills my ears, and Margot pulls away as Matty, Michael, Reyna, Margot's parents, Lance, Eliza, Andie, Elijah, and Bianca come down the steps toward the beach, all of them clapping and yelling out congratulations.

Margot laughs and looks down at me. "I love you, Jaxson Payne." She holds up her hand, and I slip the ring onto her finger.

"I love you, too, Margot. And I promise I will spend every day of my life being a man deserving of your love."

SWOON! I LOVE A BEAUTIFUL SECOND CHANCE AT LOVE story, and both Jaxson and Margot were so deserving of another shot at their happily ever after! I hope you enjoyed it, too! If you did, please consider leaving an honest review.

The series continues with Perilous Healing, the final book in the Coastal Hope series! Turn the page for a sneak peek!

Perilous Healing

CHAPTER 1

SILAS: TEN YEARS AGO

Sweat clings to my damaged body like a second skin. There's not a single part of me that doesn't burn, but as I make my way down the damp, concrete hallway, I know that if I were to stop—even for a moment—it would mean death.

I escaped once, I'll never escape again.

The guard who'd let me go told me that I needed to run. That the door at the end of the hall would be unlocked when I reach it, but that if I didn't get out soon I'd never leave this place. He told me I'd die here.

And I believed him even as I wasn't entirely sure he wasn't merely a figment of my starved, beaten mind.

But as soon as the chains had fallen from my wrists and ankles, and he'd reached down to pull me to my feet, I'd known that this is my one chance to escape. My moment.

So even as every movement is yet more torture, I continue pushing forward.

I step on a clump of concrete breaking away from the tunnel floor and hiss through clenched teeth as it bites into the soft flesh of my bare foot. Warm blood trickles from the injury, but I have nothing to wrap it. Even if I did, I can't risk the time it would take to do so.

Two hundred yards. According to the guard who helped me escape, that's how long I have to go before I'm pushing through a door and taking my chances in the deep jungles surrounding the area I've been held in since I was captured almost a month ago.

I have to make it home. If not for me, then for my entire team who didn't survive our initial contact with the American crime boss we were here to stop. My command has to know what happened. They have to know so they can act.

Still, people will say I'm lucky. But to me, luck would have been bleeding out on the ground before they ever brought me back into the compound. Then, I wouldn't carry the weight of everything that was done to me over the past three weeks.

A woman's scream rips through the stale air, and I sink against the wall, hiding in the shadows. My heart pounds, my head burning with an ache I'm sure will split me in two if it doesn't stop soon.

"Is that all you've got?" she yells. *American.* Though I'm not surprised. The compound we're in belongs to one of the most notorious drug runners in the U.S. Most of the guards are American, except for the one who let me go.

"You let him die!" a man bellows.

"And I'd do it again!" she retorts, then cries out once more as the resounding crack of a slap echoes down the hall. I clench my hands into fists, then take a deep, steadying breath and wait for it to be safe. I should just leave. Continue sneaking out, but if I do—if I leave this woman behind—what kind of man does that make me?

Save her. The two words come to me clear as day, surely my conscious telling me that I can't leave her here.

Even if I don't know her, I have to save her.

Even if it means we both get caught, I have to take her with me.

A door along the wall opens and two men stalk out.

"I'm going to go find out what we're to do with her. My guess is, they'll want her head."

"Shame, it's a pretty head," the other replies.

The door begins to swing closed, so I retrieve the chunk of concrete I stepped on, then rush forward and catch it before it locks shut, then wait to make sure the men keep walking. One thing I've learned, arrogance does not equal intelligence. If they are so arrogant to believe they are untouchable here, they won't notice something as simple as a door not closing when it should.

Sure enough, they keep walking, so I prop the door open with the concrete and turn.

I'm standing in what is clearly a surgical room of some kind, with a hospital bed streaked with blood, and an assortment of medical tools and supplies. The woman is chained to a chair, blue scrubs streaked with blood. Her dark hair falls like a curtain in front of her face, though her breathing is steady enough that I know she's alive. There's a tray of sharp tools to her right, so I reach over and grab a scalpel.

"Come for more?" she demands, then looks up at me. I'm pinned beneath a mossy green gaze, though both eyes are streaked with red. Her face is bruised and bloody, a large scratch scraping down one side of her cheek. "Who are you?"

"Chief Petty Officer Williamson, Ma'am," I say as I rush forward and cut through her bindings. "I'm getting out of here and I'm taking you with me."

"Just like that?" she asks, rubbing her wrists as I free them.

"Just like that," I reply.

"You don't even know why I'm here."

"I know you're not supposed to be and that these men are going to kill you."

"And you can't let that happen."

"No ma'am, I can't."

"So you're Boy Scout, then." She stands.

I study her, trying to decide whether or not I've made a mistake. "No, I'm a Seal."

"Navy," she replies. "You're all boy scouts." She looks me up and down. "You look pretty bad yourself."

Glancing down at my blood-streaked bare chest and what's left of my uniform pants, I can't argue her. I don't even know what my face must look like, likely even more battered than hers does. "I'm not trying to win any beauty pageants," I tell her. "Now, are we going or not?"

"Let me grab some things." She rushes to the side and grabs a blue bag, then stuffs the supplies from the tray inside. "Ready."

Keeping the scalpel in my hand, I creep toward the door and peer out. The hall is still empty. Remaining in the shadows, I creep alongside the wall, trying to pay attention to any sounds I might hear coming from either side.

There's yelling somewhere, though it's so distant I can't quite make out where it's coming from, but I still pick up my feet faster, moving as quickly as I can through the hall until—up ahead a door awaits.

Freedom.

"Shut everything down!" someone screams from behind us. "We have two escapees!"

I reach back and grab the woman's hand, then yank her forward as I sprint toward the exit. If they shut it down, we'll never leave this place. I know it deep down in my soul. So I run.

Even as my feet sting.

My muscles burn.

My head pounds.

I hit the heavy door and shove it open, then close it softly behind and sprint into the trees. It's dark overhead, so watching where we're going is an impossibility. Behind me, I hear yelling, but it just forces me to run faster, pushing my body as hard as I can.

But it's not a maintainable speed, so I can only hope we can outrun them before I lose it.

I'm not sure how long we run, but by the time dawn is breaking, I no longer hear anyone behind us. So, choosing a large tree to take cover against, I let myself rest. My breathing is ragged, my body numb from the chill in the air and likely the amount of blood I've lost over the past few hours since two of my crudely stitched stab wounds have re-opened.

"I need to look you over," the woman says as she kneels in front of me and opens the bag of stolen supplies. "Otherwise you're going to die before you can get us out of this place."

"You're a doctor?" I ask.

"Trauma surgeon," she replies. "Bianca Theodore at your service. Though I normally treat Rangers, I think I can make an exception for a Seal this time around." She flashes me a smile that I know is meant to be disarming, as she slips into a pair of gloves she pulled from the bag. "This is not going to feel great," she warns, then gently presses against one of the wounds in my side. I hiss through clenched teeth as pain shoots up through my body. "Yeah. So listen, I know we just met and all, and I hate causing pain to people who just saved me, but you should know—this going to hurt—badly."

Perilous Healing

CHAPTER 2

BIANCA: PRESENT DAY

Body slick with sweat, I take out the frustrations of yet another sleepless night on the heavy bag swinging before me. I don't know why I'm surprised, it's not like I've had a solid night of sleep in, well, ever.

A childhood of nightmares blossomed into an adulthood of the same.

Round and around we go.

"You're here early."

I stop hitting the bag and turn to face Michael Anderson. I've known the man for years, and a long time ago there were moments when I thought I'd been in love with him. Of course, I wasn't. He was just the first man who'd ever been kind to me without wanting something else in return.

Now we're close friends and co-workers, and he's happily married to a woman I absolutely adore.

"Wanted to get a work-out in before the meeting this morning."

He arches a brow. "Wanna try that again?"

I should have known better. We served together overseas, with me as a medic who saved his life on more than one occasion. I know that he struggles with the weight of his past, too, though I imagine being married to his high school sweetheart has lessened a bit of it.

The two of them are perfect for each other and if I ever hoped for that kind of connection, I might be jealous. "I couldn't sleep. But that's nothing new." Not one for vulnerability, I turn back toward the bag and slam my fist into it.

Michael comes around and holds the bag for me as I slam my fists into it, then spin and land a kick. "If you want to talk about it we can."

"Nope. Not interested. Thanks though." With one final combination, I take the gloves off and grab my shaker bottle with the BCAA mixture I still haven't finished drinking. Amino acids first thing in the morning is a necessity when I'm hitting the gym, but I'm more than ready for coffee.

"Bianca, you can't keep it all bottled up."

"It's worked for me for the past thirty-five years," I call back as I head toward the door.

"See you in a bit."

"See you then!" I call back, then step out onto the street.

The sky is darker than it should be, and I imagine it's due to the hurricane that's heading our way. The worst one Maine has seen in two decades, according to the newscasters.

All around me, I see the preparations being made. Windows boarded up, patio furniture put inside. But I'm not worried. I've faced down things far more terrifying than a hurricane and survived. And even if this is the thing that takes me out, well, then I guess I won't have to worry about much of anything anymore.

Slinging my backpack over my shoulders, then grip my cup and take off on the run that will bring me home. Since Hope Springs, Maine, is a small town, I run to the gym every morning, then use the three miles to unwind after my workout.

I've made it a habit to push my body to its limits each and every day, never again wanting to be found inadequate to protect myself.

As it does every year, the darkness ebbs closer into my mind, but I shove it back. I won't let the past consume me. Never again. Especially not today.

My muscles are liquid by the time I reach the pier that sits beside Hope Springs' church. While I don't ever imagine I'll find myself going in for a Sunday service, I do stop at the pier and stare out over the sunrise.

Pale blue waters crash against the light sand as the world is painted in rays of purple, orange, and gold.

It's beautiful.

Even if I can't make myself believe in anything, I can believe that.

"Morning, Bianca." Pastor Redding comes to stand beside me. He's dressed in shorts and a t-shirt, his grey hair sweaty at the temples.

"Morning. Coming back from a run?"

"What gave it away?" he asks with a laugh.

I smile. Even if I don't occupy a pew every Sunday, I can appreciate the kindness of the man beside me.

"Are you doing okay today?" he asks.

"Why do you ask?"

His expression reflects curiosity rather than judgement. But there's an understanding in his gaze that makes me feel—well—like he cares. Which is a new one for me. His wife has the exact same effect on me, and given that she owns the bakery in town, avoiding her is impossible.

I like cupcakes too much.

"God guided me to this pier this morning," he says. "I felt like I needed to run back by here rather than my usual route, and I can't help but believe that it's because you were going to be here."

"Listen, I appreciate you asking, but you know I'm not—"

"I know," he replies. "But even if you're unsure, He still knows and loves you."

The truth is, I don't know what I believe. But I've seen so much evil it's impossible for me to wrap my mind around the fact that there's a greater purpose to it all. "I'd like to believe that. I really would."

"Do you want to talk about what troubles you? Just friend to friend," he replies with a smile. "And it will never leave this conversation."

"Never?"

"Never," he replies.

"Today's my birthday," I reply. "And I haven't told anyone."

"Why not?"

"It doesn't feel like a day to celebrate," I admit. It's the day everything went wrong. The day my innocence was shattered, and I saw my life for what it was—a lie. A dangerous, blood-stained lie.

"Every birth is a miracle," he says. "So birthdays are absolutely worth celebrating. Is there no one who knows? What about your parents."

"Don't have them." It's not a lie given they're both dead, but it still feels wrong.

"Well then." The pastor smiles at me. "Let me be the first to say happy birthday, Bianca. And while I will keep your confidence, you really should tell someone. You deserve to be celebrated."

I pull away. "Thanks, Pastor Redding. Have a good day."

"You, too."

As I turn away, I can't help but remind myself that if he knew anything about me, he'd know just how false that statement is.

"MORNING!" LILLY, THE WAITRESS AND PARTIAL OWNER OF Hope Springs Diner, greets as she sets a mug of steaming coffee down in front of me.

"Morning. You look rested."

She laughs. "Baby finally slept through the night and now I'm not entirely sure what to do with all of this energy I have."

I laugh softly. "Glad to hear it. He's a cutie. Alex brought him by the Security office last week when he'd dropped off the coffee for our meeting."

"He's perfect and Sarah is just already such an amazing sister."

"She's a sweetie, too, so I can imagine." I'd wanted kids at one point, but I'm not bitter even knowing it's an impossibility. It just means I get to spoil the children of my friends. Which is something that was also an impossibility until I'd moved here to Hope Springs after Lance Knight—a former Army Ranger I'd saved when we'd both been in the service —called me in to help track Michael after he'd gone missing.

Once I'd seen what Lance had built here, though, I knew I wanted to be a part of it. Even if I didn't ask to come work for him until a few months ago.

"You want your usual?" she asks.

"Pancakes, eggs, extra crispy bacon and a side of crunchy peanut butter. You know me well."

Lilly grins and makes a note on the order pad she carries. "It's my job both as your friend and local diner owner. We'll get this right out." She turns and leaves the table so I take a drink of my coffee and stare down at the e-reader I brought with me.

Some probably thing I'm reading a pulse-pounding suspense.

Or a swoony romance.

But in reality, it's the Bible that is currently down-loaded, I just don't want anyone to know that I'm searching for answers. For understanding. Because letting them know that means I also have to admit that I've found none.

That right now, it all just feels like words on a sheet of paper.

I turn it on and start reading where I left off in Exodus, but I haven't made it even a page when the bell dings over the front door.

I can feel him before I see him.

The blood-sizzling, bone-deep awareness that comes from being anywhere in Silas Williamson's vicinity.

The nightmares come flooding back.

Being lost in a hot jungle.

Closing up the same wounds over and over again because his skin was so tattered it wouldn't stay closed.

"Bianca!" Little Eloise, his four-year-old niece rushes over and wraps her arms around mine. I have to pull it free just to hug her back.

"Hey, sweet girl. How are you today?"

"You know, it's my birthday."

I grin at her as she smiles up with eyes that are so like

Silas's, she could be his daughter. Likely because her mother was his twin. "Is it really?"

She nods. "I'm five today."

I give her a high five, loving that I share my birthday with such a wonderful little girl. "Happy birthday, kiddo."

"Thanks! When is your birthday?"

My gaze lifts to Silas. He's the only one who knows… but does he remember? He's not even looking at me, so I'm assuming not. "Today is your day, Kiddo."

"Eloise, we need to get some breakfast before I drop you off at the library." Silas's deep voice resonates with a part of me that I tried really, really hard to separate from myself.

He makes me feel safe.

Scared.

Hopeful and hopeless.

Everything I carry for him is a walking contradiction, but I know that's only because he knows everything the others don't. Secrets that I'd wanted to die with me in that jungle.

He could have buried me with them, but he's kept each and every one.

Our connection is volatile now, but it wasn't always like that.

I meet his gaze. "Morning."

He grunts in response but doesn't speak to me. Silas is a man of few words, sure, but with me he prefers to pretend I don't exist. I'm just glad he hasn't told Eloise she can't be kind to me because losing her happy smile would break my already tattered heart.

"Can we eat with Bianca, Uncle Lassy? Please?" She puts her hands together and sticks her bottom lip out in a pout. "It's my birthday, please, please, please?"

He looks at me like he's hoping I'll tell her no, but I'm not that kind. "Okay. As long as it's okay with her."

"Fine by me. Come on, kiddo." I scoot over and she climbs onto the booth beside me.

"Morning, lovely!" Lilly greets, setting a coloring page and some crayons in front of her.

"Morning, Lilly! It's my birthday!" Eloise greets.

"It is!" she exclaims. "Happy birthday! Special birthday pancakes coming right up."

"Yay!" Eloise claps her hands together and starts coloring as Lilly turns to Silas.

"Morning, Silas, what can I get for you?"

"Just coffee, thanks."

"No problem." Lilly leaves the table so I pick up a crayon and start coloring the page alongside her.

"Uncle Lassy is taking me to the arcade downtown. We're going when he's done with his meeting. It's going to be *so* fun because we're going to do the dance off game. And Mrs. McGinley said I get to help her re-shelve the books at the library! I love books." As Eloise keeps chattering happily, I sneak a peek at Silas who is staring out the window of the diner.

His expression is hard, uncomfortable, as it always is when we're near each other. Which makes it even more awkward given we share either side of a duplex on the other side of town.

I know why he hates me.

I hate myself most days.

But it doesn't take away from the fact that I wish, for once, he'd look at me like he did all those years ago. Back before he knew the truth.

Perilous Healing

CHAPTER 3

SILAS

"We have two installations this afternoon," Lance announces as he checks his clipboard. "Michael is flying out next week to head a protection detail in L.A., and Jaxson will be out of town until the end of the month, though he's handling some of our digital work from there." He writes something on his clip board, then sets it aside and withdraws some large black radios form a box beside him. "These will work should the cell towers go down with the hurricane. We have plenty of food, water, batteries, blankets, and medical supplies to help the town should we get hit hard."

"News said it will be hitting sometime tomorrow morning," Elijah says. "I helped Mrs. McGinley board up her library, and we've taken care of Doc's place and the church, too."

"Good." He turns to me. "You prepared?"

I nod.

"How about you?" he asks Bianca.

"I'll be getting my windows boarded up as soon as I get home," Bianca replies.

I have to force myself not to steal a glance at her. Just once. Sitting across from her this morning was torture because even as I despise everything she is and the lies she told me, I still find myself drawn to her.

Like a moth to a flame—she would destroy me. If I ever let her that close again.

"Great. Caleb is coming in for an onboard interview this afternoon. He's going to come on as one of our techs."

"Yeah?" Bianca sounds so thrilled I steal a glance at her now. She's beaming at Lance, her emerald eyes bright with joy. "That's wonderful!"

"He finally caved," Lance replies with a grin. "I've been trying to get him to come on—even if it's just part time—since he moved here."

Up until about two years ago, Caleb was living in the swamps of Florida, completely off-grid. Something that came in handy when Michael—who'd been shot—and Reyna, Michaels' now wife, stumbled into his homestead desperate for aid.

He'd been there to offer it, and we'd found them tended to and safe.

After that, he'd made the choice to leave the swamps and re-locate here, though he's still maintained a good distance from most of the residents as he tries to acclimate to being around people again.

Still, he's a good man, and one I'd trust to have my back.

"Glad to hear he's coming in."

"We're growing, that's for sure," Lance replies. "With the number of new clients were taking on, as well as the monitoring for our current ones and the aid we lend to Sherriff Vick as needed, the helps is definitely appreciated."

I doubt Lance ever thought his calling would turn into a large business like this, but it certainly has, and now Knight Security is the fastest growing private security company on the East Coast.

"Elijah, any news to add?"

"Nope." The tech lead crosses his arms. "We've had a relatively quiet month, no break-ins, so nothing to report on that end."

"Good. Let's hope it stays that way." Lance sets the clip board down. "All right, let's end in a prayer." He bows his head, and although I'm not a praying man, I do the same. "Dear, Lord, we thank You for this day, for the ability to help others, and for Your guidance and discernment in moments of trial. Please be with us as we navigate this hurricane and keep us grounded in Your light. Please protect those in the path of this storm and guide us so we can help those who need it most. In Your Holy Name we pray, Amen."

"Amen," Elijah and Michael reply at the same time.

"All right, hope you all have a great day. Silas, can I talk to you for a minute?"

In lieu of vocally responding, I push up from the desk I was leaning back on and walk over toward his desk. Elijah, Michael, and Bianca all clear out of the lighthouse, shutting the door behind them.

"You're on monitor duty today, huh?" I ask, dropping down in the chair beside his desk.

"That I am. At least for a few hours. After Caleb leaves, I'm headed home to be with Eliza and the baby. I'll be monitoring the systems from there."

"Nice. What's up?"

"I'll keep it brief since I know it's Eloise's birthday today."

"Appreciate it," I reply.

"I mainly just wanted to check in and see how you were doing. You've seemed a bit strained lately and I wanted to see how I could help." I'm not surprised the former Army Ranger and Captain sensed something was off. The man picks up on everything.

"Just settling in still," I reply. It's not a complete lie since ever since Bianca moved here full-time and started working for Knight Security, I found the rug pulled out from under my feet. I still feel like I'm trying to adapt to seeing her every day.

But I can't tell Lance any of that because I've kept the fact that I know her a secret for many reasons. None of which I care to explain to him at the moment.

"You're sure that's all it is?"

"It is."

He nods. "Thanks for letting Eloise come to church with us yesterday. Did she have fun in Sunday school?"

"She did. Thanks for taking her. She's been asking to go but I just—"

"Couldn't make it."

"Yeah. That's it." I reply, running a hand through my hair. "Is that all? I need to go pick her up and get her to the beach before she drives Mrs. McGinley up the wall with questions."

Lance chuckles. "Sure thing. Let me know if you need anything, okay? I know you like to keep your personal life under wraps, but I'm here if you need me."

"Thanks. I know you are. See ya."

The sun is warm on my face as I step down the steps of the lighthouse and toward my truck that's parked in the lot. When Lance and I first met, I'd practically been dead, having just been rescued after a month of running for my life in the jungles outside Calvers' prison camp.

He'd been in the hospital after suffering his own near-death experience and happened to be walking past my room when he felt—as he calls it—drawn to come talk to me. He'd spoken to me about God, about faith, about surviving, and I'd struggled to have an open mind.

It didn't keep me from feeling my own draw toward him, though. He spoke with such confidence, such hope, that it lit a bit of my day up. We'd gone our separate ways, but I always intended to catch up with him.

And then Sierra died.

My twin sister's sudden passing, alongside her husband Rick, made for another hit to my weary soul. It wasn't until I was back home in Montana that I found that I had been made guardian of Eloise.

At first, I'd said no.

I'd never even met the child as I'd hidden myself away in a mountain cabin, refusing to come see her even after she'd been born. Sierra was so upset at my staying away, but how was I supposed to explain the darkness in my soul? The weight that I carried? How could I have told her all the ways I struggled to cope with civilian life once I made it home?

It was when I went in to sign the papers to relinquish custody of her that I'd felt someone—or something— knock the wind from my lungs. And as I paused, trying to catch my breath, I'd seen Eloise sitting in a playpen at the children's services building, crying.

One look is all it had taken for me to realize what a mistake I was making by walking away.

And I haven't looked back since.

I get into my truck and pull out of the lighthouse, making my way toward the bakery so I can pick up two cupcakes for Eloise and I tonight. I've had custody of her for three years, now, and every year I've done my best to make her birthday special.

Since my parents are gone, Ricks, too, is just the two of us against the world.

Silas and Eloise.

And I'll die before I let anything happen to her.

So distracted by my thoughts, I don't even notice Bianca's car sitting outside the bakery until I've parked right alongside it. Dread burns a hole in my stomach, and I shift my truck into reverse, ready to bail, but when I see her sitting at a table in the corner, a single cupcake in front of her, I throw the truck back in park as memories assault me.

I know what today is.

It's Bianca's birthday, too.

And truth be told, I'm probably the only person in this town who knows it because she confessed to me that she hated today. That her birthday was the start of everything in her life falling apart.

She's in pain.

The thought hits me in the gut and I lean forward to rest me forehead against the steering wheel. I can still see her, sitting on the jungle floor, her hair wet as rain poured down on top of us. The droplets on her cheeks were either rain water or tears, but her pain—it hung heavy in the air around us.

So I get out of the truck.

Kyra Redding looks up from behind the counter and smiles at me. "Hey, Silas! I just finished Eloise's special cupcakes." She lifts a small white box and sets it on the counter.

"Thanks." Reaching into my pocket, I pull out some cash and set it on the counter as I take the box. "No change, thanks. You need help boarding up the windows?" I ask, noting the plywood leaning against the wall.

"I appreciate it, but NAME and Henry Acker will be coming by to meet Felix. The three of them are putting them up."

"Have them call if you need additional hands."

"Will do," she beams. "Thanks." Her phone rings so she quickly excuses herself.

I glance over my shoulder at Bianca. The cupcake in front of her is untouched, undoubtably a lemon with white frosting and sugar crystals, as her mother used to make for her each year, and she's reading something on a tablet.

I don't know that she even realizes I'm here.

I could probably just slip out through the door—but when her brow furrows at whatever it is she's reading, and the small scar at the corner of her eye catches my attention, I'm thrown right back into thar jungle.

I may despise what Bianca did.

But I cannot deny who she was.

So, I make my way over to her. "Enjoy your birthday."

She looks up at me now, green eyes shining. "You know better than that.'

"It's still your day."

"No," she replies, "It's not."

"Then what's with the cupcake."

She looks down at it. "Tradition." Her gaze lands on the box in my hands. "Those for Eloise?"

"She wants spaghetti for dinner."

"Nice. Good meal."

"Yeah. Well. I'll see you around." I turn to leave, but as I'm doing so, I note a man standing across the street from the bakery.

He's not looking into the windows, but rather down on his phone. He's dressed casually, in jeans and a grey t-shirt, but the gold watch on his wrist captures my attention. I can't make out the brand, but it's far too upscale for a man who dresses casually.

"He's been out there all afternoon," Bianca replies.

I look down at her, noting the worry on her face. "You're afraid."

"Not afraid," she replies as she stands. "Just curious. Excuse me." Taking her cupcake and tablet, she leaves the bakery after waving goodbye to Kyra.

I remain where I am, watching the man with the golden watch as he puts the phone up to his ear and starts walking—in the opposite direction of where Bianca went.

It could be nothing.

It's probably nothing.

But I can't shake the feeling that something other than a hurricane is heading to Hope Springs. Something that's been a long time coming.

KEEP READING PERILOUS HEALING! GET YOUR COPY TODAY!

A WOUNDED VETERAN WITH A BROKEN SOUL. A HEALER WHO **trusts no one.**

Former Navy SEAL Silas Williamson has come face-to-face with more evil than most.

Shortly after returning home from being held captive overseas, his twin sister and her husband suddenly pass away, leaving him the sole guardian of his four-year-old niece.

After moving to Hope Springs to work for Knight Security, he's hoping for a quiet place to raise the little girl. And most of the time…it is.

Bianca Theodore has certainly suffered through her fair

share of dark times. As a military trauma surgeon, she's saved more lives than she can count. But she's not just a healer. A long time ago, she took the life of a man she'd been charged to save.

Someone with ties to the former Navy SEAL she now works alongside.

And after years of hiding…those who know she's responsible have finally found her.

As Bianca faces the nightmares of her past, she turns to Silas, who is haunted by his own. Together, they stand a chance at surviving the coming battle, but only if they turn to the One who can bring them the peace they so desperately crave.

If you're looking for a sizzling (but not spicy!) romantic suspense with a protective hero struggling with his faith, a talented surgeon fighting to survive, a small town that protects their own, and a team of wounded veterans turned private security officers, then Perilous Healing is for you!

THIS CHRISTIAN ROMANTIC SUSPENSE DEALS WITH:
-Coping with trauma
-Discovering your worth
-Seeking God in everything
-Healing from your past

. . .

The Coastal Hope series can be enjoyed in any order!

Get your copy today!

A wounded veteran with a broken soul. A healer who trusts no one.

Former Navy SEAL Silas Williamson has come face-to-face with more evil than most.

Shortly after returning home from being held captive overseas, his twin sister and her husband suddenly pass away, leaving him the sole guardian of his four-year-old niece.

After moving to Hope Springs to work for Knight Security, he's hoping for a quiet place to raise the little girl. And most of the time…it is.

Bianca Theodore has certainly suffered through her fair share of dark times. As a military trauma surgeon, she's saved more lives than she can count. But she's not just a healer. A long time ago, she took the life of a man she'd been charged to save.

Someone with ties to the former Navy SEAL she now works alongside.

And after years of hiding…those who know she's responsible have finally found her.

As Bianca faces the nightmares of her past, she turns to Silas, who is haunted by his own. Together, they stand a chance at surviving the coming battle, but only if they turn to the One who can bring them the peace they so desperately crave.

If you're looking for a sizzling (but not spicy!) romantic suspense with a protective hero struggling with his faith, a talented surgeon fighting to survive, a small town that protects their own, and a team of wounded veterans turned private security officers, then Perilous Healing is for you!

This Christian Romantic Suspense deals with:
   -Coping with trauma
   -Discovering your worth
   -Seeking God in everything
   -Healing from your past

The Coastal Hope series can be enjoyed in any order!

Get your copy today!

Get your hands on Alex and Lilly's story for free today!

As a travel photographer, my life has been one adventure after the next.

Every location I visit a far cry from the small town I grew up in.

A place I'd been desperate to escape after my ex broke off our engagement and joined the military.

However, home has a way of calling you back.

Three years after my mother's death, I find myself returning to Hope Springs.

But I'm not the only one who came home.

The man who practically left me at the alter is here, too.

And he's determined to heal what he shattered all those years ago: me.

Grab your free copy today!

Founded by veterans, Knight Private Security is your best bet when it comes to safety.

God blessed us with a desire to help others, which is precisely what we do.

Whether you want to ensure your loved ones are safe at home, protect your business, or need security for an event, we are just what you are looking for.

Highly trained and ready to protect you at all costs, our team will risk everything to ensure you are shielded from whatever danger you face.

MEET THE TEAM

Lance Knight (*Founder/Private Security Specialist*): Captain. Army Ranger. His career in the military ended when he was shot multiple times and a bullet fractured his spine.

Elijah Breeth (*Tech Specialist*): Staff Sergeant. Army Ranger. After an IED nearly ended his life, he left the military behind, but still wanted to serve the community.

Michael Anderson (*Private Security Specialist*): Staff Sergeant. Army Ranger. Grew up in Hope Springs, and after getting out of the military, he began working as a bouncer in various night clubs. Now, he's returned to his home town, though travels as his position as a private security specialist demands.

About the Author

Jessica Ashley started her career writing romance novels for the secular world, before deciding she wanted to use her love of storytelling to help bring people closer to God.

She is an Army veteran, who now resides in Texas with her husband and their three children (whom she homeschools).

You can find out more about her and her books by visiting her website: www.authorjessicaashley.com or by joining her Facebook group, Coastal Hope Book Corner.